SOUL
SHaDOWS

SOUL SHADOWS

Alex Woolf

First published in 2013 by Curious Fox, an imprint of Capstone
Global Library Limited, 7 Pilgrim Street, London, EC4V 6LB –
Registered company number: 6695582

www.curious-fox.com

First published in 2011 as a serialised eBook by Fiction Express
(www.fictionexpress.co.uk)

ISBN 978 1 782 02015 8
17 16 15 14 13
10 9 8 7 6 5 4 3 2 1

A CIP catalogue for this book is available from the British Library.

Cover designed by Steven Mead

Cover images: Shutterstock – © andreiuc88; © Benjamin Haas

Typeset in Palatino 11 pt

Printed and bound by CPI Group (UK) Ltd, Croydon, CR0 4YY

To Paul Humphrey and the whole team at Fiction Express for their help and encouragement, and to über-bloggers Jenni (*Juniper's Jungle*) and Zoe (*Bookhi*) for their fantastic comments.

One

Estelle Grant stood at the white picket gate of the cottage and stared out across the meadow. The late afternoon light lay on the warm, summer air like pale wine – heady and sweet. A breeze ruffled the green expanse. She wanted to run through it, feel the silken grass and buttercups against her feet. She wanted to run until she collapsed, out of breath, in its long, welcoming fronds. Yet she held fast to the gate, awed like a long-caged rabbit suddenly offered a garden to play in. The silence was unsettling. Estelle was from the city. Her ears had been acclimatised since babyhood to the hum of crowds and traffic. In her life, grass was something you found in public parks, full of screaming kids, cigarette ends and rubbish.

But it wasn't just culture shock. There was something else about the scene that disturbed her – something not quite right. The light was strange, wasn't it? Almost nauseating, as though a photographer had gone mad with his filters. Then there was the wood. The trees rose out of the horizon on the far side of the meadow like a dark, menacing army. The area closest to the wood lay in deep shadow. The wood cast its shadow over the breezy, playful grass like a warning.

The shadow, now she looked at it, made no sense. The sun was behind her. It was in completely the wrong part of the sky to create the shadow. So what was producing it? A cloud? But there were no clouds today, just a smoky brown haze at the horizon where the sky met a line of metal towers – grain silos she assumed – way off across the fields to her right. The shadow on the meadow was a mystery. She began to worry that she was hallucinating – a side-effect of her medication. She would have called Dr Kirby, only she didn't want to sound even more deranged than she already was. Less than a day she'd been here. What would he think if she called him up now and started raving about a rogue shadow on the meadow? He'd send for the men in white coats. She'd be back in hospital before sunset. No, she had to make a go of this. It was kind of Dr Kirby to lend her his cottage for a week, and sweet of him to have such faith in her. She was determined to repay him by getting through this stage of her treatment without fuss or complaint.

Estelle went back inside the cottage, relieved to be away from all that peculiar light and shadow. She examined herself in the hallway mirror. The usual round, pale face with its thin lips and big rodent eyes stared back at her. There was a touch of pink around her nostrils – a result of an earlier hayfever-induced sneezing fit – but otherwise she looked no madder than usual.

"I recommend that Estelle spends a week entirely on her own," Dr Kirby had said to Aunt Lucy, her guardian. "It's called exposure therapy and it's the next step in her treatment." Aunt Lucy had agreed, and so had Estelle. If she was ever to get over the trauma of being locked in an attic by her mad mother for weeks on end when she was fourteen, then she had to find the courage to face that kind of loneliness again. And what lonelier spot could there be north of the Sahara and south of the Arctic than this cottage in the middle of nowhere, with just the meadow, the creepy wood and those distant silos for company? Dr Kirby had stocked it up with enough food for the week, so there was no need for any shopping trips to the local village – no need, in fact, for any human contact whatsoever.

"If you're feeling desperate, just call," Dr Kirby had said – her phone, which fitted so snugly in her jacket pocket, was her tenuous link to the outside world – "but do try to get through this on your own, Estelle." She was determined to try.

Psychology textbooks littered the sofa in the cosy front room. Guiltily she shoved some of them aside and sat down. She had promised to use this time to catch up on her studies, but what she really wanted to catch up on right now was one of the daytime soaps she had become mildly addicted to while in hospital. She switched on the television and was soon immersed in the love lives of healthy, bronzed teens – they were her friends, sort of. If only they'd been there for her when she was in the attic.

After the soap, she watched the early evening news. Then she made herself a herbal tea – lemon grass – and sent a text to Aunt Lucy. No mention of light and shadows, just a cheery description of the cottage, supplemented by photos of the front room, kitchen and bedroom. Text message sent, and not yet hungry enough for food, she tried to settle to some work. But concentration was difficult. The quiet bothered her – it seeped into her bones like damp. She tried playing some music – Adele, Eminem, Rihanna – at background volume, but her mind kept wandering down avenues suggested by the lyrics. "Not Afraid" by Eminem took her back to darker times when she'd listened to it almost incessantly. In those hospital days, listening to that track, she'd dreamed of her old friend Sandor Watts, and hoped that he might, once again, come to her rescue.

He'd been her best friend once, but they'd gone their own ways. Sandor had joined the army; she'd got sick in the head. But she'd never forgotten him. He still held a place in her heart, and if she had to summarise in one word what she felt about Sandor Watts, it was trust. She trusted him. He was the one who'd saved her. The school and the social services had believed her mum when she told them that her daughter had gone abroad to live with her father. But Sandor hadn't. He broke into the house one night, smashed in the door to the attic, and got her out of there. He carried her in her wretchedness, in her drooling feeblemindedness, to his caravan.

He saved her life, but he couldn't save her mind. Sandor didn't know how to deal with her fragile, broken spirit. She would cry for hours, threaten suicide. At other times, she'd fall into hysterical, demonic laughing fits. She made a pass at him once, which he'd gently rebuffed, and which she'd a thousand times regretted. When she did finally try and kill herself, and was sectioned, she sensed Sandor's relief that she was no longer his responsibility. By the time she had her second breakdown last year, he was off fighting his own battles with the Taliban. She never expected to hear from him again. But just a month ago he'd written to her, out of the blue. It was a very short letter telling her he was home on leave, living in a small town called Edgebourne. He'd included a phone number.

She couldn't, could she?

No, Estelle. Dr Kirby would not approve. And the last thing Sandor needed was her back in his life. In his letter, he'd hinted at mental troubles of his own. He didn't know about her second breakdown – probably assumed she was now a fully functioning human being. If she started blabbing to him about freakish light and shadows, he'd soon wish he was back in Helmand.

Gradually, the macabre light faded from the window, and the unnatural shadow on the meadow was subsumed by the all-embracing dark. Not in the mood for cooking, Estelle helped herself to some cheese and crackers, then took a bath. She smothered the silence with a combination of her iPod and her own terrible singing. Finally, she climbed into bed. The sheets, she was gratified to note, were much softer than hospital bedding.

The following morning was overcast, yet warm. Estelle took her cup of coffee out into the tiny front garden and checked the meadow. The shadow continued to darken the far side, looking strangely normal, as if it had every right to be there. It seemed a bit larger this morning, and ever so slightly closer to the cottage. She knew she ought to go and check it out: solve the mystery, put her mind at ease – *just a different shade of grass, Estelle, you idiot!* – but for some reason she recoiled from the idea.

Instead, after breakfast, she donned her walking boots and followed the road east. At length, she found a footpath, which took her through some fields and alongside a stream. By now, the clouds had gone and the sun was shining. She found a pleasant grassy patch, where she lay down. But however much she tried to relax, her mind still buzzed and chattered with random, stupid thoughts. She tried reading the novel she'd brought. She'd found it on a shelf of mainly non-fiction books in the cottage – a copy of Mary Shelley's *Frankenstein*. But she found the old-fashioned writing style quite hard-going, and a book wasn't the same as having someone to talk to. Her nose tickled and her throat itched from hayfever. At least her ears were becoming attuned to the sounds of the country: birdsong, the lazy drone of midges, wind rustling through foliage. How had she missed those sounds yesterday?

A few hours later, as she was opening the front gate of the cottage, Estelle hesitated. How odd: here, there was no birdsong; no gentle lowing of cattle. Even the midges failed to disturb the dense silence. She realised that yesterday had been the same. It wasn't just the lack of city sounds that had bothered her: it was the lack of any sounds at all! Was everything dead around here? She didn't turn her head to check the shadow – she knew it would be there – but made straight for the cottage, closing the door quickly behind her.

She switched on the television – some trashy quiz show – and turned the volume up high. The sight of the textbooks on the sofa gave her a stab of guilt. The top one was called *Introducing Psychology*. The two "o"s in the second word became a pair of eyes that stared at her accusingly. After sweeping the books violently onto the floor, she stretched out on the sofa, placing a cushion under her head, and let the sounds and pictures from the television wash through her.

At six, when her soap-star friends were gone for the day, she yawned, climbed to her feet and went into the kitchen. She found herself a breadboard and a sharp knife and began peeling and chopping vegetables. Cooking would relax her, and the smells it created would eventually drum up an appetite.

The soup was soon bubbling away on the stove and its aroma stirred not exactly an appetite, but memories, at least, of a warm, cosy childhood when they were still a proper family, before her dad left and her mum went crazy. She stood there in a pleasant fog of reminiscence, and the little country kitchen, with its pine fittings and shelves filled with colourful crockery and earthenware pots, felt very homely and safe.

But then, for some reason, the wooden spoon in her hand stopped stirring. Had she felt something? Hesitantly, she continued to move the spoon through the thick, yellow-green liquid. The happy, homey feeling had gone. The soup was now the colour and texture of a slimy, stagnant pond. It reminded her of the pale, queasy late afternoon light she'd seen yesterday on the meadow. She was crazy, wasn't she? How could her mood, her vision, just change like that? There did seem to be an unusually yellow cast to the light. Could the bulb be faulty? Or was it her eyesight? She thought about calling Dr Kirby. A few words in his reassuring brogue would do the trick, then she'd be fine. Her heart was visibly palpitating beneath her shirt. She considered taking her meds, even though it wasn't yet time.

No, Estelle! No meds. No Dr Kirby.

She took a deep breath and wiped an itchy trickle of sweat from her forehead. "You can do this," she said out loud, and she forced herself to try some of the soup. Mmm! Not bad. Just plain old leek and potato, but not bad. A pinch of salt and a sprig of parsley and it would be perfect. At least her tastebuds weren't failing her!

A sound made her hand freeze in the act of reaching for the salt. It was like a breath. She spun around. The kitchen was hazy in the yellow light. Had there been a flicker of movement at the window? She turned back to the soup. Just pour in the salt, she told herself.

No! Check the window!

The air felt heavy around her feet, as if a thick flood of the soup had overflowed onto the floor. She dragged herself unwillingly across the room and peered out of the window. Nothing. Just the outline of a shivering hedge and the faint gleam of the lonely road twisting off into the distance. The sound must have been the pipes: perhaps the boiler coming on. She wasn't used to this cottage yet, or its noises. She took a few deep breaths and waited for the shaking to stop.

The slurping sounds she made while drinking the soup, and the clink of the spoon against the bowl, sounded abnormally loud. She scooped it into her mouth as fast as she could, barely tasting it, just wanting to finish so she could get out of the kitchen. When the bowl was empty, she scraped back her chair and carried bowl and spoon to the sink. Even though it was still early, her only desire was to go to bed.

The curtain in her room was too thin to shut out the

summer evening light, and that madness before, in the kitchen, had left her too wired for sleep. So she lay there, book open, her eyes taking in nothing, for maybe an hour, thinking about her mum and dad in the good old days, and Zac, her beloved King Charles Spaniel. Eventually, she must have nodded off, for she found herself in her local park, walking Zac and smiling at the little children on the swings. But then the busy park became an empty meadow, and a worn track led to a wood of tall trees. The light in the wood was sallow and unhealthy. It made her stomach churn. She called for her dog, who had disappeared from view. She wanted to leave, but she had to look for him. Then she realised that Zac was dead anyway, and she was lost. A sound drifted out of the trees, a forceful, whispering respiration, almost a sigh.

Her eyes flipped open. She was fully awake, and hot beneath the thick covers. The night was silent as a tomb, but the sound remained like a ghostly memory in her ears. Had she really heard it?

Moonlight glowed through the curtain and pooled on the bedspread – bloodless, waxen, ash grey, the colour of death.

What was that?!

Her fingers tightened on the damp sheets.

A slow exhalation of breath. It sounded close.

She squeezed her eyes shut. Her lips emitted a faint moan as she tried to press herself further down into the bed. "Go away!" she murmured into her pillow.

She waited, her body in a paralysed kind of flinch, unbreathing, mouth shaped like a cry for help. A minute went by like this – and as the period of silence lengthened, gradually her muscles started to relax. Her eyes opened a fraction and her fingers unclamped themselves from the sheet.

She had to get out of here.

Estelle turned very slowly in her bed. The moonlight looked normal again. No dark shapes were lurking in the corners of her room or silhouetted behind the curtain. She reached for her jacket and her phone. Her thumb was on Dr Kirby's number, about to press, when she hesitated. It was 2.14 in the morning. He lived in the city – two hours away. He would try and talk her into waiting it out till morning. Worse, she might be persuaded!

Then she thought of Sandor.

Edgebourne was less than an hour away.

His phone number was in the letter.

The letter was in her bag.

Hurriedly she rose, got dressed and ran downstairs to the front room. Scrabbling frantically in her bag, she found the letter and pressed the numbers carefully into her phone. It rang for a long time. She imagined him sprawled asleep in a cramped space, surrounded by a mess of clothing and dirty pots and pans – even though she knew he'd sold the caravan years ago. Still his phone rang. Perhaps he was out with his parents – or a girlfriend? Her heart sank at the thought. At last, to her huge relief, his tired voice answered.

"Sandor," she blurted. "It's me. Estelle."

"Hullo, Es," he croaked, and she pictured him rubbing his eyes, trying to wake himself up.

"Sandor, I'm sorry, I know it's late. I need your help." Her words came in a flood. She found herself rambling, telling him about the shadow and the noises before she'd even said where she was. Eventually, he interrupted, asking for the cottage's address. She gave him the name of the local village, Delhaven, and how to find the cottage from there. She didn't mention why she was there and he didn't ask. As she expected, he didn't ask anything, just told her to lock all the doors and windows, shut the curtains and wait for him. He'd be as quick as he could.

After he'd rung off, the silence crept up on her again, like a sinister cat. She tried to ignore it as she carried out a quick tour of the cottage, checking handles and locks, closing curtains. But when she curled up under a blanket on the sofa, the silence curled up with her. She would have relished the bark of a dog, the hoot of an owl, a chorus of crickets – anything that declared the normal functioning of nature out there in the big dark. But it seemed the only living thing for miles around was her.

Sandor, please be quick!

She remembered the quiet, dusty gloom of the attic that had been her prison cell for twelve long weeks, and how she'd got through the days by talking to herself, as if she were two people – one mature and brave, the other younger, more fearful. In these conversations, she tried to reassure herself that things would be OK – they'd survive.

"And we'll do it again, little one," she heard herself whisper. "Just keep believing it'll be OK, and it will be." But she wasn't as good at this as she'd been at fourteen – couldn't quite picture herself as anything other than one lonely and very scared person. And the silence, that big, horrible feline presence, kept muscling in on her attempts at conversation. The silence was amplifying things that weren't normally heard – things that shouldn't be heard, like the sounds of her own body. Soft thumps and gurgles of digestion and blood circulation were becoming gradually, horribly audible. It revolted her – she was nothing but a sack of frightened flesh and fluids.

Her internal symphony was smothered by a sudden sound: a loud sigh that erupted out of nowhere. It sent freezing nails of fear into her neck and back.

She pressed the cushion to her face.

What was that noise? Who or what caused it?

The minutes crawled by. Estelle didn't move a muscle. Faintly, the chorus for "Not Afraid" played through her stunned brain.

"It's going to be alright," she whispered eventually. "Don't be scared. Sandor will be here very soon, I promise."

And if he isn't? It was over an hour since she'd called him. He should have been here by now. Maybe he hadn't believed her. He'd witnessed her delusions before.

She should call the police. Dammit, why didn't she do that before? They were paid to respond to loonies.

Quickly, she withdrew the phone from her pocket and pressed out the three-digit number.

The female operator answered: "Emergency. Which service, please?"

"Police," croaked Estelle.

"I'm sorry?"

"Give me the police."

There was a longish wait, and a man's voice came on the line.

"Hello. Sergeant Wilson here. How can I be of service?"

"I –"

The phone went dead.

Frantically, Estelle redialled. Nothing.

The screen on her phone indicated "No Service".

Something had happened. The phone had been working fine, and then… nothing.

She was completely cut off.

Something groaned.

This time, Estelle screamed. Before her eyes closed, she thought she saw a shape silhouetted against the curtains, darker than the night, framed in the anaemic gleam of the moon. She lay there, frozen, waiting for what was bound to follow: the sounds of breakage and entry, the horror of the thing revealed, finally, dripping its evil on the rug, on her textbooks. Meanwhile, an insane, terrified voice bellowed curses at the room. It was some seconds before she realised that it was her own voice and she worried that she may have flipped again.

Almost immediately after that came the sound of gravel popping and the wall above the fireplace shone with the twin beams of a big car pulling up outside.

Estelle leapt from the sofa and ran to the door. She pulled Sandor's tall figure towards her, crying with relief as she embraced him.

"Es," he whispered into her hair. He smelled faintly of leather and engine oil.

"You were ages!" she cursed him. "What took you?"

She let him guide her to the kitchen. Sandor prowled the room, his big hands opening cupboards and unscrewing jars in the search for coffee. The years of army service had left their mark on him – in both obvious and subtle ways. His long, dark, shaggy locks had fallen victim to the military buzz cut. His eyes were darker than she remembered – haunted, perhaps, by battlefield memories, and his face seemed harder and more chiselled in its lines, as if engraved by sharper tools.

As he moved about the kitchen, he questioned her: "Any further noises?"

"I heard something just before you arrived," she said.

He broke off what he was doing and shifted to the window, parting the curtain slightly so he could see out. "Same kind of sound as before?"

"Sort of," she replied.

"How come you're here on your own?" he asked, still keeping watch at the window.

"Therapy!" she laughed.

He frowned at her. "You've got to be joking."

"Exposure therapy," she explained. "I had another breakdown last year. I've been in hospital. I've been getting better, but my psychotherapist decided I needed to spend some time alone, so he sent me here. This is his cottage."

"That's the maddest thing I ever heard," cried Sandor. "You had three months of solitary confinement and he reckoned the best way of treating you was to give you more of the same! He's crazier than you are!"

"I was doing well," she said a little defensively. "I wasn't clingy or anxious like before. I wasn't throwing myself at men," she added with a smile, hoping to convince him once again that her long-ago pass at him had merely been a symptom of her illness. "I wanted to do this. I wanted to prove to myself that I could do it."

"Fair enough," he grunted – Sandor knew all

about setting and passing personal challenges. "Still, I don't blame you for going nuts out here. It's a bit bloody... quiet!"

Estelle laughed again. But then she reconsidered his words and felt hurt by them. "I'm not nuts, Sandor. Well, maybe I am. But I didn't imagine those noises. Or that shadow."

"I know you didn't," he said, and he pulled a gun out of his pocket and placed it on the table. Clean-lined and functional with a gleaming black surface, the sight of it lying there next to the salt and pepper was a little shocking – but also gratifying. It was a mark of his faith in her.

The kettle began to whistle and Sandor poured himself a cup of strong black coffee. "Want some?" he offered.

She shook her head.

"I nearly drove off the road a couple of times on the way here," he muttered. "Haven't slept properly in a while... Tried calling you to let you know I was on my way, but your phone was dead."

"I know," she said. "When you didn't show, I called the police – it cut out before I could tell them where I was."

"Didn't trust me, eh?" smirked Sandor.

"I was scared, you idiot!"

He checked his own phone, and frowned. "That's strange. Now mine's not working either. Phone mast must be down." He took a slurp of his drink. "Ah well, we'll soon be out of this crazy place. How soon can you get your stuff together?"

"Give me five minutes," said Estelle.

She was rising to go when the air was ripped by a

bone-juddering howl. It came from the front of the cottage – rising then falling, like a yell of anger declining into anguish. She screamed.

Sandor became a blur of movement. Before she knew what was happening, he'd already picked up the gun and was rushing to the door. Without hesitating, he charged into the night.

Estelle ran as far as the entrance hall and was stopped short by a loud thump and a clatter of metal on gravel. She couldn't see Sandor through the half-open door, only the dull gleam of his gun where it had fallen on the path.

"Get the gun, Es!" she heard him cry. His voice was a breathless croak, as if he'd been punched hard in the gullet.

The gun was just a few metres from where she stood, but the thought of going out there and retrieving it terrified her. Whatever had Sandor would get her, too, and then they'd both be done for. Instead she ran to the kitchen, where the large chopping knife she'd used earlier still lay on the board. As she picked up the knife, her eyes were caught by a flash in the window: another pair of headlights was slowly approaching along the road that led past the cottage. With the knife in her hand, she ran back to the entrance hall. The front door was now closed.

"Sandor!" she cried.

She pushed open the letterbox and pressed her ear to it. She could hear his breath whistling.

"Don't… come… out… here."

"Sandor, please, what's going on?"

She wished she could see him – the tremor in his voice scared her almost more than anything. She wanted to open the door, but her hands had gone numb.

There was a bump, like a heavy sack falling to the ground. The front door shuddered.

She heard him give another wheezing, throaty cry. "Don't... come... out... here. Stay... inside." His voice was going up and down, no longer controlled. "Es!" he shouted, and then, in a whisper that was worse than any scream: "It's... it's... horrible."

TWO

Estelle cowered in the hallway. Sandor was just inches from her. They were separated only by the thickness of a wooden door. Yet his whispered words were like messages from the far side of a dark, fathomless abyss. Whatever was out there, attacking him – killing him! – was beyond her imagining, and the dread of confronting it had immobilised her as surely as if a physical weight had pinned her to the spot.

"Sandor," she whimpered, not even sure he could hear, "I'm so sorry."

From outside there came a deep guttural groan, followed by a squelching sound, and a horrid image entered her mind of the creature feeding on her friend.

Sandor – her best mate since childhood. She couldn't bear it!

She had to do something. Hadn't he come to rescue her from her attic prison all those years ago when she'd given up hope that anyone ever would? Tonight, he'd done the same again, rushing out to confront the thing at the door with no thought to his own safety.

She had to be like him. She had to find some of that inner steel.

But what if he was already dead?

Well, even so – even if it was too late – she had to try. She owed it to him.

Estelle wiped the sweat from the palm of her right hand and took a firmer grip of the knife. She placed her left hand on the iron knob that raised the latch on the door. Her breath came out like a sob as she watched the latch slowly rise.

No, I can't do this!

Do it, Estelle! Push open the door.

She began to push, but something was obstructing it.

Sandor's body?

She swallowed, then leaned her full weight against the door. There was a soft thump and it swung fully open.

She struggled to make sense of the scene before her, or the parts at least that were illuminated by light from the hallway. It was not what she had expected.

Opposite her, on the path, was Sandor. He was crouching, looking down at another figure lying in a hunched posture at his feet. Slowly Sandor raised his head and looked at her. She saw the blackness spreading through his eyes and the slow drawing back of his lips into a grotesque smile. The sight sent needles of ice into her blood. It looked like Sandor, but it was not Sandor!

She backed away, but the figure was immediately on its feet, whipping its arm at her. The arm seemed to bend as it moved, as if made of something more flexible than bone. She felt a staggering blow to her elbow and the knife flew out of her hand. It arced glintingly through the air to land in some thick bushes to her right, lost from view and out of reach. The thing's arm flailed again and suddenly she was on her knees, cheek pressed against the gravel of the path, reeling from a detonation of pain in the back of her head. Flashing circles radiated outwards from her stupefied consciousness like earthquake aftershocks.

And there, lying in the dead centre of the circles, like a dart in a bullseye, was Sandor's gun.

Something rough brushed against her back, then tightened around her throat.

The gun was so close, she could almost reach out and…

She felt a powerful upward yank that almost cut off her air supply. The thing lifted her up so that her feet rose clear of the ground. She hung helpless, suspended like a rag doll. A string of drool dribbled from her lower lip. She could sense the creature examining her. She almost gagged as its breath wafted across her face like a warm gust from a putrid swamp.

What she had seen just now, when the thing had raised its head and looked at her, had scared and sickened her half to death. Its face was an obscene perversion of her friend's, his strong, handsome features distorted to a freakish degree. At first it had looked just like Sandor, but then the smile had expanded into a gigantic grinning rictus of long, sharp, gumless teeth. His dark irises had swollen into huge, shiny black hemispheres entirely obscuring the whites of his eyes. As his eyes and mouth had grown, the skin of his cheeks had cracked to form black fissures. The creature had killed her dear friend, copied his beauty and made it hideous. Now it would surely do the same to her.

Her throat was tight in the thing's grip and every

breath was a struggle. She couldn't move her head, but with her eyes, she sought out the crumpled figure lying on the path – the real Sandor. She would spend her remaining seconds thinking of him. To her surprise, she noticed that Sandor was moving, trying sluggishly to raise himself up on his arms. He wasn't dead! There was still hope. More surprising still, she saw something dangling from her fingers. The gun! She must have grabbed it as the creature had hauled her up.

Enfeebled by the blow to her head and the difficulty she was having breathing, it took Estelle a second or two to seat the gun properly in her hand and locate the trigger. But before she could raise it to shoot, she felt herself being lifted higher, hot breath and needle-like points pressing down on the skin of her neck. Pain flared as the teeth began to penetrate. She felt the warm wetness of her blood on her skin and the rough lick of the creature's tongue.

She could see the thing's legs below her. Her gun hand was swaying drunkenly. If she could only steady herself for long enough to aim. Realising she couldn't and she'd run out of time, she closed her eyes and squeezed hard on the trigger.

The bang came sooner and louder than she had anticipated.

It was almost exceeded in volume by the screeching howl that followed. The pressure on her throat suddenly ceased and she fell hard onto the gravel. She coughed and noisily gulped down air. When she looked up, seconds later, the gate was open, the creature was gone and it was Sandor – the original version – smiling down at her.

He was in a bad way. The smile was doing a poor job

of masking his evident pain. The red mark on his throat would soon grow into a nasty bruise, but the real damage was to his left leg. She saw the dark hole in his thigh, the blood stain on his trousers and more blood on the path where he had been lying.

She raised herself up onto her knees and embraced him. After the stench of that monster, Sandor's sweat was like perfume, his breath in her ear a lullaby. She clung to him for a while without moving, just relishing the fact that he was still alive.

"Nice shooting," he whispered.

"Has it really gone?"

"I think so. I watched it stagger away in the direction of that wood. What the hell do you think it was?"

"Nothing human… or animal," she murmured. "It looked like – at first, it looked like –"

"I know," he interrupted, as if not wanting her to complete the sentence.

The pain in the back of her neck and throat was subsiding, but her head still felt very tender and sore. She must have groaned a little, because Sandor suddenly broke away and looked at her. "Are you OK?"

"I'm fine," she reassured him. "But you're not."

Estelle stood up. An attack of giddiness made her stagger a little, but she tried to rebalance herself before he noticed. "We have to get you to a hospital right now," she said, eyeing the gash in his leg. "You've lost a lot of blood."

"Not sure I can drive," grimaced Sandor, letting the smile-mask slip for the first time.

"I'll drive," said Estelle. Aunt Lucy had given her a few lessons last year. She was sure she'd be able to remember.

Sandor tried to get up, and failed. With Estelle's help, he made it the second time. She supported him as they hobbled down the path, through the gate and over to Sandor's silver SUV.

As she helped him into the passenger seat, she noticed, further up the road, heading towards Delhaven village, the receding tail lights of a car. She wondered briefly why she hadn't seen it pass by the cottage – and why the driver hadn't stopped to help them. Then her attention was drawn to a dent in the SUV's left-side front fender. It looked quite serious – touching or close-to-touching the wheel. She wondered if it had been inflicted by that passing car, and prayed the damage wouldn't prevent them from driving.

"Where'd you get that?" she asked Sandor, as she climbed into the driver's seat.

"Happened on the way over here," Sandor grunted, handing her the key. "It's fine, don't worry." Breathing a small sigh of relief, she inserted the key into the slot and twisted.

Nothing.

The engine didn't even turn over.

She tried again, and again nothing. Sandor leaned across her and tried turning the key himself.

Estelle was starting to feel panicky again. First the phones, now this. What was going on?

Sandor was already out of the car and limping over to the bonnet. He opened it, and then stared. His shocked face scared her even more.

"Battery's gone," he said.

"Gone?" she cried, getting out of the car. "How could

it be gone?"

"Someone's stolen it. The cables that were attached to the terminals have all been cut."

She stared at the mess of severed cables and the empty space where the battery should have been.

"But who –?" she began. Then she remembered. "I saw a car heading towards Delhaven just now. And before I came out of the cottage, I saw a pair of headlights in the kitchen window. Whoever was in that car must have done this while we were fighting off that thing." She clutched the back of her head, which was throbbing again. "Oh, Sandor! What's happening? Is someone trying to stop us leaving here?"

Before he could reply, they both heard a sound. It was like a distant sighing howl, and it came from across the meadow.

"Come on," said Sandor. "Let's get back indoors."

Estelle found a first aid kit in one of the kitchen cupboards. Sandor examined the bottles and then told her what to do. After boiling some water in the kettle, she poured it into a shallow glass salad bowl and then added a few splashes from a bottle labelled "Povidone-iodine". She poured about half of this solution into another, smaller bowl, into which she placed a pair of tweezers. Then, with great care, she helped Sandor take off his trousers. All around the bite mark on his leg, the flesh was becoming swollen and shiny red with infection. Bits of fabric had embedded themselves in the wound.

When the iodine-water mixture had cooled, she used the sterilised tweezers to remove the pieces of cloth. Then she dipped cotton swabs into the water and used these to soak the wound. Sandor's breath jerked inwards as she applied the first of these. After ten minutes or so, when the skin around the wound had softened, Sandor instructed her to use the tweezers to peel open the edges of the wound.

She glanced up at him, concerned.

"We have to get rid of all the infection," he told her through gritted teeth. "I don't want to think about what kind of germs that thing might have been carrying."

"Can I give you some sort of anaesthetic?"

"I've checked," he said. "There's nothing in the box. I'll be OK. Just do it."

Trying hard to keep her hands steady, Estelle used the tweezers to grasp one of the tender flaps of flesh at the edge of the wound, then slowly peeled it back. Whitish-yellow pus dribbled out.

Her stomach heaved at the sight. Sandor emitted a strangled groan. The muscles in his leg tensed.

She wiped away the pus with a cotton swab, before continuing her way around the wound's edge, repeating the process.

"Deeper," he hissed. So she probed the deeper parts of the wound to see if any pus was hidden there. His body had become rigid, but she could tell he was observing everything she was doing.

A sudden loud whine from outside the window made her jump. The tweezers jerked in her hand, making Sandor gasp in pain.

She stared at the window, terrified that she might see the creature's face out there.

"It's the wind," Sandor reassured her in a strained

whisper.

Nervously, Estelle returned her attention to the wound. When she was sure no more pus remained, she soaked it with more of the iodine-water mixture.

"You'd make a fine nurse, Es," Sandor murmured after a while. "Not to mention a pretty sharp shooter. We could use you in the army."

She was pleased to see the pain in his eyes had lessened.

"I'd fail all the psychological tests," she smiled.

"You've been pretty solid in the head department so far."

"I'm trying to hold it together," she said. Actually, she was surprisingly calm. She put it down to Sandor's presence.

"What was that thing out there, do you think?" he wondered.

"I don't know. But it seemed sort of... flexible, like nothing human or animal." She frowned. "While I was watching, its face changed completely from normal to... horrible. And it had these very strong, whippy arms."

"Yeah, I noticed," he grinned, feeling the bruise on his throat. Then his face became serious. "Something happened on my way over here," he said. "I think it may have something to do with the thing that attacked us. I was about halfway between the village and the cottage, where the road winds through part of Delhaven Wood. I nodded off for a second, and woke up with a bump, front wheel in a ditch, the fender parked in a tree. I got out of the car to inspect the damage. I was groggy, I admit, and probably not thinking too clearly. But I swear that as I stood there, looking at the front of my car, this truly crazy thing happened. There was a strange sort of yellow light in the forest – not moonlight, something else. It was coming from a source much closer to the ground, casting these big shadows everywhere. Anyway, as I was standing there, my own shadow seemed to... move." He looked sharply at Estelle, as if willing her to laugh – but she was too intrigued.

"Why didn't you tell me this before?"

"Hey, you were freaked out enough as it was." He shrugged. "It's mad, I know. But I swear it's true. The ground sort of swelled up, as if something was coming out from underneath it, or as if the shadow itself was forming into something – something solid."

"What did you do?"

Sandor smiled ruefully. "What do you think I did? Stick around to take pictures? I dived back into my car, reversed out of the ditch and drove full pelt out of there."

"So you think that thing that attacked us might have been your shadow? Is that it?" She couldn't help frowning in disbelief. This was the maddest thing she'd ever heard of.

Sandor looked annoyed. "It was you who started all this stuff about shadows," he reminded her.

"Sure, I saw an odd shadow on the meadow, but it never got up to introduce itself..." She sighed. "Look, after what happened tonight, I'm prepared to believe almost anything – aliens, genetically modified superbeings, you name it – but homicidal shadows, Sandor! Think about it. A shadow is just an absence of light. It's not a thing, it's the very opposite."

"That's enough with the swabs," said Sandor stiffly.

"Now dry it with some of that sterile gauze."

She could see she'd irritated him, so she said no more, simply followed his instructions. When the wound was dry, she smeared antibiotic ointment on some more sterile gauze and placed this inside the wound, before dressing and bandaging it.

By now, the cold, grey light of dawn was illuminating the kitchen. Estelle had never been more glad to see it. She couldn't be sure they were any safer, but somehow the madness they had faced seemed to recede in daylight. She yawned, suddenly feeling immensely tired.

"Get yourself to bed," Sandor ordered her.

"But we should go," she mumbled. "Start walking to Delhaven."

"There's no rush," he said. "Get some kip. I'll wake you up in a few hours."

"What about you?"

"I spotted a comfy-looking sofa in the front room, which'll do me fine," he said, hoisting himself to his feet.

The bedside clock read 10.54 when Estelle awoke to an eyeful of bright sunlight – she'd forgotten to close the bedroom curtains – and the smell of frying bacon. She'd taken some pain killers before going to bed and her head was feeling a lot better for them. The bacon made her nostalgic for those brief weeks she'd spent living with Sandor in his caravan. Aunt Lucy was a vegetarian, and these days her breakfasts never got more exciting than muesli or toast with her aunt's home-made rhubarb jam. As for hospital food, everything, including the bacon, tasted as if it had been boiled for five hours.

She checked her phone in the faint hope that normal service had been restored. It remained resolutely dead. After dressing, she went downstairs. Sandor was standing by the stove, cooking. His gun nestled in a shoulder holster, which he wore over his faded red T-shirt. His left hand was resting on a knobbly old walking stick while his right tossed the fried eggs.

"Hello!" he said cheerfully. "Found this stick in the hallway. I'm sure your good friend the doctor wouldn't mind if I borrowed it."

"Suits you," she said admiringly. "You look like a true war vet... By the way, that smells delicious."

Sandor handed her a plate of bacon, eggs and toast, then set his own down on the table opposite her. She noticed he was moving with more ease than earlier.

"Feeling better, then?" she enquired.

"I feel great! You?"

"Better than I was a few hours ago, certainly," she said between mouthfuls. "Better for knowing we're heading back to civilisation."

"Yeah, I was going to talk to you about that," said Sandor. "I'm just going to slow you down, Es. Why don't you go on ahead and wait for me at the village? There's sure to be a pub or a café where I can meet you."

"No way," she replied emphatically. "We're walking every step of the way together, side by side."

At just after twelve o'clock, they stepped out of the cottage into a warm, hazy blue day. Sandor paused at the front gate and stared for several seconds. The brooding shadow now seemed to hang over almost half of the meadow. "You were right about that shadow," he frowned. "The sun is right above us, and there are no clouds." He shook his head. "Come on. Let's get the hell out of here."

Delhaven village was three kilometres away, on the other side of the forest. The first part of the journey took them through fields of crops that barely moved in the still air. The world was silent, but for the squeak of their shoes and the scrape of Sandor's stick on the road. It was like walking through a picture. "I don't like this quiet," remarked Sandor at one point. "It's like being on patrol when you're expecting an ambush at any moment."

They had been walking for about fifteen minutes, and had managed perhaps a kilometre, when Sandor suddenly broke into loud song.

Oh, the Grand Old Duke of York,
He had ten thousand men,
He marched them up to the top of the hill,
And he marched them down again!

His voice was even worse than hers. It was raucous, and somehow managed to miss just about every single note. Cacophonous and rowdy, his singing nevertheless did a very necessary thing: it shattered the awful density of silence that had accumulated around them, and cheered them both up immensely. She joined in for the rest of the song, and for several more rounds, singing louder and more stridently than she'd ever dared to before, confident that however dreadful she sounded, Sandor was worse.

By the time the duke had been marched up and down the hill for a fourth time, Sandor and Estelle had reached the part of the road that wound through the forest.

"That's where I crashed my car," said Sandor, pointing to a tree by the side of the road, with a deep scar in its bark.

The cooler air prickled the bare skin of her arms with goosebumps. Estelle found herself instinctively moving faster, leaving Sandor trailing in her wake.

"I'm sorry," she said, slowing down again.

She had noticed that Sandor was now wincing at every step. "You go on ahead if you want," he assured her. "I'll be fine. Buy me a pint at the Dead Dog, or whatever the local here is called."

She smiled tightly, appreciating his effort to cheer her up. "No, I'm staying with you," she vowed – but she couldn't help wishing he'd speed up just a little, at least while they were in the forest. Peering ahead, she tried to discern sunlight at the end of the long tunnel of trees, but the road wound and twisted incessantly, and she could never see more than fifty metres in front.

All around them was that strange light again. It reminded her of her first sight of the meadow two days ago. It shone greasily on the bark and leaves and on Sandor's face, coating everything with a silvery, waxen residue. She glimpsed black pockets of deepest shadow between the trees, and the odd bright flash that almost hurt her eyes. Dark shapes, real or imaginary, seemed to dart into the corners of her vision, then vanish before she could see what they were. She noticed her own shadow trailing faintly to her right, and was reminded of Sandor's ridiculous story.

"The shadows," he murmured, as if reading her thoughts. "They were similar to this last night."

He pointed leftwards where a silvery-yellow gleam was faintly visible through the trees. "That's not sunlight," he said. "The sun is much higher. That's something else."

"Please, can we go just a bit quicker," said Estelle, hating it that her panic was starting to show.

"Don't think I can, Es," panted Sandor. "But you go on, love. Seriously. Here." He took the gun from his belt and presented it to her.

It was a tempting offer. If she ran, she could be out of this awful forest and in the village in twenty minutes. Then hopefully she could persuade someone there to drive back up the road and pick up Sandor.

"I'll be back here with wheels as soon as I can," she said, taking the gun. "You sure you'll be OK?"

"Just dandy. I'll whack anything that moves with this stick!"

"If you tried that, you'd fall over."

"Nonsense," he said, lifting his walking stick and swiping the air with it.

"Sandor!"

He lost his balance, then regained it, then lost it again, toppling heavily onto his wound.

He groaned.

"Oh, you idiot!" cried Estelle, and she ran to help him up.

Then she stopped. Sandor was lying still, but his shadow had definitely just moved.

Now, come on, Estelle. That didn't happen. You must have seen your own shadow and thought it was his.

Hesitantly, she returned to him and bent to help him up. This time she almost fell over in shock. His shadow wasn't just moving, the entire portion of road on which it lay was rising. The tarmac surface bulged upwards by at least a metre, as if transformed into something soft and pulpy, like clay.

Sandor was as transfixed as she. They both stared as the rolling, undulating tarmac began to form itself into the rough shape of a human being. Estelle recognised the crude contours of a head, torso, arms and legs. Then more details materialised on the seething black surface: a nose, ears, eyes, the first hints of hair and clothing. All of it was still the uniformly dark colour of the road, but as they watched in horrified fascination, colours began to emerge: flesh tones for the face and arms, pale red for the T-shirt, blue for the jeans. The thing began to move. With disturbing agility, it rose up out of the trench-shaped pothole it had created. The creature had Sandor's face, his physique, even his walking stick, but it moved with a writhing suppleness that reminded Estelle of a snake. Its torso twisted and its limbs seemed to warp as if boneless. Sickeningly, the thing turned its head 360 degrees, while its body remained facing them. When its eyes lit on Sandor, they widened enormously and were flooded with black. The mouth grew monstrously big, revealing long razor teeth. With frightening speed, it snaked towards him.

Sandor, anticipating this, was already backing away. With Estelle's help, he regained his feet, and they started to make their escape along the road as fast as his hobbled state would allow. But before they had ventured three paces, Sandor pulled up sharply.

Estelle, who'd been focusing on the creature to their rear, turned to face ahead. The sight that greeted her very nearly stopped her heart.

The thing standing in the road before them wore a face she'd seen a thousand times – she encountered it every time she looked in the mirror.

"Estelle." The word, perfectly pronounced, dropped from the doppelgänger's mouth. It spoke her name like a wish, almost like a prayer.

Estelle opened her mouth to scream, and the girl-thing seemed to copy her, except that its mouth went on growing and growing, like a distortion in a nauseating hall of mirrors. Its shiny beetle-black eyes gazed hungrily back at her. Saliva dripped from needle-like teeth, as fresh soil from the forest floor began to show between the cracks in its cheeks.

The creature lunged towards Estelle. Before it could grab her, she raised the gun and fired. It staggered backwards, groaning, its clownish grin turning into an even uglier scowl – Estelle could see that the bullet had passed clean through its abdomen. A cascade of loose soil poured from the bullet hole. She fired three more shots into her double, sending it spinning into the ditch.

"Come on then, you slimeball!" she heard Sandor cry. "I'm ready for you."

Estelle turned to see him leaning against a tree, jabbing his stick at his own double, just about managing to keep it at bay.

"Get out of here, Es!" shouted Sandor.

"I'm not leaving you!" she cried, and, hoisting up a heavy fallen branch from the side of the road, she swung it hard into the back of the creature's head.

The branch partly embedded itself in the thing's

cranium. It fell backwards, unbalanced by the weight.

"Come on," she cried, tugging Sandor's arm. But he shrugged her away and began limping into the forest.

"Where are you going?"

"We'll be safer off the road," he gasped. "More places to hide."

But these things came from the wood, didn't they? This is where they live!

"No, Sandor, I don't want to go in there!"

He didn't hesitate or slow down. Meanwhile, in the ditch to her left, her double was starting to recover. Two of the bullet holes had already closed up and disappeared. To her right, Sandor's look-alike was struggling to free itself from the branch.

She began to run along the road, but images of Sandor dying alone in the forest kept flashing through her mind. Unable to stomach the thought of leaving him, she veered off the road, leaped the ditch and plunged into the wood after her friend.

The trees grew so thickly in this part, it was hard to see more than a few metres ahead. There was also less sunlight. Instead, everything gleamed with a sickly yellow glow.

"Sandor! Where are you?"

"Estelle!" came a faint call from somewhere off to her right.

She began running in that direction. Twigs caught in her hair and clothes and scratched at her face. She stumbled over roots. There was no clear path, just a haphazard zigzag between the trees – sometimes she was forced left, sometimes right, until she was no longer sure where she was going, or how to get back to the road.

She heard the snap of some twigs to her rear, and stopped, heart hammering in her chest.

"Sandor?"

A scraping sound.

A footstep? It sounded close. Any second now, one of those things would be on her again. Maybe both of them. She had to hide, but where?

In front of her was an enormous old oak with sturdy branches close to the ground. It seemed to invite her to climb it. Estelle had climbed a lot of trees in her younger days. She placed her hands on the lowest branch and heaved herself up onto it. From there it was easy enough to reach hold of the next branch up. Soon she was sitting astride a smaller branch, her back resting against the trunk, a good five or six metres from the ground.

From this vantage she could see a fair distance across the forest. She could see where the road wound through the trees, and beyond to the village of Delhaven, nestling in the valley below. It seemed not too far. If she ran – really ran... But she might get lost again down on the ground. And those things moved very fast...

Then her eye fell on something else. In a clearing some fifty metres away to her left, she glimpsed a structure of some kind: a white-walled building behind a wire fence. She could get there easily: just a short sprint. Even if it was an abandoned ruin, it could offer her a place to hide out. But her deepest hope was that there would be people there – normal, sane, friendly people, with phones and computers...

"Estelle!" came Sandor's voice. She assumed it was his voice, and was about to call back, but then she stopped herself.

These things can talk, remember?

She peered through the branches to her left, and there stood her friend, by a tree stump, about halfway between herself and the white building. He was scanning the forest, searching for her. He looked and moved just like Sandor, so he probably was Sandor. Yet there did seem to be something different about him – she couldn't exactly say what. Perhaps it was nothing – just her fear making her imagine things. Of course it was Sandor.

Wasn't it?

If only she could be sure…

Three

Estelle peered at the figure below her more closely. Suddenly she knew what was wrong about him. That "thing" last night had bitten into his left leg, but this Sandor was holding his walking stick in his right hand. That was it. With these evil living shadows they had somehow created, it seemed everything was reversed, as with a mirror. She locked this revelation safely away in her memory, thinking it might be useful: until they got angry and started showing their horrid teeth and eyes, they looked pretty much exactly like their originals – except for this mirror effect.

Evil living shadows.

The idea of it was just too bizarre. When Sandor had suggested this last night, she had dismissed it as fantasy. If she could only find him again, the first thing she would do would be to apologise. But the real Sandor was out there somewhere in the forest, probably getting further away, while she was stuck here, trapped by his shadow!

After standing by the tree stump for a moment, the shadow-Sandor moved closer to Estelle's tree. Watching its swift, gliding movement, any doubts she may still have had about its identity were immediately dispelled. No human could have moved like that, let alone one with an injured leg. Earlier she had compared its movement to a snake, but that was wrong: a snake used more muscular effort, was more earthbound. This creature moved in a light, almost ghostly way – just like a shadow, in fact.

The thing hesitated beneath her branch. If it looked up now, it would see her, and that would be it: no escape possible. She shrank back as far as she could against the trunk, trying to blend into the tree, wishing she'd put on something other than her Soul Cal pink T-shirt, and praying that the twig her foot was currently lodged against didn't suddenly snap.

Finally, after a long, sweat-glazed, tense-muscled moment, she watched the thing move on, sliding swiftly into the forest and out of sight. Estelle breathed out slowly, and began climbing down. The thing had headed in the approximate direction of the road and the village, so she went the other way, towards the white building she had glimpsed from her treetop lookout.

In less than fifty paces she had entered the clearing where the building stood. It was certainly no ruin – in fact, it looked as though it had only been erected yesterday. The painted walls gleamed and the fresh gravel that surrounded it sparkled. The single-storey, flat-roofed structure had a plain, functional design: all clean, straight lines and right angles. The uniform surface of the walls was broken only occasionally by a tiny, dark-tinted window. The building was small – not much bigger than a large house in terms of the area it covered. And yet whatever was going on within those bare, anonymous walls was deemed important or secret enough to surround them with a high fence of sharpened steel posts, topped by what looked like electrified razor wire. The slowly swivelling security cameras mounted on the roof added to the atmosphere the place exuded... of quiet paranoia.

Estelle began circling the fence, hoping the building wasn't so determinedly secretive that it didn't even have an entrance. She had got halfway round when she found one, a heavy steel gate, almost hidden behind a large sign saying:

GOVERNMENT PROPERTY
AUTHORISED PERSONNEL ONLY

Next to the gate stood a very ugly, stunted concrete structure about three metres high and two metres wide. From a small black slit near the top came a harsh, low voice.

"Halt! Don't come any closer. Identify yourself."

She stopped. "I'm Estelle Grant," she said in a quavering voice. "I've been staying in a cottage nearby. My friend and I have been attacked." It felt good to be saying these things to another human being, even if she couldn't see his face. She didn't mention that the creatures that had attacked them were their own shadows, worrying that if she said anything that crazy, they might not let her in. "I've lost my friend," she added. "And – and I'm pretty scared. Can you... Do you think I could come in?"

When no reply came, Estelle took a hesitant step closer.

"Halt!!" screeched the voice. "Did I tell you you could move?"

"No, but..."

"Throw your gun to the ground."

Estelle slowly removed Sandor's gun from her pocket and threw it away from her.

"Now go and stand in the middle of the road, just in front of the gate."

Bemused, Estelle did as she was told.

Suddenly, a dazzling bright light shone down from above. The light sizzled on her skin and turned the patch of tarmac she was standing on into a blazing square of white. The briefest glance aloft would, she was sure, render her permanently blind. Then, equally abruptly, the light was switched off.

From within the concrete bunker, she heard the crackle of a radio and the voice of the guard: "We have an unauthorised visitor here, Professor, requesting permission to enter. A young female. Says her name is Estelle Grant. We've scanned her and she's F.A.B."

"OK, send her in," came a deeper voice, laden with static.

A light flashed and the gate slowly slid open.

"Proceed to the reception area," said the guard.

Estelle didn't need a second invitation and she dashed through the gate. A glass door swished open automatically as she approached the establishment, admitting her into a small room as plain and severe as the building's exterior. Not a single picture enlivened the room's blank white walls. There was a smell of new carpets, and the only furniture – a desk and four chairs – looked like they'd arrived straight from the factory that morning.

Into the room strode a tall man. He wore a long white coat over a dark suit.

"Hello, Miss Grant. I assume it's a Miss?"

"Er, yes."

His face was smooth, his smile tight, his eyes cold and of a blue so pale as to be practically colourless. They seemed made for looking through microscopes, rather than at people.

"I'm Professor Robert Mitchell. Pleased to meet you."

He gave her hand a brief, cool squeeze, as if testing a piece of fruit for ripeness.

"You've caught us rather on the hop, Miss Grant," said the professor in an impatient tone. "We're just setting up. The rest of the staff won't be starting until next week, and that includes the receptionist." He eyed the empty desk ruefully. "I can't offer you a coffee, as I've absolutely no idea how the blasted machine works."

He looked at her as though their caffeine-free state was her fault. Bizarrely, she felt the need to apologise.

"I'm sorry, Professor. I realise you're busy, but I just need to make a phone call to the police, and to my aunt, and maybe to my therapist, and –"

"I'm afraid that won't be possible, Miss Grant."

Estelle stared at him disbelievingly. "Don't tell me your phones aren't working either."

"We have a working phone line. I just can't allow you to use it."

His expression was as cold, as indifferent, as moon rock.

Was this man, this government scientist or whatever he was, really denying her the right to…?

"Perhaps you don't fully understand, Professor," she said, trying to maintain a reasonable tone and keep the tremor out of her voice. "This is an emergency. My friend and I were very nearly –"

"No, it is you who do not understand, Miss Grant!" he snapped with a sudden flash of annoyance. "You and your friend have created a mess. An unholy mess, which we're now going to have to try and clear up. What's your friend's name?"

"Sandor. Sandor Watts. He's been wounded in the leg."

"Badly?'

"I'm afraid so."

"Well we may just have to accept that he's a goner," Mitchell muttered almost to himself. Then he turned briskly and pushed open the swing door he had just come through. Leaning his long, lanky body into the corridor, he shouted: "Sergeant Farrell!"

Mitchell turned back to Estelle. "You were attacked, too, I take it?"

"That's right. I –"

"How many of them?"

"Er, two."

"One of each?"

"Sorry? What?"

He leaned into the corridor again. "Sergeant Farrell! I want you this minute!"

Returning his attention to Estelle, he enquired: "You each generated a single shadow, right?"

Estelle was struggling to keep up. So he knew about the shadows! "Y–yes. I mean no. Sandor… *generated* another one last night."

A squat, muscular man in a black uniform dashed into the room. "Yes, Professor?"

"Ah, there you are, Sergeant. I'm afraid we have three

more shadows on the loose, courtesy of this young lady and her boyfriend."

"He's not my boyfriend!"

Mitchell ignored her. "Two male, one female. The boyfriend's also still at large. Answers to the name of Sandor Watts. Got a leg injury." He turned to Estelle. "Which leg was it, by the way?"

"Um... the left leg."

'Got that, Farrell? The F.A.B. is injured in his *left* leg. How many men do you have available?"

"Currently six out on patrol, Professor, plus four here on base. I'll alert the patrol unit right away."

"Good man. I want updates every half hour. Understood? And don't take any unnecessary risks."

After Farrell had marched off, Mitchell turned back to Estelle: "Take a seat." He pointed to one of the chairs.

"Not until you tell me what's going on," insisted Estelle, who couldn't help feeling riled by his bossy, ungracious manner. "What is this place?" she demanded. "What kind of people are you?"

Mitchell simply held out the chair for her. "Sit!" he ordered.

Sighing, she sat down.

The professor cleared his throat and paced around a little, before turning to her. "I can't say I like this situation any more than you do, Miss Grant," he said tersely. "It's just bad luck, you see – terribly, terribly bad luck, that you and your boyfriend stumbled upon something you shouldn't have."

"He's not my boyfriend."

"Delhaven Forest is publicly owned woodland,"

Mitchell blithely continued. "So it's a tricky place to fence off, and the problem, until very recently, was so small, and the wood so remote and unvisited..."

"Why can't you let me use your phone?"

"Of course we're going to fence it off now. We'll stop any other members of the public wandering in here. But that doesn't solve the problem of you, now does it, Miss Grant? And nor does it solve the problem of Mr Watts. I can only hope that by the end of today, we'll have dealt with the mess you two have made. Until such time, I'm afraid you will have to remain as our guest here."

Estelle stood up, outraged. "You're keeping me prisoner?"

"It's hardly prison, is it?" Mitchell said, looking indignant. "I may not be able to offer you coffee. But we have a decent canteen, not to mention brand-new shower and washroom facilities. You'll be very comfortable, I assure you."

"You can't do this!" she exclaimed. "I have rights. As a citizen..."

"Indeed you do," the professor agreed. "And when you leave us, you will be able to tell the whole story, which I shall, of course, deny."

She slumped back into her chair. "Who are you? What is this place?"

Mitchell took the chair opposite her, clasped his hands together over his knees and looked her in the eyes. "We're a government facility conducting research into the health risks of radiation from domestic electrical devices."

"Really!" snorted Estelle in disbelief. "If that were true, you wouldn't be ringed with all this security and have armed units patrolling the forest."

"That's the official story, Miss Grant. And that's the story I shall be telling the media, should you decide, when all this is over, to go public with any of what I'm about to say." He sighed. "However, there is little point in concealing the truth from you, as you know too much already – in fact, it sounds as though you've had first-hand experience of the real subject of our research."

"The shadows?"

The professor nodded gravely. "We've known about all this for a while. We've known, for example, that the light in this wood is... different. And that those who walk in it don't cast a shadow exactly, but something else – something that I have described as a photographic negative of their own souls: a sort of 'soul shadow', if you will. If you remain stationary in this light for even a short period, the soul shadows can acquire physical substance."

"I don't think that's the right name for them, Professor," interjected Estelle. "The things that attacked us had copied our bodies, not our souls. They didn't seem to have any... humanity in them."

Mitchell didn't look pleased with the interruption. "We're still studying them," he said curtly. "We don't know what their intelligence is yet, nor their level of *humanity*, as you call it – and I hardly think it's fair to make such judgements on the basis of your extremely brief acquaintance with the phenomena."

Estelle suppressed her irritation at Mitchell's patronising attitude. She was intrigued by his mention of the light in the wood – so that was the sickly yellow glow she'd seen. "What exactly is this light that makes the shadows come alive?" she asked.

"We call it, for want of a better term, zeta radiation," replied the professor. "For the first few years, our research was carried out in a few temporary cabins here on this site – that is, until we were lucky enough to obtain funding to build a permanent facility. All was going very well until about a month ago, during the final stages of construction, when something happened – we're still trying to figure out what. You see, the zeta radiation has always been weak, and the soul shadows never had much strength or durability. They were objects of scientific curiosity, but they weren't dangerous. For some reason, the radiation intensified and, as you've discovered, the soul shadows have become deadly. There were a few... accidents... involving some of the construction crew – which is why we erected that fence and guardhouse outside, and recruited the services of a private security firm."

"It's a bit of a coincidence though, isn't it Professor?" said Estelle sceptically. "You build your facility, and immediately the radiation gets stronger. The two have to be connected."

"Maybe so," he said gruffly. "Although I don't see how."

"Do you even know the cause of the radiation?"

Mitchell stood up. "I've said enough," he said abruptly, and walked to the door. "I hope you understand why we have to keep you here for now, and why we can't let you make any phone calls. This is top secret work we're engaged in. If it gets out, it could cause a general panic, which the government is understandably keen to avoid. Once we have eliminated all the soul shadows in this forest, and any evidence they ever existed, then you'll be free to go. And if you speak to the press after that, it'll simply be your word against ours. We'll have what the politicians like to call 'deniability', and that, as any politician will tell you, is a very useful thing to have."

"And if I swear to you now that I won't say a word?"

Mitchell shook his head. His expression had hardened again. "Not good enough, I'm afraid, Miss Grant. I'd like to say I trust you, but it simply wouldn't be true. Now, I must get back to work." He led her through the set of swing doors into the corridor and pointed. "Down there you'll find the canteen. Mrs Hollins will be able to sort you out with some lunch should you want some. There's also a recreation area with a television and some magazines. I will see you in a little while." Before Estelle could say another word, Mitchell had marched off in the other direction and disappeared around a corner.

Estelle wandered down the corridor, past the non-working coffee machine, and into the canteen. The counter was brand new, like everything else, and entirely devoid of food. The single window had bars on it. She crossed the room and tried opening it, but it wouldn't budge. While she was standing there, she saw a black-uniformed guard walk by along the gravel path next to the fence. He was accompanied by a large German Shepherd on a short lead.

"Can I help you?" came a low female voice to her rear.

Estelle turned. A mature woman in a blue uniform was leaning out of a doorway behind the counter. She was holding a large cardboard box.

"You must be Mrs Hollins?" said Estelle.

The woman looked at Estelle warily. "Did the professor

send you?"

Estelle nodded. "He said I could get something to eat here."

"I've got nothing fresh," said the woman frostily. "Won't have anything fresh in till Monday. You can help yourself to crisps and nuts. Or we've some tinned fruit salad here in the back."

With that, she bustled away.

An hour later, Estelle was sitting on a sofa in the rec room, restlessly flicking through a magazine called *New Scientist*. The remains of her meal – a bag of crisps and a tin of pineapple rings – sat on the low table in front of her. There had been no further word from Professor Mitchell; no updates, so far as she knew, on Sandor, or the killing of the soul shadows.

In her enforced idleness and her agitated frame of mind she concocted an elaborate conspiracy theory. She convinced herself that the professor hadn't really been surprised by her arrival at the Facility this morning, but that he had known about her and Sandor all along. It had been him in that mysterious car last night. He had driven past the cottage and witnessed the attack by the soul shadow. Fearing that they might survive and then blab to the press, he had stolen Sandor's car battery. And straight after leaving her, he had radioed Sergeant Farrell and told him to forget about finding Sandor – he must kill him. Those ice-blue eyes of his told her all she needed to know about Professor Robert Mitchell. For him, the research project was everything, and if people had to die for it to continue, so be it.

By this stage in her thought processes, Estelle was absolutely certain that she would never get out of the Facility alive, and it was only a case of when, and how, she would die. Would it be a mafia-type killing? Would they give her a pair of cement shoes and then throw her into a lake so she could "sleep with the fishes"? Or would she be sprayed with gold paint like that girl in the James Bond film? Knowing Mitchell, she'd probably be fried from the inside by some super-high dose of radiation. Yes, that would be more his style.

And who would miss her? Not her mother, that was for sure! Aunt Lucy would no doubt shed a few tears. Some of her old schoolfriends might be sad for a day or two. But, truth be told, she hadn't really made much of a mark on the world in her eighteen years. She rather doubted there would be a big fuss when the news crept out that she'd disappeared. No Facebook tribute pages for her. She liked to imagine that if things had been different – if her life hadn't been so disrupted by the divorce and her mum's madness and her own breakdowns – she might have forged deeper relationships with people. Sandor was the one exception. He'd vanished from her life for four years, but the bond between them was so deep, it hardly mattered. He was alive – she was sure of it! – and he would survive this nightmare, and she'd continue to exist in some way after this, in his memories.

A knock at the door interrupted these contemplations. She jumped. *Here it comes*, she thought miserably.

But it didn't come. Instead, the face that appeared at the door was a friendly, cheerful, smiling face. It was a man in his thirties; unshaven cheeks, receding hairline. He bounded in.

"Well, hullo there! You must be Estelle. I'm Derek Atkins."

She gave him her hand, which he shook enthusiastically. He was short and not exactly thin, and his amiable exuberence was an immediate tonic for her spirits. If she was going to be killed by anyone, Derek would be her preferred choice of assassin.

"I'm one of the researchers here," Derek told her. "We're just a skeleton team at the moment. The rest of them are arriving next week." His eyebrows rose and fell excitedly as he spoke, as if he was telling her the most astounding news. "I'm like a kid in a toyshop right now, playing around with all this brand-new state-of-the-art kit." He looked at her. "Hey, do you fancy a tour?"

Estelle couldn't help smiling. He had big, eager puppy-dog eyes. Not at all like an assassin in fact – more like a geeky scientist with a secret romantic side, who'd never managed to find himself a girlfriend. She immediately spied an opportunity.

"I'd love it," she grinned.

For the next half an hour, Estelle allowed herself to be shown around the "kit" in the lab. The room was filled with metal boxes, trailing wires, monitors, pipes, metal stands and clamps gripping bottles of different-coloured fluids. She was bombarded with terms like "beamlines", "electron storage rings", "synchrotrons", "vacuum chambers", "crystallography" and "diffractometry", and she kept smiling and nodding and praying that he wouldn't ask her if she had any questions.

The inevitable query eventually arrived. "So, Estelle, is there anything you'd like to ask?"

Those puppy-dog eyes again! He was so hoping to have found a fellow geek. Of course the only question on her lips was: "Can you help me get out of here, please?" – but she sensed the need to play the game a bit longer, really win his trust, before landing him with that one. Then she remembered a curious term the guard had used just after showering her with bright light. "What does F.A.B. mean, Derek?"

"F.A.B.? That would be flesh-and-blood. It's just a short-hand term we're using here for people."

"As opposed to?"

"As opposed to… er… other things," he prevaricated.

"You mean soul shadows?"

Derek's eyebrows shot up a couple of inches. "So you know about them then, do you?"

"Oh yes!" She pulled down her T-shirt at the back to show him the teeth-mark scars.

He gazed at her bare neck for perhaps a tad longer than was strictly necessary. The tip of his tongue licked his top lip. "Heck, that looks like a mature one…" he murmured. "You were lucky to survive."

"So is this where you research them then?" Estelle asked, turning to face him again. She didn't mind tantalising him a little, if it helped her in her goal.

Derek, still slightly mesmerised by what he'd just seen, finally blinked and refocused. "Soul shadows? Oh no! Not here. This is where we do all the official stuff: testing domestic appliances, that sort of thing. It's real research, don't get me wrong, and it's what we'd show the press or the public, should they ever get wind of this place. But soul shadows research goes on down there." He pointed to the floor. "Hey! Why don't I show you?"

Estelle decided to test out the man's sense of loyalty. "Are you sure Professor Mitchell wouldn't mind?"

Derek tapped his nose. "Who's going to tell him, hey? Hey?" He waggled his eyebrows at her.

This subversive streak she'd uncovered gave her cause for hope. If he was prepared to go behind the professor's back on this sort of thing, then what else? But then a scary thought occurred to her. "Are there… soul shadows down there?" she asked.

"It's all perfectly safe, I promise," Derek winked.

She followed him back out into the corridor, where he summoned a lift. After a short descent, the doors opened onto a long, dimly lit subterranean corridor. The walls were bare concrete, lined with pipes.

"This place is bigger than I imagined," Estelle murmured.

Derek laughed. "You haven't seen the half of it!"

After a short hike along the corridor, they reached a large metal door set into the right-hand wall. The door didn't fill her with confidence. It was painted with yellow and black diagonal stripes and reinforced with bands of steel. A boldly lettered sign said:

DANGER!

Category A Personnel Only.

Derek slid a card through the entry scanner, and the door slowly hissed open. Estelle found herself looking into a large, high-ceilinged chamber at least as big in area as the entire ground floor of the Facility. The chamber was in virtual darkness except for a central section, which was separated from the rest of the room by a ring of closely spaced vertical steel bars that ran from floor to ceiling. This caged area was flooded with the same sallow light she had seen in the forest. It contained three male figures, one of whom looked exactly like Derek.

"Are they…" she began, hesitating at the entrance – but she knew the answer.

The soul shadows had all turned to face Derek and herself. So far, they looked like normal human beings, just curious.

"They most certainly are," said Derek, strolling in. "Impressive, huh? The world's first captive soul shadows." He gestured to the silvery yellow light filtering down from the ceiling. "That was the hard part. Reproducing the zeta radiation. It had to be perfect, or they'd sicken and die. It has a frequency of exactly 405 terahertz – that's just about on the threshold between infrared and natural light, which is probably why you feel nauseous just looking at it. We then had to chromatically distort it in all sorts of clever ways."

Derek went over to a large metal cabinet on the right-hand side of the chamber, opened the door and pulled out a tray of raw, pink flesh.

"Relax. It's animal, not human!" he laughed when he spotted Estelle's worried face.

"The zeta radiation has no effect on matter of any kind," Derek continued, as he donned a pair of blue rubber gloves. "But when it passes through certain types of organic material, like human tissue for instance, it changes. The substance of whatever it hits next – a floor for instance – is chemically transmuted into an almost perfect replica of the person the radiation just passed through. *Et voilà*. A soul shadow. Amazing when you think about it!"

He picked up the tray and approached the caged area. "Now watch this!" Estelle edged further into the room, scared yet curious to see what was about to happen. As Derek came closer, the eyes and mouths of the soul shadows distorted and grew bigger. They howled and rushed in their horribly quick, lithe way to the edge of the cage and stuck their grimy hands through the gaps between the bars, groping towards Derek and his tray.

"I'm sorry to say they're smelling me, rather than the meat," said Derek. "That's what's exciting them. Human flesh sustains these beasts. It prolongs their lives."

Particularly aroused was "Shadow-Derek", who was jumping up and down and screaming and sticking his arm out as far as the bars would allow. Estelle noted once again the mirror effect – Shadow-Derek's hair was parted on the right – the opposite side to his original.

The real Derek turned back to Estelle, grinning and raising his eyebrows. "See this one! He loves me, doesn't he?! They have this weird attachment to their originals, their progenitors, as we call them. It's not exactly love in the sense that we mean it. If I let him out now, he'd eat me. Still, it's rather sweet, don't you think?" As Derek tossed the first piece of meat through the bars, one of them – Shadow-Derek – caught it, and the other two immediately leapt on him and began trying to tear it from his grasp. One of them stuck his fingers into Shadow-Derek's chest, and something that looked like porridgy sawdust began leaking from his mouth. It seemed for a moment as though they'd actually kill him. Then real Derek threw several more pieces in, and the other two skittered across the floor to seize their own food.

"It's not their preferred diet," beamed Derek. "But we can't give them that – for obvious reasons!"

Estelle was rapidly going off her new friend. His enthusiastic manner was quite endearing when focused on things like synchrotrons and Geiger counters, but now, in the context of these caged monsters, it seemed more like sadism. But she tried, despite her fear and revulsion, to appear as if she was enjoying herself. If she was ever going to persuade him to help her escape, she had to maintain the illusion of camaraderie between them.

"Now watch,' said Derek, and he moved to a control panel opposite the cage. He pressed a few switches, and the pallid yellow zeta radiation in the caged area was suddenly split by shafts of brilliant white light. The soul shadows roared with pain as the shafts struck them. Their black eyes widened and their enlarged mouths vomited up the meat they had just eaten. As the beams began to rove like lights on a dance floor, they tried to escape them by moving around, but the lights always caught them. One of them hurled himself against the bars in a desperate effort to escape. Another rolled himself up in a tight little ball, offering as little of himself as possible to the burning beams.

Derek was laughing. "It can't kill them," he guffawed. "They're too mature for that. But it sure burns!"

"Stop it!" yelled Estelle. She couldn't help herself.

"Switch off the lights."

Derek turned to her, frowning. "Hey, are you actually feeling sorry for the brutes? They'd eat you, you know. They're complete monsters."

"I – I just don't… like seeing anything in pain. That's all." To her relief, Derek switched off the beams. The creatures moaned pitifully and rubbed their blistering skin.

Estelle had seen enough. Now she just wanted to get out. There was no way she could ever convincingly befriend a man like this, so she decided to risk all with a plea from the heart. "Derek, would you do me a favour? Would you help me get out of here? I know the professor doesn't trust me, but I promise I'd never tell anyone about this set-up of yours. I don't actually care what you're doing here. I really don't. But I'm scared. I miss my aunt. I miss my life. I just – I just want to go home."

The tears at the end weren't entirely faked.

"Hey, Estelle, sweetheart, don't cry, love." Before she knew it, Derek was standing next to her, arm lightly enclosing her shoulder. "Of course I'll get you out of here. If I'd known you wanted to leave, I'd have offered to earlier. You only had to ask."

This was a big surprise, and a happy one. "But – but won't the professor be angry with you?" she sniffed.

"Hey, leave all that side of things to me, sweetheart. Don't you worry about a thing. Derek'll sort you out."

She didn't much care for the arm around the shoulder or the "sweetheart" business, but it was a hell of a lot better than watching him fry soul shadows for kicks. She could scarcely believe she was about to get out – out of the

Facility, out of the forest!

She allowed him to lead her back through the door of the chamber and further along the corridor to a small underground carpark. There were spaces for about thirty cars, but only two were parked there, plus a formidable-looking armoured personnel carrier. "This way, love," said Derek, guiding her to one of the cars, a small white Fiat.

Estelle still felt wretchedly nervous. This was all too good to be true. It had to be a trap. She kept glancing over her shoulder, as she climbed into the car, and as Derek reversed slowly out of the parking space, expecting to see the professor arriving, flanked by a row of soldiers all pointing their weapons at her. But no one arrived to stop them as they proceeded up a long, dimly illuminated ramp that ended in a steel gate embedded within rock. Derek opened his window and slid his ID card through another scanner, and the gate began to rise. A slowly widening strip of daylight flashed into her eyes, and that was when she allowed herself the first delicious sense of hope that all of this might soon be over. When the gate was fully open, Derek accelerated out of the tunnel and onto a narrow black road twisting through the forest. Glancing behind her, Estelle saw the tunnel entrance sliding shut to become, to all appearances, a natural grassy bank. The secret entrance had taken them a good thirty metres beyond the Facility's perimeter fence, which was now swiftly receding in their rearview mirror.

"Where can I take you, my lady?" he smiled, waggling his eyebrows at her. "To the village? To Edgebourne? What, pray tell me, is your desired destination?"

There was no way this man had ever had a girlfriend!

But she would happily bear his company – and his eyebrows – for the next hour if it meant getting a ride to Edgebourne.

The trees flashed by on either side. He was driving extremely fast. Soon they would see fields!

"You mean you'd really take me all the way to –"

She never managed to finish the sentence.

There was a violent bang on the car roof. The roof actually bulged inwards by about ten centimetres. Estelle's mouth went dry. Her fingernails dug into the seat cover. Tyres screamed as Derek went into a swerve and nearly crashed into a tree, before bringing the car to a skidding standstill at an angle in the centre of the road.

"What – what was that?" croaked Estelle.

Derek didn't say anything. He peered upwards at the huge bulge in the roof, and she saw his adam's apple bobbing in his throat. His face was tight with fear.

She knew as well as he did that there was something still up there. They could hear its groaning, wheezing breath.

Derek, his eyes still fixed on the bulge above his head, seemed to have turned to stone, except for his hands, which were madly trembling.

"G – get out of here!" Estelle screamed.

This snapped him out of it. His foot slammed down on the accelerator, and the car screeched away. As they raced along the road, filthy fingers with long, yellow nails suddenly appeared at the top of the windscreen, and then a face – a smiling horror of piranha teeth and black, pitiless eyes.

Derek began to scream. The car, still flying along at top

speed, began to slalom crazily as his hands went into a frenzy. Estelle saw he was trying to shake the thing off, but it was clinging on with ease – the usual physics of motion and momentum didn't seem to apply to these creatures born of shadows.

"No!" cried Estelle, as she saw the front of the car rising up. Suddenly they were off the road and flying up a bank. She grabbed the wheel, trying to pull it back the other way, but it was too late. There came a neck-jarring, metal-crunching whump as they collided with a tree. She flew forward, knocking her head with a hard smack against the windscreen.

Pain bloomed in her temples like a monstrous black flower. She lay there dazed, but did not lose consciousness. She wished fervently she would – wanted so much to slip away from this terrifying reality into nothingness. But all the time she lay there, feeling the warm wetness trickling down into her eyes, she was aware also of the breathing that grating, squeezebox breath – of the creature still close by. Slowly, achingly, she raised her head. She dreaded seeing it there, squatting like a demon on the concertina'd bonnet. But when she actually looked, it was nowhere in sight. Derek was moaning with pain, moving sluggishly. The steering wheel seemed too low down. In the collision, it must have collapsed onto his legs, trapping them.

Where was the creature? The loudness of that awful respiration told her it was only centimetres away – just outside the car. But where? Next to Derek's door, perhaps?

No! Next to your door, Estelle!

The dark shape rose up silently beside her, like smoke. Its black eyes glistened, its nostrils quivered with the smell of her. Only the window glass shielded her from those claw-like hands, those teeth. And what a meagre shield it suddenly seemed! She watched, helpless, as the soul shadow drew back its pale hands and then battered them against the glass. The bang was loud, like a balloon-burst in her ears. She screamed. The car shook. But the window held.

That incessant tortured breathing was driving her insane. The in-breath was like a scarcely human metallic growl; the out-breath like a quiet scream. Again it threw its hands against the window. The car rocked, and this time spider cracks spread through the glass. The demonic smile widened in triumph. Estelle shrank back, trying to squeeze herself between the front seats and into the rear of the car. Derek was moving more urgently now, frantically trying to free his legs from the steering wheel. Estelle cast around for some kind of weapon, but there was nothing – not even a pen.

She heard the shattering, and felt the rain of splintered glass on her arm and leg. Again she screamed, as the hands with their horn-like fingernails groped at her T-shirt. She tried to push it away, but it grabbed her wrist, and hauled her closer to the window. Her cheek was now jammed in the angle between the door frame and the roof. In the distant background she could here a rising tumult of engine sounds, clashing gears and squealing tyres. Her left arm and shoulder were out of the car, being stretched painfully. The creature's breathing had reached a hysterical pitch. She could picture its jaws poised over her flesh, preparing to bite.

SLAM!

Estelle felt an overwhelming force propelling her across the car, into Derek, who cried out in shock and pain. Something huge had cast its shadow over her side of the car. She shivered, nursing her stretched and bruised arm, trying to work out what had just happened. Then she heard more clashing gears and the roar of an engine. An eight-wheeled armoured personnel carrier, like the one she'd seen earlier in the underground car park, was reversing away from the bank where Derek's crashed car was perched, back down onto the road. The soul shadow was still there, leaning in through her window, but its eyes no longer gleamed and its mouth was slack and immobile. Black mud-like matter was seeping out from its nostrils and between its lips. She reached over and pushed it away. It slid lifelessly to the road. She saw now that its body had been completely flattened by the impact of the crash.

So dazed was she by all of this that she was now convinced she was dreaming, especially when she saw Sandor looking down at her from the turret of the APC.

"Sandor?"

"Hello, Es!"

It wasn't a dream – it was real! Sandor had come to her rescue again!

But he looked grim.

"Get out of there, Es, and climb in," he said urgently. "Quick as you can now. We can't hang around. There are soul shadows further up this road and they're closing in fast. The patrol that found me bolted after we were attacked. I managed to rescue one young corporal, but he's seriously injured. Needs medical treatment A.S.A.P. He tells me there's some sort of facility up the road, is that right?"

Estelle glanced across at Derek. He looked back at her with frightened eyes as he struggled again to lift the steering wheel that was pressing down on his thighs. She tried to help him, but the whole steering column had collapsed and couldn't be shifted by hand.

"Don't leave me here," he pleaded.

Estelle turned back to Sandor. "The driver of this car is stuck, Sandor. The steering wheel, it's jammed against his legs."

Sandor lifted himself flinchingly out of his turret and hopped on his good leg onto the road. After limping his way around the car, he leaned in through the driver's window and tried wrenching the steering column upwards, but to no avail.

"We've got a hydraulic cutter in the APC," said Sandor. "But it'll take time. The shadows'll be here any minute, and I reckon young Hynson will die from loss of blood if we don't get him to a surgeon in, like, ten minutes."

"But he was helping me to escape," Estelle pleaded. "We can't just leave him here."

In the silence that followed, they heard a whisper in the trees up ahead. Estelle hoped it was only the wind.

FOUR

Sandor limped back to the APC, beckoning Estelle to follow him. He glanced briefly at Derek, then leaned close and whispered to her: "I can't see what choice we have, Es. There are about six of those things heading our way, and they're strong and unbelievably quick, like nothing I've ever seen! If we stay here and try to fight them off, we'll probably all be killed, your driver included. Our best bet is to drive on to the Facility, get young Hynson to a doctor. Then I'll gather up some reinforcements and come back here to try and rescue your friend."

"We can't go to the Facility, Sandor!" Estelle cried. "That's where I've just escaped from! The senior man there, Mitchell, tried to imprison me. He was scared that if he let me go, I'd spill the beans about the soul shadows."

"Imprisonment is better than death, in my book!" said Sandor.

"It might be death back there, too! You should have seen the way he looked at me. I wasn't a person to him – I was a problem to be dealt with. I swear he looked like he wanted to kill me!"

Sandor stared at her, shocked.

"Who do you think knocked out the phone mast?" she persisted. "Who do you think stole your car battery? We're not going to get out alive if we go back there!... Now, what sort of weapons have you got?"

Sandor bit his lip and frowned. "A couple of GPMGs, some combat shotguns... But Es, this is crazy..."

She grabbed his arm. "We've got to try, Sandor." Nodding towards Derek, she added: "For his sake as well as ours. Now just show me what I'm supposed to do."

He gritted his teeth, and she could see he'd made up his mind – she just hoped it was to agree with her. "Get in there," he ordered, gesturing to the open hatch in the APC's roof. "Bring me two machine guns and a shotgun, plus some ammunition."

Relieved, Estelle clambered up the vehicle's side and swung herself down into the interior. On a low metal bench lay Corporal Hynson, a fair-haired boy, no older than her, with a big gash in his right side. He was moaning feverishly to himself, scarcely conscious. Someone had tried to staunch the wound using a bandage and a belt as a tourniquet, but a dark red pool had already started spreading onto the bench. As she cast around for weapons, he must have become aware of her presence because he began crying out to her, calling her "Julie".

"It's OK," Estelle soothed, wishing she knew his first name. "You're going to be fine." Her eyes alighted on a rack of guns at the far end, and some belts and boxes of bullets. She grabbed two heavy black machine guns and passed them up through the hatch. Sandor was waiting there to grab them. Then she passed him as much of the ammunition as she could carry, and what she assumed was a shotgun, though it looked more like a very long pistol with a double barrel.

"Thanks... for... for coming back, Julie," Hynson gasped. She gave him a tight smile and started up the ladder. Halfway up, she hesitated and went back to him, bent down and kissed his cheek. "I'm so proud of you!" she said. Then she remounted the ladder and stepped onto the small gunner's platform so that her upper body was out of the hatch. Sandor had loaded one of the machine guns for her and placed it on its tripod, pointing into the forest, so all she had to do was take aim and pull the trigger.

"Place the stock firmly against your shoulder," he advised. "Good... Now, when you see them, aim for their bodies, and fire in short bursts. You'll be surprised how little pressure you need to place on the trigger. There's a bit of a kick, but you'll get used to it."

She watched him hop down and pass the shotgun through the window to Derek, murmuring instructions to him, which she couldn't hear. Then Sandor went and laid himself on his stomach a few metres in front of the APC, and placed his eye to the sight of his own GPMG.

The trees ahead rippled in the breeze, and Estelle flinched, half expecting to see something horrifying tear through their branches. Again, she became aware of the unearthly silence of the forest – not a bird or insect to be heard, only the faint moaning of Corporal Hynson below. The primitive whimpering sound he was making reminded her of a dying animal. *Basically, we're just like animals, she reflected, except that animals aren't so vain or stupid that they think they can fight this thing – they got the hell out.* Was she crazy to have persuaded Sandor to make a stand?

A sudden howling drowned out these thoughts. Her heart jumped painfully at the sound, which seemed to come from all around them. Sweat poured off her, making her hands slippery on the gun.

"Enemy approaching at 11 o'clock," said Sandor.

What was he talking about? They were coming now!

Then she understood what he meant and adjusted the angle of her muzzle by a few degrees, towards the left-hand side of the road.

She squeezed her hands into fists to try to stop the shaking, then blinked away the sweat from her eyes. When she reopened them, it was in time to catch movement from two different directions: one from where Sandor had predicted, and another, moving rapidly towards them from about 2 o'clock.

The things, when they emerged, looked at first like ordinary, black-uniformed soldiers breaking out of the trees – so much so that she hesitated. But then one of them seemed to elongate towards them, its legs stretching like rubber, and suddenly it was close enough for her to see the glint of its sharp teeth.

Flames burst from Sandor's gun, piercing the forest silence with a rat-tat-tat-tat. The soul shadow fell back, daylight apparent through the numerous holes in its shirt. The other one, meanwhile, was almost upon Derek. Estelle squeezed her trigger before aiming properly. Her ears and shoulder were battered by a series of what felt like metallic hammers as her bullets cracked harmlessly through the trees. Feeling a little dazed and bruised, she peered once more through her gunsight to see more soul shadows coming down the road. The forest was now echoing with the staccato of Sandor's gun. A deafening blast from the car announced Derek's entry into the firefight – and only just in time, for a soul shadow had got as far as his car door before staggering back, a huge hole in its stomach.

Placing the butt more firmly against her shoulder and taking careful aim at one of four soul shadows now converging on them, Estelle pulled the trigger. This time she was ready for the juddering noise and violence of the gun, and as she saw the creature fall to pieces in front of her, a semi-hysterical jubilation overtook her. She screamed – it seemed to help! – as she lined up another one in her sights, and blasted it to a similar state of disintegration.

After that, Estelle seemed to move into a different plane of consciousness, no longer thinking or worrying; no longer aware of anything except the next target in her sights, and the quiet thrill of seeing it torn to shreds in the fire unleashed by her finger. She felt calm, like she'd had a double dose of Prozac, yet brutally efficient; she knew exactly what to do next.

She must have dispatched a dozen of the things before something nagging at her brain finally broke through her trance-like euphoria. The soul shadows, she realised, weren't dying – or at least they weren't staying dead. Their wounds were closing up, and they were dragging themselves to their feet and lumbering back into attack. Some seemed to have reverted, at least partially, to their pre-shadow state, their damaged appendages now resembling tree roots or compacted grass or soil. At the same time, she noticed that her ammunition belt was rapidly diminishing in length. Sandor had placed a second belt next to her, but she didn't have a clue how to reload, and even if she did, there would be no time to do so before one of the monsters was upon her.

Again Derek's shotgun discharged. This time his car windscreen exploded and the steering wheel burst upwards through it. The door swung open and Derek, having used the gun to free himself, gracelessly scrambled out and staggered away back up the road towards the Facility. For a plump, short-legged man, he moved with surprising speed.

There's gratitude for you, thought Estelle. We stay here to save his life, and now he runs away, leaving us at their mercy. But before she could suggest to Sandor that they might think about making a tactical retreat of their own, there came a sudden, menacing growl to her left. Estelle glanced up and was stunned to find herself looking, at close range, into the empty black eyes of a soul shadow.

Evading Sandor's fire, it must have clambered onto the APC's roof and was now grinning hungrily at her. She tried to raise her weapon, but its long arms snaked towards her, hands like fanged jaws snapping tightly shut around her wrists, imprisoning them. Hard yellow nails dug into her flesh. The thing's mouth grew cavernous, as if it meant to take her entire head inside it.

"Sandor!" she croaked, but last time she had looked he was surrounded, and she doubted he was even aware that she was in danger.

Then an explosion ripped the air above her. She felt herself flying backwards as globules of something hot and sticky splashed her. She landed with a painful jolt on tarmac. Wiping her eyes, she saw she was lying on the road between the APC and the wreckage of Derek's car. Above her, on the APC's roof, was her attacker, now not much more than a pair of tottering, stumbling legs – its entire upper half having exploded.

A soldier carrying a long tube-like weapon appeared above her and began helping her to her feet.

"Looks like I got here in the nick of time," he beamed. "I was part of the patrol that originally found Sandor. You must be Estelle, right?"

She nodded. He was a bright-eyed, cheerful, curly-haired boy, who seemed barely old enough to shave – but she admired his coolness, given the circumstances.

"Hey, Connor," yelled Sandor from behind her. "Stop flirting and get over here with that thing."

Connor dashed over, raised the weapon to his shoulder and fired, blowing up one of the nearer soul shadows. Estelle picked up her own gun, which had fallen to the road next to her. She smiled as Connor gave her a little wave. The soul shadows were now in a severely depleted state. Scarcely resembling humans any more, they staggered along like pieces of the forest come to life. Looking at them, she began to believe that she, Sandor, Connor and Hynson might – just might – get out of this...

But the belief swiftly died with the emergence, just then, of a new, healthy soul shadow, out of the trees to her right, just metres from Connor, yet out of his sight line.

"Connor!" she screamed. But she was too late. A long arm whipped out and grabbed him by the throat. The thing's neck telescoped outwards, bringing its head to within a centimetre of Connor's. It took a giant bite out of the young soldier's handsome face as if munching on an apple.

Connor screamed. He whirled around, and fired his gun blindly. The rocket-propelled warhead blasted a huge hole straight through the body of his assailant and continued its trajectory into the APC behind it. For the second time in as many minutes, Estelle was sent soaring through the air on a shockwave of heat. She landed on the grassy bank in time to witness the APC go up in a huge fireball.

"No!" cried Sandor. "No! No! No! No! No!"

Already, three soul shadows had converged on the stricken Connor. Hearing his agonised cries, Estelle ran to pick up her weapon and then fired it at the creatures surrounding him. Connor's cries abruptly ceased, and Estelle realised, with sickening awareness, that it was she who had finished him off.

She couldn't believe the charming, fresh-faced lad who'd arrived out of nowhere to save her, was now dead. And poor Hynson, too. What a waste of young lives!

Meanwhile, Sandor seemed to have gone completely unhinged. He had picked up his now empty weapon and was swinging it wildly at the soul shadows while screaming terrifying curses at them like some axe-wielding Viking warrior. These damaged versions were less mobile than their healthy counterparts, and most were sent reeling on impact. Yet even Estelle could see that Sandor's strategy was doomed. No sooner were they knocked down than the things got up again. At some stage, he would tire and one of them would get him. She examined her own weapon and noted that she too was out of bullets.

"Come on, Sandor!" she called. "We have to get out

of here!"

"Not until I've killed every last one of these yellow-blooded scuzzbags!"

"You're not killing them, you stupid...!" Then she sighed. "Oh, hell!" She hefted her weapon and launched herself into the fray, and soon both of them were standing in the middle of the road, swinging their guns like baseball bats as the six or seven remaining creatures attempted to close in on them.

"I'm sorry, Sandor!" Estelle gasped. "I should never have dragged you into this."

"No regrets!" puffed Sandor. "Except for young Hynson. I promised him he'd see his sister again."

"Julie?"

"Yeah. I shouldn't be so broken up about it, only a similar thing happened to me in Afghanistan." He swung his gun, despatching another shrub-like shadow. "A friend of mine – a close friend – I watched him die. I shouldn't keep making promises I can't honour... Hey, how did you know she was called Julie?"

"You didn't break your promise, Sandor... He saw his sister, or thought he did..."

She felt the burn of unexpected tears – why was she crying? She knew why. For her own messed-up life, and the emptiness at its heart. But if Hynson could have his final wish, why couldn't she?

"Will you make me one last promise?" she heard herself say.

"No, I'm retired."

"Promise, if we get out of this, you won't run away from me again."

He stopped and stared at her.

"Sandor! Watch out!" She swung at one of the beasts, which had got to within centimetres of him.

He returned to the fight without giving her a reply.

Estelle was tiring. Pulses of excruciating pain were running through her limbs with every movement. She would have appreciated something from Sandor, now they were nearing the end. She didn't expect the big L word or anything – that would hardly be his style – but something about not leaving her again would have been nice, and then she could die believing he meant it.

Her wrists and neck ached. The gun felt as heavy as a ship's anchor. She didn't want to fight any more. The thought of dying, though, without knowing – without even being sure that she meant anything to him – was heartbreaking. She had to make him tell her. What did pride matter now?

"Sandor, I have to ask you something –"

A screech of brakes, and then a loud female voice screaming: "Get in! Get in!"

Estelle turned to see a black Range Rover halted at the side of the road, next to the charred wreckage of the APC. The woman at the wheel was calling to them. Estelle dropped her gun and staggered over to the car, opened the rear door and collapsed into it. Sandor climbed in after. A vaguely human-shaped column of pine needles followed him and reached inside the car. Sandor slammed the door shut, and the creature's severed forearm disintegrated in a shower of dry brown needles. The car roared away.

For some moments, Estelle simply lay sprawled on the soft, shiny, tan-coloured seating, trying to get her breath back and her mind into some kind of order. The woman was talking to them, but she could scarcely hear her over the gunfire and explosions still resounding in her ears. Gradually, though, the realisation arose within her, gaining momentum like a joyful musical crescendo, that they were alive – they were getting out! Treetops sped past the window, offering flickering glimpses of a deep blue, late afternoon sky. The branches began to thin out, and soon there was nothing but sky. The forest was behind them! She reached for Sandor's hand and felt it grasp hers. The warmth and strength in that grip revitalised her like some sort of healing drug.

The car decelerated and drew to a halt. She saw the driver open her window and a black-uniformed soldier lean in. A horrid chill settled over Estelle's heart as she remembered Professor Mitchell telling her of his plans to place a security cordon around the forest. This wasn't over. It would never be over. And they would never get out – so long as the professor wished to protect his precious secret. Questioning would soon reveal what they knew – it was too late to warn Sandor or their rescuer to pretend ignorance.

But surprisingly there were no questions. The woman showed a card to the soldier. He glanced at it, and to Estelle's relief and amazement, he waved them on. They drove for a few more minutes, and then slowed and turned. The crack of gravel could be heard beneath the wheels and the car came to a gentle stop. The woman got out.

"Where are we?" Estelle whispered to Sandor.

"This is Barbara's house," said Sandor.

"Who's Barbara?"

"Weren't you listening? Barbara Wallace is the lady who saved us."

Barbara opened Estelle's door. "Welcome to my home," she said.

She was a tall lady of dignified bearing, perhaps in her early fifties. Her dark hair was wavy and carefully groomed, and her face had a watchful sharpness, reflected in the chiselled quality of her nose, chin and cheekbones. Her skin was smooth and pale, almost unblemished but for a tiny mole on her right cheek, close to her nose.

Estelle helped Sandor out of the car and up the drive.

Her home turned out to be a cottage with white, ivy-clad walls. It had grey slate tiles on the roof and above the two sash-windowed bays on either side of the front door. Colourful pansies tumbled from wall-hung baskets and tubs on the garden path. Upper storey dormer windows peeked from beneath the heavy tile roof like sleepy eyes.

"Come in, both of you," announced Barbara. "Don't be shy... Shoes off, please."

The interior was a showroom of period features and fine furnishings, from hand-woven rugs on the glossy wooden floors to pink chintz curtains and cushions and oak beams in the ceiling. "I'm a hopeless traditionalist when it comes to interior design, I'm afraid," smiled Barbara, seeing them stare. "Now, can I get you some tea?"

While she was busy in the kitchen, Sandor made himself comfortable in an armchair. Estelle found room on a sofa next to a sleeping white cat, and listened as Sandor filled her in about what he'd learned. "Apparently, she was taking one of her regular strolls through the forest when she heard the sounds of our little skirmish. She raced back to her car and then drove over to see if she could help."

Estelle wanted to trust in their rescuer – wanted so much to believe she was telling the truth and the nightmare was over. But something didn't quite ring true about Barbara's story. It all seemed a bit too easy.

"Strolls through the forest? Do you believe that?"

"Sure. Why not?"

Estelle frowned at him. "A woman taking a walk on her own in Delhaven Forest, with all the soul shadows and armed patrols. Seems highly unlikely to me."

"It's a big forest," pointed out Sandor. "Most of it's probably quite safe."

"And would she really drive *towards* a firefight? Most people would drive *away* from it. Fast!"

"Not the people I know," said Sandor quietly.

"What about that roadblock? They just waved her through."

"Maybe the security isn't as tight around here as you were led to believe." Then he smiled. "Listen, I understand why you're still feeling twitchy, but just try to relax, will you? Anyway, we're out of danger and she's only a woman. We can easily…"

"What do you mean 'only a woman'?" Estelle snorted.

"OK, OK." Sandor quickly changed the subject. "What were you about to say to me before we were rescued?"

"Oh, that." Estelle felt her cheeks growing hot. "It was nothing."

Tea was served by Barbara in a Wedgewood tea service, with a choice of lemon or milk, and a small plate of sandwiches with the crusts removed.

"You know I've been walking in those woods for years,"

said Barbara, "and I've never seen anything unusual. It was quite a shock to find you battling those men dressed up in leaves and grass or whatever it was they were wearing. Were they eco-terrorists by any chance?"

Estelle swapped glances with Sandor. He cleared his throat. "Uh, yes. I think that must be what they were. They took us by surprise." He didn't explain the blown-up APC or the weapons, and luckily Barbara didn't ask.

"I'm just glad I arrived when I did," she said. "You didn't look like you were winning."

"Er, no."

"Would it be OK if I made a phone call?" interjected Estelle. "I think the police ought to be informed."

"Why you're absolutely right, my dear. We should inform the police. In fact, rather than bothering with emergency services, why don't we call the police station at Edgebourne. All local enquiries are rerouted there anyway. Before I call them, can I offer you more tea?"

"That would be lovely," smiled Sandor.

The tea tasted good and sweet. The ham sandwiches tasted nice and... *hammy*. Estelle found, to her surprise, that she was already on her third, and her cup was almost empty.

More of the hot, golden liquid was poured into each of their cups. The lowering sun, coming through the leaded windows, made Estelle want to close her eyes. The room was warm, on the threshold of stuffy. The sofa was soft and comfortable, the cushion smooth beneath her head, and all the fear and anxiety of the past few hours seemed to be rapidly melting away, leaving her light and happy... and tired. She yawned. Through half-closed lids, she observed Barbara come back into the room, a cordless telephone pinned to her ear. She heard her speaking to the policeman, but was too sleepy to listen properly.

"Yes, they'd virtually destroyed them… They were second or third stage degeneration… I had to pick them up, just in case… They'll be safe here… I put something in their tea… I'll bring them back to the Facility first thing tomorrow."

Something about the words Barbara was saying, and the way she was now looking at Estelle and Sandor, struck Estelle as strange or wrong, but it was hard to concentrate, hard enough not to spill her tea or to prevent her head from falling onto her…

Clatter of crockery. Hotness on her lap, spreading. Pain. Pulling. Dragging on her arms. Bump. Bump. Bump. Then darkness… soft pillows… sleep.

"Wake up, Es! Wake up!" It was Sandor, his voice an urgent whisper in her ear. Her eyes were so heavy, it was like breaking open ancient coral-encrusted shells just to look at him. She glimpsed his concerned face in the darkness. "You were right about Barbara Wallace," he said. "She's a baddy and no mistake. She drugged us. I've been awake for hours waiting for you to come round."

Estelle tried to sit up, but her body felt so sluggish, she immediately collapsed.

"I'm sorry, Es," said Sandor softly. "I should trust you more, I know. You're pretty shrewd when it comes to judging people's characters."

Too right! thought Estelle groggily, before sinking back

into semi-consciousness.

When she managed to force her eyes open again, she saw they were in a small, book-lined study containing, among other things, an ornate roll-top desk. She was lying on a mattress on the floor.

"I realised just in time," Sandor was saying. "I was given a benzo once that tasted like sweet corn starch. I caught the same flavour in her tea. Threw most of it in a pot plant behind my armchair. Then I faked unconsciousness. Otherwise we'd both have woken up back at the Facility."

"She's working for the professor then?"

"I reckon so."

Estelle vaguely remembered a phone call, just before she lost consciousness.

They'd virtually destroyed them... I had to pick them up, just in case...

She rubbed her forehead, trying to puzzle out what that could mean. In case what?

"Come on, Es." He was helping her to her feet.

"What time is it?"

"About five in the morning. We have to get out of here before she wakes up."

Groggily, she slipped on her shoes and followed him out of the room and into a hallway. To their left was a windowed door through which they could see the dim silhouettes of a back garden – plants and a half-constructed greenhouse beneath a grey, pre-dawn sky.

"This'll be safer than going out the front entrance," whispered Sandor.

He tried the handle. The door was locked.

"Front door?" suggested Estelle.

"That'll be locked, too," said Sandor despondently. "She wasn't taking any chances... Wait here, I'll see if I can find some way of breaking out of here." He opened the door that led to the front of the cottage.

"Be careful."

Soon after he'd gone, Estelle heard a creak on the stairs. She retreated into the study and concealed herself in the shadows, praying that Sandor had heard the sound too and had found a place to hide.

The door Sandor had just gone through started to reopen. Who was coming through? It couldn't be him, back again already.

Estelle scurried back to her mattress, where she collapsed into feigned sleep. The study door creaked open and the soft pad of footsteps approached where she lay. A breath rattled in her ear. She could barely refrain from flinching at the thought of what...

A softness brushed her cheek. Her eyes flickered open, and she let out a sigh of relief, tinged with irritation.

The cat!

Sandor leaned in from the hall. "Come on, Es. You can catch up on your sleep later. I've got the door open."

On the floor, by the open door, lay several discarded paperclips, a kitchen knife and a store card.

Estelle looked at Sandor, her admiration tinged with disapproval. "Is that something you learned in the army?"

"No. That's from a mis-spent youth."

The garden was as well tended as might be expected, having seen the care lavished on the cottage. Leafy vegetables were lined up in neat rows in front of bamboo teepees supporting bean plants. A meandering herbaceous border of pink, yellow and white flowers, intermingled with bushy shrubs, surrounded a well-trimmed carpet of lawn.

Sandor led the way to the bottom of the garden, past the half-completed greenhouse and a wisteria-covered brick outhouse, to the back fence. He peered over.

"There's a lane behind here," he reported. "I'm sure it'll lead us back to the main road, and then to the village."

He was about to launch himself up and over the fence when they both heard a noise: a soft knocking sound that seemed to come from very close by.

"What was that?" Sandor wondered.

Estelle shivered. "Don't know and don't care. Can we just get out of here, please?" She brushed past him and placed her hands on top of the fence.

"Wait," said Sandor. "I think it's coming from…" He walked back to the outhouse and placed his ear to the wooden door. "…here."

"Sandor, forget it!" Estelle almost shouted. "Whatever it is Barbara Wallace is keeping trapped in her garden shed, I really don't want to know about it. Can we please go now?"

Sandor looked about to acquiesce, when he was stopped again by another sound – a faint cry.

"Help me!"

The voice sounded female, and it was definitely coming from inside the little brick building.

He tried the door handle. It was locked. He glanced at Estelle. "We have to help her," he said.

"Why? Why do we have to help her? Why can't we help you and me for once by just getting ourselves out of here?"

Sandor looked disappointed in her – which hurt her to see. "Remember your driver friend," he said. "I was ready to leave him to his fate, but you persuaded me that we should make a stand there – save his life. You did the right thing."

"Yeah, and a fat lot of gratitude he showed us for it, running away as soon as he had the chance."

Again that look of disappointment. "We don't do these things for gratitude, Es."

She scowled at him. Irritatingly, it didn't seem to affect him in the slightest.

He rammed the door with his shoulder. The door held firm. He tried again, then again, with the same result.

Estelle waited in the shadows by the fence. She didn't know what she feared more: being discovered by Barbara Wallace or finding out what manner of person or thing Sandor was about to set free.

Sandor found a gap near the bottom corner of the door where the wood had partly rotted. He limped back to the half-built greenhouse. Next to the frame structure was a pile of glass panes and a stack of metal poles. He picked up one of the metal poles and hefted it in his hand. Appearing satisfied, he carried it back to the outhouse. He inserted it part way into the gap at the bottom of the door, then used it as a lever to force the door open. Sandor put all his strength and weight behind it. There was a loud crack as the screws holding the door's hinges burst from the frame.

Sandor pulled open the door. He immediately staggered back, his legs almost giving way beneath him. Pallid yellow light shone out from the interior, projecting its oily tinge on nearby foliage and on Sandor's shocked face.

"What? What is it?" cried Estelle. But then it was her turn to gasp as through the door stepped a frightened, bewildered Barbara Wallace.

The thought hit both of them simultaneously: she had to be a soul shadow! Yet she didn't look or act like a soul shadow. She didn't bear her sharpened fangs at the sight of them, blacken her eyes or stretch herself in any hideous, rubbery ways. She just remained a very ordinary-looking human woman, identical to the one who'd rescued and then drugged them yesterday. Except… slightly different.

Estelle recalled the mirror effect and searched for any telltale signs. She pictured the original woman: her skin unblemished except for that tiny mole on her right cheek. *This woman's mole was on the left.*

"Run, Sandor!" Estelle cried. "She's a soul shadow!" She began scrambling over the fence.

"Stop! Please!" said the woman, and her voice was so gentle and ordinary, that Estelle allowed herself to drop back into the garden and face her.

"I know this must be confusing," said the Barbara lookalike. "Well, I assure you I'm as confused as you are. You see, I –" She stopped and smiled at Sandor. "Thank you for rescuing me, by the way, young man. Allow me to introduce myself. I am Barbara Wallace."

"No," said Estelle. "We've met Barbara Wallace. She looks like you, but she's not you."

"The woman you met is an imposter," the lady calmly asserted. "I don't know where she came from, but she broke into my home two nights ago and locked me in here. I think she wants to steal my identity." She held out her hand.

Sandor hesitated before shaking it. "I'm Sandor," he said.

Estelle eyed the proffered hand suspiciously, but decided not to shake. "I'm Estelle," she said simply.

A light went on in an upstairs window of the cottage.

"Oh dear, she's awake!" cried the woman. "We must get away."

She and Estelle ran to the fence, but Sandor stayed put.

"Don't you want to reclaim your property?" he enquired, a note of scepticism in his voice.

"Yes, but not now. She has a gun!"

As if on cue, the still, dark air was split by a sound like a small cannon.

Barbara – the original Barbara – was standing at the back door, her face a picture of rage. She was aiming a large shotgun at them.

Estelle felt Sandor lifting her into the air and pushing her over the other side of the fence. She tumbled down a short bank onto the stony lane as another gunshot blew a big hole in one of the wooden slats, sending splinters flying everywhere. The other Barbara bounced down next to her, followed by Sandor, who landed awkwardly and clutched at his bad leg. Fresh blood had appeared on the thigh of his jeans.

Two more shots, fired in quick succession, shook the fence.

"Lucky she's a poor shot," gasped Sandor as the women helped him to his feet. Between them they supported him in a running, hopping stumble down the lane.

"Your car," he panted.

"She has the key with her," said the Barbara woman.

The lane followed the backs of half a dozen houses. Upper-storey windows were now ablaze with light as curious neighbours leaned out to see the cause of the shooting. At the end of the row of houses, the lane forked. They paused here, relieved to note that the original Barbara seemed to have given up the chase. The left-hand fork curved back towards the forest, while the right-hand one went through a meadow, crossed a stream and then met with the streetlights of the main road. The lights of the village could be seen about a kilometre away.

"If we follow this to the main road, she'll find us with her car," warned Sandor. "Our best bet is either to go back into the forest, or else cut through the meadow and head for the village through a back route."

"The forest would be safest," suggested Barbara.

Estelle immediately vetoed that option. "I'm never going back there," she vowed.

Barbara frowned in thought. "In that case, there is a place we can go to in the village. There's a man there called Carl Henrison. I know him well. He'll be able to help us." She glanced to her left, towards the eastern sky, where the first pink rays of the sun were twinkling through the treetops. "We'd better be quick, though," she added. "That woman will find us very easily if we're still out in the open in daylight."

Sandor nodded. "OK, let's go." He removed his arms from the shoulders of the women and limped off the lane into the long grass, embarking on a course midway between the two forks.

Estelle looked at the other woman and shrugged. They

began following him. Estelle's shoes and the lower legs of her jeans were soon damp from the dewy grass.

"Your friend doesn't want our help?" asked Barbara.

"He's very independent," said Estelle.

"Are you involved with him romantically?"

"No!" Estelle replied, slightly irritated. "Why does everyone always assume that?"

"I'm sorry," Barbara backtracked. "I thought I saw something in your expression when you looked at him, but I am very bad at intuiting these things."

"We're friends, that's all."

They walked in silence for a while. Then Barbara asked: "Tell me, my dear, why do you fear the forest?"

"Because it's full of shadows that kill. Not to mention a rather dangerous professor with his own private army."

Barbara nodded.

"What do you know about it?" Estelle asked.

"I've heard all sorts of rumours," said Barbara, shivering a little. "Carl knows a lot more than I do. But I can tell you one thing, young lady: there were no shadow creatures in those woods before the professor arrived and built his Facility."

Estelle nodded. "That's what I thought – the professor created the soul shadows."

"I can't be absolutely certain, but it does seem to be the only likely explanation."

"And this other Barbara who turned up at your cottage? Is she your soul shadow?"

"Maybe." She gave a short, dry cough. "I've heard the mature ones are more resilient to daylight. They're also harder to tell apart from humans. They act just like us.

You have to really interrogate them before you discover how shallow their knowledge is." She coughed again, and shivered. "Excuse me. It was very chilly in that outhouse. I may have caught a cold." Looking again at the brightening sky, she said: "Do you suppose there is any chance that we could go a little faster? We're very exposed out here. I'm sure there will be men with dogs here very shortly."

"I'm afraid this is Sandor's top speed," said Estelle.

Sandor accepted Estelle's help fording the narrow stream. He put his hand on her shoulder as he hopped across. She also had to help Barbara, who suddenly seemed quite frail. By now the sun had cleared the tops of the trees. It illuminated the misty meadow and gleamed on the water's surface.

As Estelle helped Sandor up the bank, he nodded towards Barbara. "She doesn't look well." Barbara was now hunched over, coughing.

Estelle went over to her and placed her arm around her. "We're nearly there," she encouraged. "You can rest soon."

When Barbara looked up, Estelle got a real shock. Her face seemed to have aged dramatically. The flesh sagged where before it had been firm and smooth. As the rays of the sun hit the woman's face, Estelle thought she saw something falling from her cheeks. Was it tears, or a trail of dust?

"The mature ones," croaked Barbara. "Are more resilient to daylight. But it's still agony to them. They're also... harder... to tell apart... from humans." She coughed once more, and now Estelle was absolutely certain something was sliding off her face, and it wasn't tears. "We become more like humans... But we never stop desiring you!"

spluttered Barbara. Estelle backed away, moving closer to Sandor. Barbara, now almost bent double, looked up at them. It was clear she was in agony. Part of her face – the side most exposed to the sun – was fast disappearing: crumbling into dusty fragments, swiftly dispersed by the breeze. "One thing can save me," she groaned. "But I shall not obey that call..." She fell to her knees. "My flesh hungers for yours." Her eyes had grown big and black within her twisted, pain-wracked face. Her mouth was stretching wide like elastic, and Estelle saw sharp teeth pushing through behind the dark lips.

"Run!" screamed Shadow-Barbara. "Get away from me!"

Estelle stared, horrified, but did not move. Neither did Sandor. Shadow-Barbara was long past posing any threat. Much of her had by now disintegrated into powder and was swirling around the meadow. What remained resembled a windblown stump, about a metre tall, her head a series of concave surfaces, with deep eye sockets and a giant black scream for a mouth. Below her tiny neck, her limbs were fast becoming fused with her trunk to form a rough pillar.

They watched in awed silence as she gradually crumbled away to nothing. Eventually, Sandor asked: "What happened to her?"

"Soul shadows thrive on that special kind of light in the forest," Estelle told him. "Daylight is poison to them."

Five

The rising sun fanned its rays across the meadow, igniting the breeze-blown stalks of grass and burnishing the surface of the stream to a pale copper. Sandor's face glowed with sweat. His brow was furrowed from the effort of dragging his wounded leg for over a kilometre across rough ground. But as he and Estelle stood there on the bank of the stream, arguing about their next move, he refused to act the victim. To her frustration, he also refused to acknowledge the importance of finding a place of refuge where he could rest and regain his strength. He was, to his core, a soldier and a tactician. And stubborn. As far as Sandor was concerned, their next move should be to return to Barbara Wallace's house and force her to reveal what she knew. Perhaps there was some merit to the idea in theory – if they'd been carrying weapons and he was fully fit. But they weren't, and he wasn't.

He was also being irrational. Barbara Wallace's soul shadow had advised them to seek help from a man in the village, Carl Henrison. Sandor's instinctive hostility towards soul shadows had led him to dismiss this suggestion out of hand. His prejudice prevented him from seeing that it might just be their best hope.

Estelle had used all the arguments she could think of, and a few choice insults – she'd called him pigheaded and illogical – but he remained implacable. So Estelle took the only option left to her. It was unsporting, she knew it, but what choice did she have? She turned on her heel and began walking towards the village.

"Estelle!" Sandor shouted. "Come back here."

"Try and stop me," she called over her shoulder, knowing full well that, in his current condition, he didn't have a hope.

"Where are you going?"

"To find Carl Henrison."

"You're going to trust the word of that monster-woman?"

"Yup!"

"I'm warning you, Es! This is a very bad idea."

Estelle gambled that, whatever she meant to him personally (and that remained an open question), Sandor would never actually abandon her while he believed she was in danger. Glancing back, she observed with a mixture of relief and guilt that he had reluctantly begun hobbling after her. She slowed down enough to allow him to catch up a little, while taking care to remain just out of his physical reach. They followed a route to the south-west, roughly parallel to the main road, heading for the village through a field dotted with buttercups.

"I take back what I said before about wanting you in the army," she heard him grumble. "This kind of insubordination would not be tolerated."

"And who put you in charge?" challenged Estelle, secretly amused.

"You asked for my help, Es…" He paused, breathing heavily as he levered himself across a small ditch. "It's my fault, of course," he added. "I should have laid down the ground rules at the start. You want my help, then you have to do things my way."

She stopped, angry now, and turned on him. "Sandor, I'm not a fourteen-year-old kid any more, so stop treating me like one! I called you because… because you're the bravest and truest friend I have. I needed you, and you came, and I can't tell you how grateful I am. But now you're acting like I'm some private in your platoon. I'm your friend…" She came closer, wanting to reach out to him, but still fearful of how he might react. "I feel so guilty," she said. "You're supposed to be home on leave. I know you've had your own nightmares to deal with from your time in Afghanistan. You didn't need this. And now… And now I sort of see it as my duty to get you out of here – to get us both out of here. We're not fighting a battle. This isn't warfare. It's survival. Going back to that woman's house and confronting her is not going to get us out of this."

Tentatively, she touched his arm. He didn't pull away, but after a long moment, he smiled. "You have grown up, haven't you, Es?"

She gave his arm an affectionate squeeze. "Let's go."

Crossing a stile, they entered a field of green, unripe wheat, bordered by a heavily rutted track. They followed the track past the line of giant silver silos Estelle had glimpsed on her first morning at the cottage. By now,

Sandor was panting with exhaustion, but he waved aside her suggestion that they stop and rest. They passed a barn and some storage sheds, but saw no one. Estelle's plan was to try and avoid the main street of the village, where they might be spotted, and head straight for Carl Henrison's house, if she could only find some local person who could give them directions.

The path eventually took them alongside some garages and then a garden behind a dilapidated stone house. A blonde lad of about seven was inside a wire mesh chicken house near the back of the garden, collecting eggs in a basket. Four or five chickens clucked and strutted around his feet.

"Morning," Sandor called out to him.

The boy stared at them.

"Are your mum or dad about?" Estelle asked.

"They're in bed," said the boy shyly.

She smiled, trying to put him at his ease. "You don't happen to know where Carl Henrison lives, do you? I've heard he has a house somewhere in this village."

The boy shook his head. "I could ask my dad?"

"Ask me what?" came a gruff shout from the patio next to the house. A short, stout man stood there, still in his dressing gown and pyjamas, and just lighting his first cigarette of the day.

"Good morning to you," said Sandor amiably. "We're looking for Carl Henrison."

The man frowned. "What do you want with him?"

Sandor looked quizzically at Estelle.

"We're old friends," she said quickly.

"If you're old friends, you'll know where he lives."

The man was slowly approaching them across his shabby, yellow lawn, his face creased with suspicion.

"We wanted to surprise him," said Sandor. "We haven't seen him in years."

The man stopped when he reached the fence, and treated Sandor to a mean stare. He barely came up to Sandor's chest, but he more than made up for it in girth. He turned to the boy. "Off you go now, son. Take those eggs inside and help your mum make us some breakfast."

As the boy made his way back to the house, his father returned his gaze to Sandor, entirely ignoring Estelle. He leaned in close, so that his nose almost touched Sandor's chin, and said under his breath: "I hope you don't mind me being blunt with you mister, you bein' a friend of his and all, but we don't much like Carl Henrison around here. We don't like the way he goes around stirrin' up trouble about the Facility. What Carl Henrison fails to appreciate is that that place has been good for Delhaven. It employed a lot of people from the village during the construction, and it's going to employ a lot more now that it's built." He took a long drag on his cigarette, keeping his eyes fastened on Sandor. "I'll grant you, there were some accidents. A few people got hurt. And we've all heard the rumours about them things in the forest. But the people at the Facility have taken steps to make things safer, and the village has decided to give them the benefit of the doubt. Life's been tough around here since the factory in Edgebourne closed. The village has been slowly dyin'. So when a new employer pitches up offering jobs, we're not goin' to give them the cold shoulder, understand me? We're not going to make a fuss over a few accidents, or call in the press like

Carl Henrison was threatening to do. We're going to take them at their word." The man nodded to himself, then turned away and began plodding back the way he came. Halfway up the garden, he stopped and looked back over his shoulder at Sandor. "You can tell Carl Henrison from me, Jack Hollins, that he's not welcome here. If he stays, I won't be responsible for the consequences."

"Where can we find him, so we can pass on your message?" asked Sandor.

"Church Street, third house on the left," said the man as he trudged back towards the house.

Staring down at them from an upstairs window was a woman Estelle recognised from the previous afternoon: Mrs Hollins, the woman in the Facility canteen.

"Looks like you were right, Es," murmured Sandor. "Henrison sounds like our man."

He peered down the lane. "I guess this eventually joins with the village high street. From there, we should be able to find the church and, presumably, Church Street."

"We'll be quite exposed," said Estelle.

Sandor shrugged. "I can't see we've got a lot of choice."

They continued past several more houses before reaching a junction with the high street. On the far side of the road, past a small grassy traffic island with a signpost perched on its summit, stood a church. It had an uncared-for look, with its steep, mossy roof, black, arched windows and weathered old gravestones in its yard, many of them stunted and tilting at odd angles, as if gradually sinking into the long grass. To the right of the church, almost opposite to where Estelle and Sandor were standing, was a narrow road lined with brick-terraced dwellings. A small sign near the corner of the road confirmed that it was Church Street.

Sandor swiftly grabbed Estelle's elbow and pulled her behind a low wall. "What is it?" she whispered.

"I saw a couple of those blackshirts further up the street." He nodded to his right.

"Blackshirts?"

"You know, those guards in charge of security at the Facility. They must be searching for us."

"How will we get across the road?"

Sandor peered out from their hiding place. "We'll have to wait for them to move on."

He kept lookout for a further two minutes, then gave her the signal to run for it. She dashed across the road, stopping at the far corner. Visibility was better from this side. After a quick look up the now empty high street, she beckoned for him to join her. Sandor hobbled across as fast as he could.

The third house on the left was not unlike its immediate neighbours with its blue door, single lower-storey window and two upper-storey windows – but there the similarities ended. While the houses to either side boasted polished brass door-knockers and letter boxes on their shiny doors, and pretty window boxes beneath their sash windows, the third house on the left was a mess. Its dirty bricks had been crudely daubed with some words, no longer legible. The panes of the sash windows were all smashed, and the windows had been boarded up from the inside.

The sound of a vehicle in the high street diverted their attention from the house. Sandor limped across the road and planted himself at the corner. "It's OK," he called.

"It's just a van delivering newspapers."

Estelle tried knocking on the dirty blue door. "Hello-oo!" she called brightly. "Anyone at home?"

No answer came.

Then she noticed a button on the wall to her right, and below it a small speaker. She pushed the button and waited.

Again, no answer.

"Blackshirts approaching," Sandor called in a low voice.

Estelle looked around for somewhere to hide. There were no convenient alleyways on the terraced street. She pushed the button again, as Sandor cast an exasperated glance in her direction.

Finally, the speaker next to the door crackled into life. "Yes? What do you want?" came a frail, well-spoken voice.

"Hello, is that Mr Henrison?"

"It might be," came the wary reply.

"Mr Henrison, we desperately need your help. Can you let us in please?"

"Who the devil are you?" The voice quivered with fear and distrust.

"We're… we're refugees" – it was a word she'd often heard on the news, and it seemed to fit their circumstances – "… from the forest. We're being hunted by people from the Facility. We were told you could help us." She looked briefly at Sandor, who was frantically signalling at her.

"Look, I'm sick and tired of your games, you people," said the voice. "I just want to be left in peace, alright?"

"They're going to be here any second!" cried Sandor in

a hoarse whisper. "Tell him about Barbara's soul shadow."

"We met the soul shadow of Barbara Wallace," shouted Estelle, unable to keep the panic out of her voice.

This elicited a short, surprised exclamation, then: "Nonsense. She must be dead by now."

"She is. But she... she told us about you before she died. We rescued her from the real Barbara's house."

"You rescued her?" The voice now seemed full of wonder.

"Let us in, Mr Henrison. Please!"

She heard footsteps approaching the corner of the street. At the same moment, there came a sound, behind the door, of latches being drawn back – at least three of them, and keys being turned in locks.

Estelle signalled to Sandor, and he began lurching back across the street, his face pale with anxiety.

The door opened a crack and Sandor shoved it back further and bundled Estelle over the threshold. He followed her in and slammed the door.

They were in a very dark corridor. The place smelled of unwashed laundry, pizza and cats.

"I say, how dare you barge your way in like this!" cried the frail voice from somewhere below her. She could just about make out a narrow, foxy face at about the level of her waist.

Was it a man or an animal?

His eyes seemed big and shiny – until she realised they were a pair of round-lensed glasses, and he looked small because he was in a wheelchair.

"I'm afraid there are a couple of black-shirted security guys coming," Sandor warned him.

"Oh-hh dear," quailed Carl Henrison. "Quick, in there both of you."

Estelle felt a pair of bony hands pushing her through a doorway. Thin, dusty shafts of morning light shone through knotholes in the wooden boards covering the window. They left most of the room in shadow, but illuminated enough to show that Mr Henrison lived in pretty dismal conditions. The only furniture was an armchair positioned near the fireplace and a battered old television in the corner. The chair's fabric had split in several places, exposing the internal padding. Beneath the pizza cartons and soft-drink cans that littered the floor was a threadbare rug. From the far side of the room, a cat gaped at them, then went back to licking at a smudge of sauce on one of the cartons. Unlike Barbara Wallace's sleepy, pampered feline, this was a thin, lank-haired, nervous-looking creature.

There came a loud knocking at the door. Estelle jumped. She sidled into the shadows, closer to where Sandor was standing, taking care not to trip on a carton. She felt better, as always, standing close to Sandor. A small sizzle of electricity ran through her as his hand closed around hers. He still liked her! Even after she'd forced him into following her plan, and after their little row on the meadow. She allowed her body to rest lightly against his.

That's all right, isn't it? If we can hold hands, we can also lean against each other. It doesn't mean anything.

"Go away and leave me in peace," she heard Carl pleading through the front door.

"Open up please," came a calm, authoritative voice.

"What do you want from me?"

"We're from Securicus, Mr Henrison. We believe

two people we wish to question may have entered your property."

"There's no one here," shouted Carl. "No one ever comes in here. You must be mistaken."

"You have nothing to fear, Mr Henrison. We only wish to talk with them."

"Like you wanted to talk with me the other week, and I ended up with two broken legs."

Estelle shivered on hearing this. She pressed herself more deeply into the shadowy corner, pulling Sandor with her. Unfortunately, this caused him to fall backwards into a bookcase. An avalanche of heavy books thumped and clattered to the floor. The noise was tremendous. Her heart stopped. She squeezed his hand so tightly, she heard him moan.

"There are people in your front room," said another voice. One of the knotholes at the window went dark, and Estelle could almost see an eye peering through.

"That's uh… Fraser, my cat," said Carl.

There was another pause. Then the original voice returned, no longer bothering with its veneer of politeness: "OK, Henrison. But if we find out you've been lying to us, we'll make sure you never walk again. Understood?"

Footsteps slowly receded up the street. After a moment, Carl appeared in the doorway. His head was mostly bald, with some gingery tufts above his ears and some more growing in an uneven goatee beneath a long, pointed nose. He was ghostly pale and his hands, resting on the push-rims of his wheelchair, were shaking.

In this man were rested all their hopes of salvation!

"They're going to kill me," Carl Henrison observed,

staring at the cold ashes in his fireplace. "This time, they're really going to kill me."

"We'll leave," said Sandor, moving past him into the narrow entrance hall. Estelle followed.

"No!" said Carl. He turned himself about and looked up at them. Behind the thick round lenses of his spectacles, Estelle saw the fear in his green eyes, but also a desperate kind of excitement. "You may be able to help," he said in his high, quavering voice. "They've cornered me, you see? Like a rat in a hole." He tapped his legs. "I can't escape. They've cut off my phone and internet access. No one outside the village knows I'm here. One of these nights, they're going to come in here and kill me." He looked at Estelle. "But you, young lady. You've still got your legs. You could make a run for it. Head for Little Darrow or North Dene, even Edgebourne. Get word out to the newspapers, the police." His hands were shaking more than before, but his cheeks had become flushed. His eyes were feverish.

"Estelle isn't going anywhere," Sandor calmly asserted. "The streets are crawling with blackshirts. There's a checkpoint at the northern end of the village, and I'm sure they've got them at every other exit. Besides, why do we need to go elsewhere? There must be someone in this village you can trust. Someone with a phone, who can –"

Carl shook his head. "The Facility owns Delhaven. They've bought its soul."

Sandor stared at him disbelievingly. "And you? How come you're different? How come they want to kill you? Who, in fact, are you?"

Carl didn't reply, only wheeled himself further down the corridor towards the back of the house. He beckoned

108

to them, and they followed him into a kitchen-dining area. The kitchen units and surfaces were stained with ancient grime. Only the coffee stains on the table, and the water in the cat's bowl, looked reasonably fresh.

"Well, if you don't believe you can escape from here, young lady, you and your boyfriend may as well make yourselves comfortable."

Estelle blushed. "He's not my boyfriend."

"Really? I think you'd make a handsome couple."

She rolled her eyes at Sandor as if to say, "Is this guy nuts, or what?" Sandor only smiled, though whether his amusement was due to the nuttiness of Carl Henrison or the notion that he and Estelle could ever be a couple, she couldn't be sure.

"I doubt we have more than a few hours' grace before they come back here in force," said Carl. He pointed to Sandor's blood-stained jeans. "That, sir, needs seeing to. Young lady, there are fresh bandages and antiseptic in the bathroom. Meanwhile, I shall sort you out some breakfast."

Carl manoeuvred himself around the kitchen, opening cupboards and extracting bowls, spoons and cereal boxes. Estelle was relieved to observe that he seemed calmer, now that he had practical concerns like breakfast on his mind – or perhaps he was just resigned to his fate. She went into the bathroom. It wasn't too bad compared to the rest of the house, if you ignored the stains in the bath and the nasty-smelling pile of laundry in the corner. In a cupboard above the sink, she found what she needed, then returned to the kitchen, where Sandor already had his jeans off and leg up on a chair. The original bandage was dirty and heavily stained with blood. She carefully unwrapped it and was pleased to see that, although the wound was bleeding again, the flesh around it looked a normal colour. She knew what to do this time, and got to work boiling up some water in one of Carl's unused saucepans, then mixing the antiseptic with water.

Meanwhile, the men ate their dry rice munchies and slurped black coffee – Carl's hospitality did not extend to milk – and Carl told his tale.

"You may find it hard to credit, looking at me now," he began, "but I was once a respected physicist, a University Research Fellow of the Royal Society and a professor at the University of Edgebourne. For ten years I worked with my colleagues Barbara Wallace and Robert Mitchell, researching new forms of radiation, with the aim of improving medical radiography. One of the wavelengths we looked at lay between that of infrared and visible light, at around 790 nanometers or –"

"405 terahertz?" chipped in Estelle, as she carried a bowl of antiseptic mixture to the table.

Carl glanced up from his rice munchies. "How did you know?"

"Someone at the Facility told me. Although he claimed it was a natural thing, this weird light – that you discovered it in Delhaven Forest and then set up the Facility to research it. Are you telling me you created it artificially, in a laboratory?"

Carl nodded. A dreamy, almost nostalgic look had entered his eyes. "Those were exciting days. We were a real team back then, motivated only by the thrill of making new discoveries. The breakthrough occurred one day about three years ago. I was working in the lab late one evening, experimenting with different ways of refracting this light, when I chanced upon a particular chromatic aberration. I can't claim credit for it – the truth is it was caused by a faulty lens. Anyway, I shone it on a lab rat and… out of the sawdust in the cage next to this rat, grew… a second rat." He looked up at Estelle. "I suppose you already know that this particular light – this zeta radiation – produced the creatures that Mitchell later christened soul shadows."

Estelle looked up from Sandor's leg in time to observe a proud little smile forming on the man's weasel-like face, and a cold fury descended over her. "You created those things," she shouted. "It's all your fault!"

"No!" Carl rebutted with even greater vehemence. "Whatever you may think, I am not responsible for what has happened. I did not create those demons in the wood. It is true that I agreed to move operations here, to Delhaven Forest, because of its remoteness. But it wasn't because I thought our experiments were dangerous. It was because what we had discovered was so momentous, so revolutionary, I needed to be sure that we could continue our work in absolute secrecy. In those days, the Facility was little more than a few cabins in the wood, and the experiments took place inside the buildings. The zeta radiation was never allowed to leak into the woods. Our plan was to exploit this new technology to try to create spare organs for transplant. That, I assure you, was the limit of our ambitions. The first soul shadows – I hate that term, but I suppose we must use it – the first soul shadows were benign, fragile, short-lived creatures. But the further we went with our research and the more we refined our zeta ray transmitters, the stronger and more durable the soul shadows became. And with strength and durability came intelligence, and the desire inherent in all organisms: to adapt and survive. They found a way – somehow they discovered a means – of surviving in the absence of zeta rays, by sustaining themselves instead on human flesh…"

"Ow!" Sandor gave a yelp of pain as Estelle dabbed at his wound a little too aggressively.

"I'm sorry!" she cried. "It's just… I can't believe you people could be so irresponsible!"

Sandor, still flinching from the pain, turned to face Carl. "Yeah, so what exactly did you do, Carl, when you discovered you were breeding killers in your little cabin?"

Carl fiddled with his teaspoon. The pride he had displayed earlier had evaporated. "My colleagues, Mitchell and Wallace, were fascinated by the new, stronger soul shadows. I was fearful of them. I believed we were meddling with forces we didn't understand and couldn't control. We decided to go our separate ways. It was a perfectly amicable divorce. They continued with their work in the wood, while I transferred my base of operations to a lab at my Alma Mater in Edgebourne. It was all fine for a while. But then I heard they were building a permanent Facility, and there were rumours of trouble on the site. Radiation had apparently leaked into the forest and soul shadows had been seen there. There had been some accidents among the construction crew, all of them people from this village. I was horrified. I felt partly responsible and believed it was my duty to do something. First I tried talking to Mitchell and Wallace, but they didn't return my calls and emails. So I called a village meeting. I urged them to campaign to have the Facility shut down.

The denizens of Delhaven weren't interested. They'd been promised jobs at the Facility, and received assurances that things would be safer from now on. Of course I knew that these assurances were worthless. Mitchell and Wallace had no idea how to control the soul shadows once they'd got out of the lab. I threatened to go public with the story, which is when I started facing harassment from the villagers – smashed windows, excrement through the letter box, obscene messages – really charming stuff! Even worse were the black-shirted thugs hired by Mitchell and Wallace. They cut off my phone and internet, smashed my mobile, beat me up. I became frightened to go out – stopped going to the lab, or even the local shop… And this is how you find me today, my friends: wheelchair-bound, cut off from the world, surviving on takeaway pizza."

He pursed his lips in an expression of resignation. "I believe we've reached the endgame now, though. They're going to come for me soon, maybe even tonight – they'll come for you two also – and they intend to finish the job."

Estelle had now cleaned the wound and applied a fresh dressing. While she helped Sandor put his jeans back on, Carl wheeled himself out of the room. He returned a minute later with a pair of crutches, which he offered to Sandor. "I have another pair," he assured him. "These'll help you keep the weight off that leg."

"Thanks."

Carl moved back into the corridor. "Follow me, my friends," he said. "I have a secret I want to show you, which Mitchell, Wallace and the boys in black know nothing about. It's a forlorn hope, maybe, but it might just prove our salvation." Estelle and Sandor followed him out.

They watched as he leaned forward and pushed open a door beneath the staircase. Behind it lay a small cupboard containing a broom, a mop and a few other cleaning implements. Carl backed himself into the cupboard and applied his brakes.

"Why have you gone in there?" Estelle asked, fearing that their host might just have lost his final toe-hold on reality. He didn't reply, just made an odd sucking sound with his lips. A moment later, Fraser emerged from the front room and hopped onto his master's lap.

"You expect us to hide in there with you?" wondered Sandor.

Carl ignored him and pushed a button in the wall next to him. A hissing sound followed, and the section of floor he was parked on, along with the wheelchair, Fraser and Carl himself, began descending slowly out of sight. Carl's voice called up to them: "I'll send it back up for you."

The platform soon returned, and Estelle stepped onto it, crouching slightly in the confined space. She pushed the button and began her own descent, smiling at the bemused Sandor and blowing him a cheeky kiss as she disappeared through the floor. The platform, which turned out to be supported by a hydraulically powered metal pole, landed in a brick-walled Victorian basement, filled with very modern-looking, high-tech equipment.

Carl pressed another button and the platform began to rise once more to pick up Sandor. Estelle recognised some of the equipment from the lab Derek had shown her at the Facility. She was relieved that Carl did not share Derek's tendency to want to explain how everything worked. In fact, he didn't say a word, merely waited for Sandor to arrive, then led them through the mess of boxes, cables and precarious metal stands to an arch-shaped opening at the far end. To Estelle's surprise, this turned out to be the entrance to a dim, narrow brick-lined passage.

"This is still the basement to your house?" asked Sandor, sounding similarly amazed.

"Not strictly," said Carl over his shoulder as he led the way along the underground passage. "I discovered it not long after buying this house. It connects to… well, you'll see."

He pushed open another door at the far end and entered a spacious yet low-ceilinged room of stone walls, pillars and arches.

"We must be in the crypt of that church across the road!" exclaimed Sandor.

"Clever boy!" applauded Carl. "Strictly speaking, we're in a disused annex of the crypt – one that, luckily for me, has been forgotten about for at least a generation. The door to this room was inadvertently concealed by a poorly placed tomb in the main crypt, and, as far as I know, the current vicar has no idea the room exists."

Estelle turned to ask Carl something and was astonished to find him out of his wheelchair. He walked towards her, beaming. "Surprised, my dear?"

Sandor nearly dropped his crutches when he saw him. Then his gape of surprise turned to anger. "What sort of game are you playing with us, Henrison? Why did you lie about the broken legs?"

"I didn't," said Carl, though strangely his lips didn't move.

At that moment, another Carl emerged from behind

a pillar, this time in his wheelchair. "I'm so sorry!" he sniggered. "I don't get many visitors, and I've been dying to play that trick." He gestured to the other, standing Carl. "May I introduce the other Professor Carl Henrison, or, as I call him, Shadow-Carl."

Shadow-Carl bowed graciously.

"He created me in his laboratory," said Shadow-Carl, "and this is where I live, sustained by the zeta radiation in this room."

For the first time, Estelle became aware of the now familiar yellow tinge to the light, only this had a warmer tone than the pallid glow of the forest. She eyed her own faint shadow nervously.

"It's alright, my dear," Carl reassured her. "The light in this room is sustaining, but not reproductive. Your shadow will remain a normal shadow."

"Is this one safe?" Sandor enquired, looking charily at Shadow-Carl.

"I'm perfectly safe," Shadow-Carl replied, without a hint of indignation. "The focus of Carl's work since he established his laboratory here has been to make the soul shadows strong, while retaining our original benign natures."

"Have you created others?" Estelle asked Carl.

He shook his head. "I worked by myself, so I didn't have access to other progenitors – people, in other words. And I couldn't create multiple copies of myself. This form of zeta radiation – I call it zeta-pro – is so powerful, it's dangerous to expose people to more than one dose."

"There was someone else, though, wasn't there?" said Shadow-Carl. "I wish we knew what happened to her."

Original Carl sighed. "That's a sad story. I'm afraid she's dead."

"Oh, too bad!" said Shadow-Carl. He went and sat down by a pillar. Estelle thought he looked lonely, bereft almost. Fraser suddenly appeared from somewhere and nestled next to his legs. Meanwhile, a second Fraser was contentedly rubbing his back against another pillar, close to original Carl.

"I gave you a copy of my cat though, didn't I?" original Carl pointed out.

"I suppose," conceded Shadow-Carl, idly stroking Fraser or Shadow-Fraser – there was no telling which one it was. "But you can't talk to a cat. Tell me, how did Barbara die?"

"Wait!" Sandor interrupted. "Are we talking Barbara Wallace here? Is this the lady – the creature – we met?"

Carl nodded.

"Then would you please start from the beginning. How did you ever get to make a copy of that woman in the first place?"

"I didn't," said Carl. "I was out walking in the meadow – this was back in the days when I still went out from time to time. I found her there, Shadow-Barbara. She was dying. She'd strayed too far from the forest and suffered exposure to the sun. I took her back to my lab and revived her with a dose of my benign zeta-pro radiation. She recovered, and at the same time acquired a very pleasant nature. She and Shadow-Carl got along very well, didn't you?"

Shadow-Carl nodded ruefully.

"Far better than your progenitors ever did, at any rate... Naively, I decided to show her to her original. I set up a meeting with Barbara Wallace and took Shadow-Barbara to her house. I wanted to show her what could be achieved with my new zeta-pro radiation. Barbara seemed impressed. She gave me tea, but it must have been drugged. I woke up the next day in the street outside my house. I don't know what happened to Shadow-Barbara. But you two told me you rescued her from Barbara's house?"

Sandor and Estelle exchanged glances. Estelle crouched down next to Shadow-Carl and touched his shoulder. "She was a lovely lady," she said gently. "She died very bravely... saving us, in fact."

There came a strident banging from upstairs.

"They've arrived," said original Carl, suddenly going pale. Estelle noticed with alarm that his hands were shaking again.

"What's the plan?" asked Sandor.

"Plan?" asked Carl, who seemed to have aged ten years in a matter of seconds.

"You said you had some secret that might help us defend ourselves."

"Did I?"

The thump of distant footsteps could now be heard.

"Ah yes! We must make shadows of you two, and fast! We can use them as decoys."

"Shadows? Of us?" Sandor didn't look at all comfortable with the idea.

"It's a good plan," Estelle said. "You've seen Shadow-Carl. He's harmless."

Sandor still didn't look sure.

"Follow me!" said Carl, wheeling himself back up the

118

passage that led to his basement lab. "They're bound to find us soon, so we haven't much time."

In the laboratory, they were directly beneath his house, and the sound of footsteps above was frighteningly loud. They could also hear clattering and smashing sounds as if the place was being violently ransacked.

Sweat was now pouring down Carl's face as he led them to the back of his lab. A tall object stood there. It looked like a large shower-unit, with frosted glass walls. "This is my shadow-maker," he said in a trembly voice. "In you go, young man. Quickly now." Hesitantly, Sandor slid open one of the glass panels and, with a final, nervous glance at Estelle, hitched himself awkwardly into the unit. The door closed behind him. Meanwhile, Carl positioned himself at a nearby control panel and began pressing buttons. "We won't have time to create a detailed copy," he said. "He'll lack your mannerisms, your self-awareness, and his vocabulary will be... basic. But it should hopefully be sufficient to fool those brutes."

The unit began to glow with a yellow light. Estelle crossed her arms and her fingers. Next to her, Carl was a blur of feverish activity at the control panel, pushing levers, adjusting dials and studying displays of flickering figures. Upstairs the noisy mayhem continued. She didn't imagine there could be much left to destroy.

Eventually, she heard a small hissing sound and the glow faded from the unit. The door opened and out limped Sandor... followed by another Sandor.

Estelle ran to the first one, ready to embrace him, but then stopped. "Which one are you?" she asked him.

His face broke into a grin. "I'm the original." And then

he frowned. "At least I think I am."

Carl looked up distractedly and nodded. "Yes, yes, you're the original. If you were the shadow, the wound would be on your right leg."

Sandor looked at his leg, and his smile returned. He turned to his double and grasped his hand. "Very pleased to meet you... me... whatever!"

"I'm... I'm Sandor Watts," the other Sandor muttered.

"Welcome!" cried Carl. "Happy birthday! Let's all have a party!" His face looked like it might explode with tension. "We haven't any time left people! We have to be quick! Now you, Shadow-Sandor, go down that corridor into the Sustaining Room, before you get sick." He pointed to the door that led to the crypt. Then he turned to Estelle. "You, young lady, step inside the shadow-maker."

Estelle stepped in and closed the door. A thick, glowing yellow fog swiftly enveloped her. She thought she might choke, but found she could breathe normally. It may have looked like gas, but it was actually just a very intense kind of light. It wasn't entirely inert, however. She felt its effect very faintly as a kind of pulling against her skin and even deeper than that, as if something – some essence – was being studied, copied, drawn out. It wasn't unpleasant, just slightly disconcerting. And it was over very quickly. As the strange light faded, she saw, standing next to her, herself. She held out her hand to it. "Pleased to meet you, Estelle."

Her double stared at her hand and then tentatively raised her own and shook it. "Pleased to meet you, too... Estelle."

Shadow-Estelle was identical to Estelle in every way.

Looking at her was like looking at her reflection in a mirror, except that this reflection didn't move when she did.

When she stepped out of the unit, followed by her double, she saw Sandor and Carl staring at a monitor on the far side of the lab. Sandor looked bleak, while Carl looked demented with anxiety. He was pulling at the reddish tufts of hair on the sides of his head and moaning. "I don't believe it. Oh, calamity! Disaster!"

Estelle quickly told her double to head for the Sustaining Room, then raced over to join Sandor and Carl.

"What is it?" she asked.

Sandor pointed at the screen. It showed flickery images of the front room upstairs. "This is live footage," he explained. "Carl installed CCTV cameras in each of his rooms."

The boarded-up window had been smashed inwards, its shattered remains spread across the floor, along with Carl's takeaway rubbish. The television and armchair had been pulled apart, their broken carcasses and innards adding to the mess.

"I'm so sorry," she said to Carl, placing a hand on his shoulder.

He looked up at her, frowning. "Sorry? For that? I don't care too hoots about that. They can trash the whole house for all I care. What concerns me is who's doing the trashing."

The screen changed to show the kitchen, and there, for the first time, Estelle caught sight of one of the perpetrators of the destruction. It was a black-shirted soldier who was in the process of ripping a cupboard door from its hinges. But he was moving strangely, his limbs warping as if without bones. He turned slowly towards the camera, and Estelle leapt backwards, her hand clamped to her mouth, as she caught sight of the man's eyes and teeth.

"He's a soul shadow!" she cried. "They're using soul shadows!"

"Those criminals!" screamed Carl. "Those gangsters! They've found some means of controlling the creatures, and now they're using them to inflict destruction and – I've no doubt of it – murder!"

"We can still carry out our plan though, can't we?" Sandor urged. "We can send the decoys up there. The real blackshirts must be waiting outside the house, and they'll nab them, thinking they're us. Then we can make our escape."

Carl shook his head. "I'm not sure. They must have filled the upstairs with the bad type of zeta radiation. If our doubles are exposed to it, they may turn bad, too. And they'll lead them all down here."

Then an idea struck Estelle. "What about escaping through the back way? You said there was a forgotten door to the main crypt. We could get out through the church."

Again Carl shook his head. "I told you, it's blocked by that tomb. The space is too narrow. We could never get out."

Estelle was getting a little tired of his defeatism. "Let's just try, shall we?" She strode out of the lab and into the corridor, pleased to hear the clatter of crutches and squeak of the wheelchair behind her. In the Sustaining Room she spotted the three shadow creatures sitting facing each other on the floor. Shadow-Carl was saying something, but all three looked up when she entered. She smiled at them, hoping inwardly that the door did turn out to be accessible and these kindly creatures wouldn't have to be sacrificed.

Carl raised a curtain at the back of the room to reveal a low, oaken door with a big rusty key in the lock. With some effort, he turned the key and pushed open the door. It creaked open no more than thirty centimetres before hitting a large stone surface. Estelle peered through. Sandor joined her.

"There's no way we'd get through there," he said bleakly.

"I could," said Estelle, and before anyone could say another word, she squeezed herself through the gap. It was bone-crushingly tight between the stone monument and the wall behind, but within a few seconds she had wriggled herself through it and was standing in the main crypt. She stared triumphantly back at Sandor, but he just shook his head sadly.

"I can't get through there, and I can't let you go alone," he said. "We have to stick together. I'd never forgive myself if anything happened to you."

"It's OK," she assured him. "I can run to another village and get help. Anything's better, surely, than staying down here, waiting to be captured and killed."

"No!" said Sandor. "For once you have to listen to me, Es. The exits to this village are being watched, I'm sure of it. They'll catch you."

Estelle suddenly got impatient with him. "You don't like me playing the hero, is that it? You want me to stay down here with you, so you can live up to your self-image – so that you can try and protect me in some final, pointless

123

act of self-sacrifice!"

"No, that's not it." Sandor bit his lip. "It's just... I'm scared that we'll die not knowing what happened to each other." She felt the intensity of his gaze and it surprised her. "If they get us, I want to be with you, Es. You see, I –"

"Wait!" shouted Carl, butting in just as Estelle thought Sandor might be about to say something very interesting indeed. "I've just had a crazy idea. If Estelle could break open that tomb, we might be able to make multiple soul shadows of the corpse. We could use these to help us fight the evil soul shadows upstairs!"

Sandor stared at him. "Make a soul shadow of a corpse? Would that work?"

"I don't know," spluttered Carl. "I've never tried it before. But there's no reason why it shouldn't!"

SIX

Before Estelle or Sandor could say another word, Carl had sped away on his wheelchair back up the corridor to his laboratory.

They stood there awkwardly looking at each other through the gap in the door, while the muffled bangs and crashes continued overhead.

"Is Carl mad doing this?" Estelle asked.

"Probably," said Sandor. "But what choice do we have? The soul shadows we've created won't be any match for the killers upstairs, and they could turn evil through exposure to the light up there. But a small squadron of 'corpse shadows' might just make the difference, and provide enough of a distraction to allow us to make our escape."

"I could still make a run for it, Sandor."

His eyes turned worried again. "I can't let you do that, Es."

In truth, she'd lost enthusiasm for the idea herself. She didn't want to leave Sandor now, not after what he'd just said about wanting to be with her. And she was dying to find out what he'd been about to say before Carl had interrupted.

"What were you going to say to me just now?" she asked, trying to sound as if it didn't matter much to her.

Sandor frowned, as if struggling to recall, though she didn't believe his memory could be that bad. "Ah yes, well the thing is, I…"

Irritatingly, he had become distracted again, this time by something going on in the annex, which Estelle wasn't able to see.

"Well of all the crazy things…" he began, before trailing off.

"What is it?" she prompted.

Sandor was looking at something going on to his right and whatever it was was now making him blush – a sight she never thought she'd live to witness.

"Er, you really don't want to know," he said eventually.

Estelle was now so curious about what she was missing, she almost decided to wriggle back into the annex to take a look, but was prevented from doing so by the return of Carl with a large metal-headed mallet lying across his lap. "We've no time for niceties, young lady," he said to Estelle, as Sandor passed it through to her. "You must use all your strength to smash the lid of that coffin."

The grey stone coffin was bulky, but plain, with very little ornamentation. On its side, the following words were inscribed:

The shadows are deepest where there is much light
The soul that suffers goes strong into the night
Rev. Edmund Craven (1841–1898)
May sweet Jesus grant him eternal rest

There was something faintly disturbing about the words of the epitaph. This sounded like a troubled man. Were they doing the right thing resurrecting him?

"Hurry up!" she heard Carl's voice call.

Brushing aside her doubts, Estelle picked up the mallet, raised it high and let the heavy iron head fall onto a corner of the coffin lid. It made a ringing crack that echoed around the crypt. Chips of stone flew up and a deep splinter appeared in the surface of the lid. Three more energetic blows with the mallet and the entire corner of the lid broke and fell inward with a loud clunk. Breathlessly, she continued to hurl the mallet head down until more than half of the lid was smashed. Only then did she dare to look inside.

The musty smell made her cough as she peered into the murky interior. The Rev. Edmund Craven had been dead for over a hundred years, and, of course, Estelle expected to see no more than a skeleton. She was therefore surprised to find a wizened yet well-preserved body lying amid the shattered fragments at the base of the coffin. The body was dressed in green and white priestly robes, now coated with dust. The shrivelled head had brownish, leathery skin stretched tight over a fine-boned skull. There were deep creases in the forehead between the closed eyes, as if the man had been in turmoil or pain before he died. His small, gnarled hands were clasped across his chest. "What can you see?" Carl urgently demanded. "What condition is the body in?"

"Looks pretty good to me," said Estelle. "Considering."

Taking a deep breath, she reached inside and placed her hands beneath the corpse's knees and back. Worried it might fall apart, she raised it as slowly and gently as she could. The body was very light and it was easy to lift out of the coffin. Averting her gaze from that pain-wracked face, she passed it carefully through the gap to Sandor, then squeezed herself back into the annex.

She immediately looked around to see what had caused Sandor to blush, and when she saw it, she only wanted to giggle. Shadow-Sandor and Shadow-Estelle, oblivious to all around them, were seated next to each other, leaning against a pillar, holding hands and looking into each other's eyes. That's so sweet! she wanted to say. How could Sandor not find that the sweetest thing? But Sandor's attention was now riveted on the corpse. "It's still got its skin and hair!" he said incredulously as he laid it on the floor.

"Remarkable!" agreed Carl. "Natural mummification. It sometimes occurs in crypts if the conditions are sufficiently cool and dry. So far, my friends, fortune appears to be smiling on us. Now, we must work fast. Young lady, will you please carry the body to the shadow-maker? And be careful with it!"

While Sandor went ahead, holding doors open for her, Estelle picked up the corpse and carried it down the tunnel to the lab.

There was now an eerie quiet upstairs. Estelle wondered if there was anything left to destroy. She glanced at the security monitor and saw that it was blank. "They must have found and destroyed my cameras," muttered Carl as he, too, noticed the dark screen. "I fear it won't be long before they find us."

"Are you seriously planning to reanimate that?" Sandor

wondered, staring at the corpse now propped up in the shadow-maker.

"If you mean generate soul shadows from it, then yes. Why not?" responded Carl as he fiddled around with the dials and switches on his control panel. "We've done it successfully with rat corpses, although they were, admittedly, a little fresher than this specimen."

"But you've got to have something to… generate from," stammered Sandor. "I mean, I'm no scientist but –"

"This is no time to get into arguments about metaphysics, young man!" snapped Carl. "What is body and what is soul? Just accept that there is something remaining within that decaying matter, some residual essence if you will, that the zeta rays are sensitive to and can in some mysterious way reproduce. I know as little about how it happens as you do. I have no idea what nature of shadow a corpse that old will generate, or if it will generate anything at all. But we must try! Now, if we've finished with our philosophising, would you please close the shadow-maker door."

Sandor slid shut the door, Carl pushed a lever forward and the unit filled with yellow light.

Estelle kept her eyes fixed on the glowing shadow-maker, fearful yet intensely curious to see what, if anything, would step out of it. The process seemed to take an age – Carl had decided to bombard it with as big a dose of radiation as he could safely administer in the hope of finding something to awaken in that rotten shell.

At last, the light faded and Sandor slid back the door. The corpse lay propped against the rear wall in the same position, its head lolling sideways like a broken-necked doll. The rest of the unit remained concealed behind frosted glass. Estelle, Carl and Sandor listened for any sound of movement, but all was still and silent.

"Alas," croaked Carl. "It must have been too old. I don't think –"

Then he broke off, for they had all seen a shifting of the shadows behind the closed part of the unit. Estelle jumped as a claw-like hand suddenly gripped the edge of the door. There came a soft sliding shuffle and a figure appeared at the door – an ancient, hunchbacked man in his green and white cassock.

Carl rolled forwards, ready to support it as it emerged into the light. The figure opened its eyes, which were big and scared, with the whites showing all around the blue irises. It opened its mouth and its teeth were yellow within the shrunken hole of its mouth. It emitted a hollow wail that sounded like the wind passing through a forest of bones, and a sour, primordial stench filled the room.

"Quick, help him into the Sustaining Room," yelled Carl.

Estelle hesitated. Seeing those long-dead limbs coming jerkily to life affronted her at a deep level – it looked freakish and wrong.

"For pity's sake!" screamed Carl. "The poor man's about to expire!"

She ran to support the creature, which was starting to collapse. As she placed her left arm around its thin shoulders, its long, emaciated fingers clutched at her right wrist with horrible vitality.

"Wait there with him," ordered Carl. "I'm going to try and make some more shadows. Sandor, stay here. I may need you."

The corpse shadow moved in step with Estelle in a lurching shuffle down the corridor and she had to hold her breath to avoid the acid reek of the air spilling from its mouth. When they reached the Sustaining Room, she let the creature lie down on the cool stone floor, and it seemed to find some comfort in that position – at least its eyes lost their horrified stare and the mouth became small again. She sat watching it, revolted by its twitchy little movements, tempted to put the abomination out of its misery by smashing its head in with a brick. A sudden tap on her shoulder made her flinch.

"Sorry to make you feared," came a soft, shy voice.

She had forgotten she wasn't alone in the room, and was relieved to see it was only Shadow-Estelle.

"That's OK," Estelle replied.

"Can Shadow-Estelle speak her feelings to you?"

Estelle nodded. "Yes, of course."

The girl sat down facing her. "You are Shadow Estelle's spirit-mother, yes?"

"Er, yes. I suppose you could call me that."

"Shadow-Carl is teaching Shadow-Estelle. Shadow-Carl is clever-clever."

"Yes, he is."

"Shadow-Carl teaches that you are the mother of the feelings in Shadow-Estelle. Make her heart go bump-bump-bump."

"That's right."

"Shadow-Estelle is afeared of alone-ness. Of trapped-ness. Shadow-Estelle not ever want to be alone."

Estelle felt a small sob in her chest when she heard that.

She looked into her double's dumb, innocent eyes. "Yes, I'm afraid I'm the mother of those feelings," she admitted, pressing her lips together to stop them from shaking.

"Why Shadow-Estelle is so afeared?"

Estelle reached out and brushed the girl's cheek with her fingers. "Because once, a long time ago, your spirit-mother was trapped in a room on her own. Since then she's been trying to get over it, but it's hard. I'm sorry I've passed that fear onto you."

Her soul shadow nodded gravely. Then her face broke into a smile. "Shadow-Estelle feel safe with Shadow-Sandor. He very nice."

"Yes, he is," Estelle had to agree.

"He make her heart go bump-bump-bump, but in nice way."

Estelle stifled a giggle. It was like listening to herself aged 13, or a version of herself who'd been raised by wolves and was only starting to get to grips with human society.

The girl's smile faded. "But Shadow-Carl say there will soon be war. Shadow-Carl is afeared of war. But Shadow-Sandor say he want fight in war. Shadow-Estelle is afeared that Shadow-Sandor will die, and she will be alone."

"Shadow-Sandor won't need to fight," Estelle assured her. She indicated the twitching figure lying on the floor. "We're making new soldiers to fight."

The girl took in the corpse shadow for the first time, and her smile reappeared. "Shadow-Sandor won't need to fight," she repeated to herself. "Spirit-Mother make new soldiers to fight."

"Book time!" called Shadow-Carl from the far side of

the room. He stood there, brandishing a large book he'd plucked from a shelf full of similarly bulky tomes.

"Shadow-Estelle must go," said the girl, getting up. "Shadow-Carl is teaching us more."

From the floor behind Estelle came a dry cough. When she looked, she saw the corpse shadow had sat up.

"So," he growled with a voice like a sack of nails being dragged across concrete, "the Good Lord, in His infinite wisdom, has seen fit to bring me out of retirement. Well, I suppose it was only to be expected. For this sinner, eternal rest was always an unlikely prospect." The tendons in his neck creaked like old leather as he began to examine his surroundings. Recognition dawned on his withered features, as he rasped: "It seems I have been returned to the very scene of my blasphemous undertakings. How entirely appropriate." Finally, his eyes fell on Estelle. They were an arid blue, like cracked, empty swimming pools, and she thought she saw a terrible remorse in their dark centres. He coughed once more and a small cloud of yellowish powder burst from his mouth. "Are you an angel?" he asked her. "Or a demon?"

"I'm Estelle," she replied, trying her best to hide her revulsion.

"Estelle," he repeated. "It means 'star', does it not?" He scrutinised her even more carefully, making her want to squirm. "I must say, you don't look like an instrument of divine vengeance."

"I assure you, I'm not."

"Well, then, why did you awaken me?" he barked.

She wondered how best to phrase her answer.

Well, the thing is, we needed some bait to distract the killers upstairs so that we could escape, and you just happened to be available.

"We need your help," she said finally. "This is the 21st century. We're being attacked, and –"

Edmund Craven raised a bony hand. "21st century? Are you saying I've been dead for over a hundred years?"

She nodded.

His eyes filled with wonder, and then flashed with alarm. "Attacked by whom?"

"We call them soul shadows. They look a bit like humans, but they're evil, with black, shiny eyes and sharp teeth, and they like to eat our flesh. They were created by –"

"Do not speak his name!" shrieked Edmund, his leathery cheeks twitching with horror. Then he uttered a dreadful wail and beat his narrow chest, making a hollow, dead sound like a funeral drum. "I should have known this would be the consequence," he wept. "I am to blame for your predicament, Estelle. I summoned him here, all those years ago. I and my fellow devotees, with our black magic rituals, we invited the Evil One to this place, and now he has sent forth an army of his dark-eyed minions to attack you. You, my poor young lady, are reaping the consequences of our diabolical act."

To Estelle's alarm, Edmund suddenly threw himself face down on the ground, his spindly arms thrust forwards and hands clasped in an attitude of supplication. "Dear Lord," he cried, "I thank you for granting me this opportunity to redeem myself. Through the intercession of this young lady, you have generously resurrected me so that I can put right the great harm that I did in my lifetime.

Thank you, Lord. Thank you."

Estelle's initial disgust had by now evolved into something approaching sympathy for the pitiable creature now lying prostrate before her. But she was also puzzled.

"Black magic rituals?" she said. "That doesn't sound like priestly behaviour."

He looked up at her, oily tears welling in the hollows of his enormous eyes. "For many years, I led a double life," he croaked. "A man of the cloth by day, delivering sermons from my pulpit, ministering to the needs of my flock – while by night I was the Magus of a very different institution: the Church of the Cloven Hoof we called ourselves, and we met right here, in this place. We had read our Michelet, our de Sade, our Carducci. They had revealed to us the seductive power of the left-hand path, the inverted pentagram. Oh," – he laughed – "we became quite intoxicated with that power!" Edmund's face then grew tight with contrition, as he recalled himself. "We were always masked," he said. "Never knew each other's identities, though we guessed them well enough. It was a small village, and my voice was, of course, well known. We kept our secret to our graves, and my grave was to be, quite literally, the guardian of that secret. I had my coffin built directly in front of the door to our ungodly shrine, to conceal it, so I thought, for all eternity." He bowed his head. "But, of course, one can have no secrets from the Lord."

Estelle decided it was best not to disabuse Edmund of his notion that he'd been brought back to fulfil a divine quest. There wasn't time to explain the true situation, and by allowing him to interpret his circumstances in his own way, he'd hopefully prove more co-operative.

At that moment, Sandor limped into the room followed by two more Edmund Cravens. Both corpse shadows collapsed to the floor and lay there unmoving. These ones looked, if anything, even weaker and more decrepit than the first one.

"Carl says that's the limit," Sandor told Estelle. "The third one may not even survive.

"Why not?" she asked.

He shrugged. "Basically, whatever the stuff is, in the corpse, that they're being copied from, there's not enough of it to stretch to copying any more. Or something like that."

The first Edmund recoiled in shock at the sight of his doubles. "More of me? What kind of devilry is this?" He turned to Estelle, doubts now clouding the eyes that had earlier been so full of morbid conviction. "Don't tell me that you people are also meddling in the black arts!"

"No, no," said Estelle, determined to sustain him in his illusions. "My friends and I prayed to the Lord that he would revive you to help us in our plight, and, er, Lo! – in his great generosity, the Lord said unto us... Indeed, verily he said unto us, I shall send forth a whole multitude of Edmunds to, er, do my bidding."

Edmund frowned at her. "Egad, you people of the future speak strangely!"

"Estelle?" queried Sandor, looking equally bewildered. "What's got into you?"

Before she could explain, Carl entered, looking more tense than ever. "I can hear them up there!" he warbled. "They're drilling into the floorboards now. It's only a matter of time before they find us."

"I am ready to fight," coughed Edmund, trying to get to his feet. "Lead me to the minions of the Evil One." He got as far as a crouch, but the weakness of his limbs put the completion of the task beyond him, and he soon toppled back to the floor. Estelle rushed over and helped him up, propping him against a pillar. "I trust," panted Edmund, "that the Lord will grant me the requisite strength to do my duty when the time comes."

"The time is now!" lamented Carl. "They're coming for us, don't you understand? Oh, I was a fool to think I could shadowcast a hundred-year-old corpse and send it out to fight. Look at the thing! He can barely stand!"

"Stand I shall, and fight!" protested Edmund. "Lead the way, and let me prove my worth."

"I shan't be leading the way," said Carl sadly. "In fact, my friends, I don't think I shall be going up at all today."

"Why ever not?" demanded Sandor. "Don't you want to escape?"

Carl shook his head. "See this?" he raised his hand from the push-rim of his wheelchair. It was shaking violently. "Frankly, I'm terrified. I simply can't go up there. Call me a coward if you want, I don't care. But I'm staying down here in the Sustaining Room with the soul shadows. I'll seal off the door from the lab. You two should stay down here, too. They won't find us." He shook his head manically, as if trying to convince himself. "They won't ever find us in here."

"They will!" countered Sandor. "And we'll be cornered like rats. That's no way to die, Carl. We have to fight our way out of here, like we agreed!"

"How?" challenged Carl. "The corpse shadows will be cut down in two minutes. What kind of a diversion will that be? You won't stand a chance."

"I want help," came a deep voice from the back of the room. Shadow-Sandor put down a book he was looking at and approached them. "I want help you escape," he said. "I want fight bad soul shadows upstairs."

Sandor grinned and clapped his double on the shoulder. "Good man!"

"No!" pleaded another, higher voice that Estelle immediately recognised as similar to her own. She watched as her shadow now stepped forward. "Shadow-Sandor not need to fight. Spirit-Mother say she make new soldiers to fight."

"New soldiers no good for fighting," insisted Shadow-Sandor. "I want help." He looked distraught at the effect of his words on the girl, who then broke down in tears. Estelle ran to her and held her in her arms as sobs wracked her body.

"It's OK," she whispered.

"Shadow-Estelle is afeared that – that he will d–die."

"Don't worry," Estelle soothed. "Whatever happens, I promise that I'll come back for you."

The girl immediately looked up on hearing this and ceased her crying. Her eyes were startlingly clear and trusting. Estelle had made the vow without really thinking, and now wondered if it had been the wisest thing to do.

Estelle and Sandor went to work massaging the Edmunds' ancient limbs. It may have been Sandor's over-vigorous technique or maybe it would have happened anyway, but just five minutes after being born, the third and weakest of the Edmunds quietly expired. That left an "attack party" of two Edmunds and Shadow-Sandor, to be followed up by Estelle and Sandor. Carl, who could not be persuaded to go with them, would remain behind the sealed door of the Sustaining Room with Shadows-Carl and Estelle.

When the time came for the off, the whole party reconvened in the lab. Carl had flooded the room with the sustaining form of zeta-pro radiation to give the soul shadow contingent an extra burst of vitality before their ascent. From above came a clamour of mallets and drills being applied to the flooring.

The elder Edmund looked around the lab. "This was once our little temple," he muttered. "Now it seems the setting for another form of dark magic."

"So that was your mess, was it?" grumbled Carl. "It took me ages to get rid of those blood stains and remove the pentagram carvings from the walls."

Shadow-Estelle hugged her man and then her spirit-mother, while Shadow-Carl shook hands with everyone. Then Carl impatiently shepherded them back up the passageway to the Sustaining Room. A door was slid across the arch-shaped opening, and it looked remarkably like just another piece of wall – as Carl had intended. A button was pressed and the pole descended, topped by a small square of flooring from the cupboard under the stairs.

The two Edmunds and Shadow-Sandor stepped onto the platform, and Estelle was uncomfortably aware that they were sending them to their deaths. However much she told herself that they were just shadow-creatures – not really human – that wasn't how it felt.

Sandor had gathered some makeshift weaponry from the lab. Carl had kept a couple of sharpened kitchen knives there for self-defence, and Sandor took one for himself and gave the other to Estelle. He handed his shadow the large metal-headed mallet. "Do as much damage as you can," he told him.

"Yes, spirit-father."

"Let's have none of that," said Sandor. Estelle was surprised to note that his eyes were moist. "I never had a brother," he said. "It feels great…" He laughed, and wiped his eye. "I'd be proud to call you brother."

"And I, too… brother."

"Remember," added Sandor. "The light up there is bad! It'll turn you bad like them!" He handed smaller hammers to the two Edmunds. "Kill as many of those things as you can, then get out of the house. You won't live long in the sunlight, but at least you'll die as you are now: as good… as good… men." Again, he rubbed his eye.

"Fear not, I know all about the evil light," said the older Edmund (the younger, weaker one, had yet to find his voice). "I was its captive for too long during my living years, and I remain only too aware of its allure. As for death, I welcome it. I only pray that, before it reclaims me, I will have done my duty and killed as many of those demons as my strength will allow." He made a practice swipe with the hammer, which almost sent him tumbling to the floor. Estelle caught him and helped him back onto the platform.

"Go get 'em, Father," she smiled.

Sandor pressed the "Up" button, the platform began its ascent and its cargo gradually disappeared from view.

Estelle felt awkward. She could see Sandor was in distress and wanted to comfort him, but didn't know if he'd welcome it. He gave a short, brutal laugh. "There I go, watching another young soldier go off to his death."

"He's a shadow," she reminded him gently.

"Looked human enough to me."

Much quicker than she expected, the platform began its descent, while from upstairs they heard a sudden roar of voices and sounds of clashing wood and metal.

Shockingly, a black-shirted soul shadow came into view, crouched on the descending platform – it must have leapt on as its previous occupants got off. Its black eyes fixed them in a pitiless gaze, while its giant mouth, jagged with teeth, grinned malevolently. When the creature was still halfway to the floor, its arm shot outwards, doubling in length, and it grabbed Estelle's neck. The pressure on her windpipe was intense. Her arms flailed wildly as she tried to draw breath. Then came a flash of steel, and the hand, together with a short stump of arm, dropped lifelessly to the floor. Sandor's knife flew again and the soul shadow fell from the platform, the blade stuck in its belly. He plucked the knife, which was smeared with greyish foam, from its stomach, and hauled himself onto the platform. After pressing the button marked 'Up', Estelle jumped on too.

"Remember, just get out of the house as fast as you can," Sandor murmured.

The platform arrived in the cramped cupboard, and

through the gap in the door, she glimpsed the kitchen, gutted almost beyond recognition – the walls were bare brick, the floor a giant mound of plaster fragments, broken cabinets, smashed furniture and shattered crockery. Everything was seen through the filter of a nauseating yellowish glow – the light in the Sustaining Room had been a similar colour, but didn't make her stomach churn like this. Sandor threw wide the cupboard door and began limping at a fierce pace up the corridor. There were no soul shadows in immediate view, but the sound of approaching footsteps told Estelle they were close. To her right, she glimpsed the front room, which was in a similarly vandalised state. The rear of a van could be seen, parked very close to the smashed front window, its back doors wide open so its interior was in view. The van was flooded with the same yellow light, and framed in its entrance was the unmistakable figure of Derek Atkins.

Estelle didn't have time to do anything more than observe this disturbing sight as she dashed past – she wasn't even sure if he'd seen her. Ahead of her, Sandor was manoeuvring himself around a fallen figure – the younger Edmund Craven, now as motionless as any self-respecting corpse ought to be. The elder Edmund lay slumped just beyond him, but he was still stirring. He looked up as Estelle passed him, and gave a mad laugh. Most of his teeth were missing, having perhaps been smashed out of his head by his own hammer, which lay on the floor beside him. There was a gaping hole in his chest.

"Good lady, you should have seen me," he wheezed. "I was magnificent. I came out swinging and I clouted that demon, as clean a hit as you could ever wish for."

He looked ecstatically happy. But Estelle saw that the new teeth already pushing through his shrivelled gums had a distinctly sharp look to them. Sandor spotted this, too, and dropped one of his crutches so he could drag the corpse shadow to the front door. Leaning against the wall, he pulled open the door and sunlight washed through the corridor. Estelle was about to follow him outside when she felt herself being hauled back and thrown to the carpet. A black-shirted soul shadow loomed above her, baring its teeth. A red light glowed in the centre of its forehead. She used one arm to try to drag herself out of its range, while the other struggled to extract the knife from her belt. As the creature swooped towards her throat, she drove the knife upwards into its chest. It collapsed on her, and with some effort, she threw it off, pulling the knife out as she did so. Sandor was now back in the corridor, urging her to get out. But like a nightmare, another soul shadow leapt out from the front room, once more cutting off her escape. She saw Sandor lunging at it with his crutch, prompting it to twist its head 180 degrees, while its body remained facing her. Its arm dislocated itself and flailed like a bullwhip towards Sandor, causing him to collapse in the corner by the front door.

Estelle cried out in anguish, and the creature's head jerked around to face her once more, its rattling breath coming in short, excited gasps as it studied her. This one also had a mysterious red light in its forehead, like an evil third eye. Feeling the staircase against her shoulder, she hurriedly climbed to her feet and began backing her way up the stairs. It was following her, as she had hoped it would – her only thought at this moment was to coax it away from the unconscious Sandor.

That's it. Forget about him on the floor! Come this way!

About halfway up, she turned and raced up the remaining stairs, skidded around the newel post at the top and dashed along a short corridor into a large bedroom at the front of the house. It was empty, thank goodness! The bed, like every other piece of furniture in the house, had been senselessly smashed and was now an unrecognisable heap of broken timber, springs, pillow feathers and bedding. The boards that had covered the two windows had been ripped out, adding to the general mess, but both sets of curtains, bizarrely, had been carefully closed, and were now billowing gently in the breeze.

Through a doorway in the wall opposite was a tiny bathroom, containing a shower, washbasin and toilet. A soft creak in the corridor outside told Estelle her pursuer was close. As quietly as she could she edged her way into the bathroom, closed the door and slid home the little chrome bolt. She leaned against a small patch of wall between the shower cubicle and the door, cooling her cheek against the white tiles and clutching her knife to her chest like a talisman.

Another creak of floorboards sounded, this time closer, followed by the squeak of the bedroom door. Her breath was loud in her ears and she tried to quieten it by breathing through her nose.

There were sounds of movement in the bedroom. The wall she was leaning against shook after being punched or kicked. She heard the gravelly respiration of the creature as it searched for her. Was there a tone of frustration in that sound? Why didn't it try a different room? Could it smell her? Tremors coursed through her body as the wall behind her received another hefty thump. A small cry escaped from her throat.

Did it know she was in here? Was it playing games?

The door handle next to her turned, and the door was pulled forcefully back against the bolt. The handle began rattling furiously. Soon the entire door was shaking under the frenzied attack. The noise resounded through the tiny washroom. Estelle clutched her ears and shut her eyes. "Go away!" she screamed. "Leave me alone!"

Suddenly, it stopped. She blinked and opened her eyes. Her skin was now clammy with sweat. Glancing to her right, she saw that the screws fixing the little bolt to the door and its frame were looser than before, but they had held.

The silence persisted. Had it given up?

She was about to open the door to peek out when she heard that groaning breath again, very near, and then –

BANG!

The entire door bulged inwards with the force of a massive blow. Estelle screamed. Cracks had appeared in the door at about the height of her head, and the screws holding the bolt were now half an inch clear of the door frame. Before she could even draw another breath, a second blow sent wood splinters flying. A hole had opened in the door and a yellow-clawed fist streaked into view. The fist, at the end of its pliable forearm, whipped around blindly like the head of a scourge, smashing at the interior wall of the washroom, missing Estelle's head by fractions of an inch. Terrified, she collapsed backwards into the shower cubicle and tried to close the folding door, as she watched the bolt finally give way and the door was ripped backwards.

The creature leaned into the little room and hauled back the shower door. It sounded to her ears like a hysterical steam-driven machine as its glittering black eyes feasted on her cowering figure. She glimpsed a long black tongue flickering between its needle-sharp teeth, and the red light in its forehead seemed to brighten, as if with excitement. A hand lashed out and pinioned the wrist of her knife hand against the shower tray. The other hand grabbed her left arm and hauled her painfully upwards, closer to its mouth. She felt the slime of its tongue across her cheek, smelled the fetid vapour of its breath, and prayed that death would be quick, that the teeth would find an artery, and sudden, massive blood loss would end this unbearable terror.

Instead she heard a voice calling her name.

"Estelle?"

And then the creature's head seemed to cave in from the top as a heavy black mallet head came crashing down on its cranium. The soul shadow fell backwards, revealing... Sandor. No, not Sandor: his shadow. The injury in the right leg, and the mallet, told her that. Brave shadow!

Estelle staggered to a kneeling position, and then to her feet. "Thank you," she gasped. "Thank you so much." She stumbled out of the cubicle. "Sandor will be so proud... Now we must... get out of here."

She hadn't really looked at him properly yet – just threw an arm around him and began coaxing him towards the door. It was only when he didn't move that she glanced at his face. And then, with a plunging heart, she took in the inky eyes, the ravenous, spike-edged grin spreading across his face.

"Oh no!" she screamed. "Please no! You're not one of them. You're Shadow-Sandor. One of the good guys. Don't you remember? Let's get you out of here. Quickly!" She began pulling at his arm, despite her growing fear of him, despite the yellow talon-like nails that were now pushing out of the ends of his fingers. She turned to face him, desperate to find some remnant of humanity in the void of his eyes.

"Remember Shadow-Estelle? She loves you! She's waiting for you!"

Something flickered in his eyes when she said that – some doubt or memory made him hesitate. His grin faded, his eyes softened and shrank. But it didn't last. When he turned to her again, the evil smirk was back and she knew he no longer saw her as anything other than meat. His talons bit into the flesh of her wrist. He pulled her towards him… and screamed in pain.

The curtains of both windows had been flung wide open and the zeta radiation was immediately banished in a torrent of bright natural light. There was a bustle of activity in the room. She sensed blackshirts around her – humans this time, not soul shadows. But her eyes remained on Shadow-Sandor, who had now fallen to his knees and had raised his arms to try to shield his head from the dazzling onslaught from the window. Already, his arms were disintegrating, crumbling into fine powder. She felt sad to see him like that – sad for Sandor, sad for Shadow-Estelle. It was no way for a soldier to die.

"Ahem." A throat was theatrically cleared by the bedroom door. She turned to see Derek standing there.

He was holding a bulky black box topped by a red light. "What a pleasure to see you again, Estelle," he simpered, waggling his eyebrows at her.

"Where's Sandor?" she asked flatly.

Derek nodded towards the two blackshirts stationed at the window and they closed the curtains. He came further into the room, adjusting the controls on his black box. Into the room stepped two black-shirted soul shadows. They were still and erect, like two human soldiers standing to attention – the only clue to their shadow-identity being the shiny black eyes, now mostly hooded, and the red lights implanted in their foreheads. Between them was the semi-slumped figure of Sandor, his face red and swollen from a recent pummelling.

He opened his puffy eyes as much as he could, and saw her. "Hullo, Es," he slurred. "I'm afraid they got me."

She rushed towards him but her arm was grabbed tightly by a soul shadow standing behind her. It was the same one who'd just attacked her in the shower cubicle. He now seemed recovered from Shadow-Sandor's mallet attack, yet was apparently no longer interested in eating her. In fact, as soon as she stopped struggling, the soul shadow released her arm.

Derek pressed a button on his black box and suddenly she felt the soul shadow's hands on her again. One hand slid and slithered all over her body. She tried to get away, but the vice-like grip of its other hand wouldn't allow it. When the disgusting ordeal was finally over, Derek raised his eyebrows at the soul shadow. "Find anything?" he asked. "No? That's good."

He turned to Estelle, stroking his black box

affectionately. "Brilliant, don't you think?" he purred. "Tame soul shadows. And with one flick of a switch, I can turn them back into killers."

"Why would you want to do that, Derek?" Estelle demanded. "Carl Henrison told me this whole thing began because you wanted to develop spare organs for transplant. How did that turn into creating remote-controlled flesh-eaters?"

"Oh, I don't know," he shrugged nonchalantly. "Mission creep, I guess!... We created these things. It was our responsibility, don't you think, to figure out how to control them?"

"And was it also your responsibility to terrorise a fellow scientist?"

She seemed to have struck a nerve with that question – Derek's cool façade cracked just a little. "Carl was threatening to go public on us before we had a chance to get the situation under control!" he said impatiently. "That would have killed the whole project stone dead. We've learned how to control the lab-grown soul shadows – you've seen the results here today. But the wild ones – the ones that grew from the radiation leakage in the forest – they're a tougher proposition."

Estelle was standing a short distance from one of the windows. As Derek talked, she glanced through a narrow gap that had been left between the two curtains. She could see that the window itself was smashed to pieces and was now just a gaping hole in the wall. Directly below it was the roof of the van...

"Carl wouldn't see reason," Derek continued. "He failed to see the bigger picture: the vast potential rewards, scientific and financial, of our project."

Without turning her head, Estelle glanced quickly through the broken window again. The van's roof was a relatively short jump from there. Just two quick strides, a hop through the window, another hop to the ground, and she'd be away. If she acted with sufficient suddenness and speed, the nearest guard wouldn't even have time to react.

Derek was confidently droning on, "We had him nicely pinned down here though. We'd scared him enough to ensure he'd sit tight for at least a few more weeks, until the wild soul shadows had been dealt with. But then you two had to show up on his doorstep. Thanks to you, we suddenly had a crisis on our hands. He could pass his secret onto you, and then you could pass it onto the press. Luckily, it would appear he didn't pass it on to either of you."

"What secret would that be?" asked Estelle, edging very slightly closer to the window.

Derek smiled. "He didn't tell you then, did he? It's a rather long and complex formula, and smart as you are, I don't think you'd have been able to memorise it. I'm pretty sure this one hasn't either." He gestured to Sandor.

Derek's face grew more kindly as he registered the rising anger in Estelle's. "You forced this on us, my dear. But it's over now. In fact, you know what, I'll willingly let you two go free. Call it a favour returned. You rescued me once, and one good turn deserves another. I'll let you go, and tell my bosses – the ones who ordered me to haul you both back to the Facility – that you died in the siege. You haven't got the secret, so there's no real risk. All you need to do is tell me where Carl is, then you can walk away."

"Why do you want Carl all of a sudden?" Estelle asked him. "You've known where he's been for months."

"The powers that be have become nervous. After today's little incident, they've decided the safest thing would be for Carl to be permanently neutralised."

"You mean killed? If you kill him you'll never find out his secret."

Derek laughed. "I'm afraid you misunderstand. We don't want his secret. He can go to his grave with it for all we care, just so long as he doesn't tell it to anyone else before he does. And while he's alive, there's every chance he might."

"You're talking about cold-blooded murder! What secret could possibly be worth that?"

"What do you care? You only met him this morning. Just tell me where he is and you can forget all about this whole unpleasant business... And don't tell me he's in the basement lab. We've found that and he's not there. In fact we've stripped out the entire house. But I reckon there must be some little nook or cranny we've overlooked. I know he hasn't left the house today, so there has to be some other little hidey-hole we've yet to find. Now if you could just –"

"I have no idea where Carl is," said Estelle.

Derek nodded and smiled to himself, as if he'd expected this. "Just like your boyfriend said."

"He's not my boyf –"

Sandor suddenly let forth a howl of pain. Estelle was shocked to see that one of the soul shadows supporting him had deliberately dug one of its talons deep into his shoulder. It had done so just after Derek had adjusted a control on the black box. Once Estelle realised this, her shock changed to fury.

"Boyfriend or not, I detect a soft spot there, Estelle," sniggered Derek. "But don't worry, I'll try not to be jealous, although – well, put it this way – I wouldn't shed too many tears to see my love rival entirely removed from the picture…"

Estelle felt like she might explode with rage. She wanted to rush at Derek and rip that little box out of his hands.

"So what's it to be then, Estelle?" smirked Derek. "Freedom for you and your friend, or do you want to see Sandor really start to scream? Your choice."

seven

Derek smiled at Estelle as he set out his terms, and for a moment she was reminded of the cheerful, friendly guy who'd introduced himself to her just twenty-four hours earlier when she was trapped in the Facility. He'd arrived like a gust of fresh air – geeky in a charming kind of way, and entirely harmless. Could this be the same man? Hadn't he risked his life trying to help her escape from the Facility? Or had that whole escape effort been a ruse? She recalled the way he'd casually slipped an arm around her just before they left the Facility. Maybe he'd been planning to take her to some secret den of his when they were ambushed by that soul shadow.

These speculations only served to increase her anger. She was angry with Dr Kirby for ever suggesting she should stay in his insanely remote cottage where even mobile phones refused to work; angry with herself for all the bad decisions she'd made since then, the worst of which was persuading Sandor to try to save Derek when he was trapped in that car – now she wished they'd left the horrid man to die. Irrationally, she also felt angry with

Sandor for being helpless when she most needed him, and for the ridiculous hold he had over her heart. Most of all, she felt a murderous rage towards Derek and wanted nothing more than to "permanently neutralise" that smile on his face.

She tried to consider her next move, but it was hard to think rationally when she was so churned up with anger, and the jerky, asthmatic breathing of the giant soul shadow standing behind her did not exactly aid her concentration. The easiest option would be to tell Derek what he wanted. But would she ever be able to look herself in the mirror again if she did that? Not only would she be passing a death sentence on Carl Henrison, but also Shadows Carl and Estelle, and she had promised Shadow-Estelle that she'd come back for her.

There had to be an alternative, and one that didn't involve watching Sandor getting tortured. She was standing quite close to the window, and it would be relatively easy to vault out of it onto the van roof and then bounce down onto the street. She'd be round the corner and into the High Street before the nearest guard could get off a shot. But what then? She'd be on her own in a village full of armed blackshirts and their citizen sympathisers with virtually no chance of getting away. And Sandor would still be tortured. Or, worse, her little act of defiance might just provoke Derek into killing him.

There was, however, a third option – Plan C – and a rather foolhardy and desperate one it was. Plan C went like this: she would launch herself at Derek and wrestle from his grasp the black box – the remote control device he was using to control the soul shadows. She would then use this to turn the soul shadows against him and the two blackshirts guarding the windows. There were so many things that could go wrong with this plan, it was hard to know where to start. For one thing, it would take her three full paces to cross the room to where Derek was standing, and before she reached him she might be grabbed by the Derek-controlled soul shadow behind her or shot down by one of the human guards. Even if she got to Derek, she might then struggle to seize the remote control from him, offering a further opportunity for the enemy to grab or shoot her. Finally, assuming she got to Derek and managed to snatch the remote, what then? She didn't have a clue how it worked, and might very well do disastrous things with it, such as ordering the soul shadows to kill her or Sandor. So, in summary, Plan C was almost certain to end in spectacular failure, and only a complete madwoman would even begin to contemplate it.

It didn't take Estelle long to decide on Plan C.

In a sense, it was Derek who made the decision for her. "Come now, Estelle," she heard him coax. "It's make-your-mind-up time." He gave a self-satisfied chuckle, and the sound of that throaty little laugh generated a wave of such intense loathing in Estelle that she found herself charging at him before she even properly knew what she was doing. Plan C was in motion! The element of surprise was perhaps the only reason why Estelle managed to get as far as she did before anyone else in the room reacted. Her momentum carried her straight into Derek and pushed him hard against the wall behind him, knocking the breath from his lungs and the remote control from his hand. As Estelle groped for the box on the floor, she glimpsed one of the guards raising his gun towards her.

This was always going to be the point where Plan C fell apart, she reflected bitterly. She could never have hoped to master the black box and mobilise the soul shadows in the time it took for a man to aim at her and fire. But at least she'd managed, if only fleetingly, to wipe that smile off Derek's face and replace it with an expression of utter panic – a sight she would happily dwell on for the remaining seconds of her life.

A blurry movement to her left suddenly caught her eye: Sandor, who she had assumed was virtually out for the count, let fly with his good leg and knocked the guard's pistol from his hand. There was still the other guard to deal with, of course, not to mention Derek. And Estelle found herself faced with a choice: the black box or the fallen pistol. Both lay within her reach on the floor. She chose the pistol, but as she laid her hand upon it, the first guard kicked it away. She twisted herself leftwards and reached for the black box instead, but simultaneously felt someone behind her – Derek? – grab her by the shirt and drag her away from it. A gunshot blast rang in her ears and a large hole appeared in the floor where her hand had just been.

Feeling a slight slackening in the hold on her, Estelle reached again for the black box and this time managed to grab hold of it. The surface of the box was covered in buttons and switches. She pressed four or five of the buttons at random, and flicked three of the switches for good measure. The result was immediate, and startling. The soul shadows holding Sandor lost their passivity and began to growl menacingly. One of them eyed Sandor hungrily, while the other grabbed hold of Derek, making him squeal. Meanwhile, the huge soul shadow behind her lifted up the second guard by the neck and seemed about to throw him out of the window.

In the confusion, the first guard dived for his gun and then spun into a crouch, training it on Estelle. "Hand the box back to me," he advised breathlessly. But Estelle was more concerned about saving Sandor than she was about risking her life. Desperately, she tried to focus on the controls. There were four switches, presumably one for each of the soul shadows Derek had brought with him – there were just three in the room, but maybe one had been disabled in the struggle downstairs. She didn't have time to contemplate the rows of buttons so she flipped a switch at random. Nothing happened. She tried another, and the soul shadow holding Derek immediately became dead-eyed and still. Derek shoved it aside and scrambled on all fours out of the door.

Sandor was pushing at his assailant with all his remaining strength, while leaning back to keep out of range of its teeth.

"Hand it over now, or I'll kill you," barked the guard. Estelle flipped the third switch, and Sandor's attacker, mercifully, became still.

The guard fired, and Estelle felt a scorching pain in her left forearm. She dropped the box and clutched at her arm. The guard grabbed the box, but before he could engage with its controls, he was sent reeling by a second kick from Sandor, who had hopped across the room to deliver it. The kick, from Sandor's good leg, being unsupported by the other, caused Sandor to keel over as well. But he'd done enough, and Estelle quickly regained control of the box.

The pain in her arm was severe and she expected to see blood when she glanced down, but instead saw a vivid flash of dark red on her skin where the bullet must have grazed her.

"Get out of the way!" she screamed at Sandor, before pushing down the second switch – the one controlling Derek's former captor. Sandor crawled towards the window just as the soul shadow reanimated. In its immediate sightline was the first guard, and it closed on him with frightening swiftness, grabbing him and pushing him back down on the floor.

Both guards were now in the grip of soul shadows. The hulking shadow near the window remained in precisely the same pose as when she'd last looked, leaning back with arms raised high as if preparing to hurl the second guard out of the window. The terrified second guard was vainly struggling to remove himself from the creature's grip – but the shadow, for some reason, was no longer moving. Estelle glanced down at the control panel and saw that the switch controlling that shadow was pointing neither up nor down, but was at its midway point. She moved the other switch to the same position, and the captor of the first guard became similarly rigid, holding him tightly against the floor, but thankfully not actually killing him.

"Come on!" she yelled at Sandor. "Let's get out of here!"

Sandor didn't move from the window. He'd used the ledge to haul himself halfway to vertical and had now pushed his head through the curtain to stare out of it.

"Derek's getting in the van," he spat. "The scuzzbag's running away! – Again!"

Estelle sighed. "You know, I don't actually care. Let's just go."

But Sandor wasn't listening. He had by now levered himself into a sitting position on the window ledge, facing into the room. He stared at her through his puffy, half-closed eyes. "We can't let him get away, Es," he said, and, to her horror, he tipped himself backwards out of the window.

"Sandor!" she screamed, running to the window.

She saw him lying below her, winded, spreadeagled on his back, on the roof of the van, which was now starting to pull away from the house, its rear doors still open and flapping on their hinges. Estelle had less than a second to make her decision.

She jumped...

Either too slow or too late, she landed on the sloping part near the rear of the van, and could not avoid bouncing and sliding off the back. Desperately she flung out her hands and tried to grab the edge of the roof. She was able to hold on just long enough to swing herself through the doors into the van's interior, where she collapsed in a traumatised heap.

But she was denied even the briefest moment to recover her spirits. The van, she noticed, was moving erratically. It swerved one way then the other, throwing her painfully against its metal sides. When she looked up, she realised why. Derek was simultaneously trying to drive while fending off blows from Sandor's fists coming through the driver's window from above. Vaguely she wondered what Sandor would have been like if he'd been fit. Nothing seemed beyond him. He was carrying a serious leg injury and had just been beaten to a near pulp – yet he remained as tenacious as a bulldog with a bone. His never-say-die resilience must have been terrifying to Derek, who was now cowering below the level of the dashboard to avoid Sandor's fists.

The van, with its driver now effectively blind, veered wildly towards the stone wall surrounding the churchyard. Estelle braced herself for the inevitable collision, but at the last moment the van swung hard left towards the high street. It never made it. Instead, it mounted a grassy traffic island and smashed into a signpost. After much crazy weaving, they had managed a net distance of perhaps twenty metres from Carl Henrison's front door.

Derek grabbed a gun and scrambled out of the car, firing two shots in quick succession. She prayed Sandor was OK. She could hear Derek's footsteps heading cautiously towards the rear of the vehicle. He seemed equally uncertain about whether his shots had found their target. Any second now, and he would find her. She had to act fast. She slid quietly to a position just inside the right-hand rear door and gently pulled it closed, planning to open it hard into his face. The footsteps stopped. He must have seen the door moving.

"I know you're there, Estelle," came Derek's voice, and she could hear the nervousness behind his attempt at genial self-confidence. "I've got a Walther P99, my dear. If I fire now, it will blast right through the thin wall of the van. So if you want to come through this in one piece, I suggest you step out now. It's not too late to make a deal… Oh, and in case you're wondering, your boyfriend is dead. No one's going to step in and save you this time."

He couldn't know that! He couldn't possibly know that for sure!

Numb with anxiety, Estelle climbed out of the van. She noticed that the nearby shops were shuttered, and anxious, curious faces were clustered at the windows of the apartments above.

"Good girl," beamed Derek. The gun pointing at her was wobbling. His face was pale and visibly sweaty.

She raised her eyes to the roof of the van, hoping for a sight of Sandor, but saw nothing.

"Hand it over," said Derek. Estelle noticed she was still holding the remote control and passed it to him.

"The same deal holds," said Derek. "Tell me where Carl is, and I'll let you go."

"And if I don't?" she asked.

His smile became even broader. "Then I'll have to find ways of persuading you."

"Let her go," came a weak voice from behind.

They both turned to see Carl there, at the corner of Church Street, blinking in the bright sunlight. He was leaning against one arm of his wheelchair and looking very fragile.

"Carl Henrison," chuckled Derek. "The rat resurfaces."

"I'm sick of hiding from you, Derek," said Carl. "You can do what you want to me. But let the girl go."

Derek shifted position so that his gun pointed at Carl. He put the remote control inside the van, then stretched out his arms and placed both hands around the weapon to steady his aim over the longer distance. "Goodbye, my old friend," he whispered.

"No!" Estelle screamed and charged at Derek, pushing

161

him aside. The gun fired and Carl jerked as if hit. But the bullet must have flown harmlessly wide of its target. Derek turned on Estelle, furious. Then his shoulders relaxed and he forced a smile back onto his face, albeit through gritted teeth. "I know this is horrible," he said to her, gesturing to the gun. "And it's not who I am, honestly. But this man is... dangerous." He pursed his lips, trying to find the words that he thought might help her understand. "Imagine," he said, "if you had a time machine and could go back to the year 1923, when Enrico Fermi first thought about the possibilities of nuclear fission. The entire future as it came to pass – Hiroshima, Nagasaki, Chernobyl, the arms race, nuclear proliferation – was all locked up in one man's head. You'd kill him, wouldn't you? If you had the chance? Well that's the situation we're in now, Estelle. That man over there is Enrico Fermi, and that's why he has to die!"

"You're comparing this to the bomb?" said Carl incredulously. He wheeled himself closer to Derek. "All I've done is discover a way of turning soul shadows into good-natured, intelligent human beings..."

"Yes," nodded Derek. "That's all you've done! You weren't content to stay with the project, were you? In our labs at the Facility, we managed to create shadows with the intelligence of gorillas – simple-minded creatures that would provide us with an inexhaustible supply of spare organs. But you weren't satisfied with that, were you? You wanted to play God. You wanted to create an alternative species – one to rival humankind. Well, let's think about the implications for a moment. Let's imagine such a world, shall we, Carl? We'd have to give them rights, education, homes, jobs. And do you think they'd be satisfied with that? On this overpopulated planet, there could never be enough resources to cater for two competing races. There'd be a war on a scale we can't imagine. And who can say who would ultimately win? Humans... or shadows? Perhaps you'd prefer it if the shadows won, eh, Carl?... It's a Pandora's Box, my friend. And fortunately, at this moment in time, you're the only one who holds the key."

Derek suddenly took aim and fired his gun. Carl was just a few metres away.

Estelle saw the blood flowering on his chest, the look of open-mouthed shock on his face, and his wheelchair rolling back, back, back towards the kerb.

Choking on the vomit that rose into her mouth, she ran to him, took him in her arms, tried to get him to breathe. But the glassy look in his eyes told her that it was too late.

"Murderer!" she screamed at Derek. Then she stood and looked up at all the pallid, cowering faces at the windows above the shops. "Someone call an ambulance!" she cried. "Call the police!" Pointing at Derek, she yelled: "This man is a murderer, and you're all witnesses!"

No one moved or said a thing, and Estelle began to feel dizzy. She fell to her knees. Did none of them actually care?

She felt the muzzle of a pistol pressing against her head. "This is the final act, Estelle," said Derek. "I'm really sorry. I just can't trust you to be discreet."

Craning her neck upwards, she squinted into the bright sky, trying to read his face. He was smiling as usual.

"You said you'd let me go," she snivelled.

"It was a ploy," he admitted. "An inducement. I was never going to let you leave this village, my dear. The stakes are simply too high."

She turned again to the people at the windows. They were staring down at her, at Derek, but their faces seemed to be made of stone. She'd seen more humanity in Carl's soul shadows.

Then she noticed that some of them had started to look animated. They were looking at something behind Derek, and pointing. One of the nearest sash windows opened. "Watch out!" yelled a man.

Derek looked up. "Wh–?" he began, then he collapsed.

Behind him, like a beautiful moon eclipsing the sun above their heads, rose Sandor. Estelle stood up and embraced him, enjoying the soft press of his lips on her hair, where seconds earlier she'd felt the colder kiss of a gun.

He was alive! Oh, joy!

Blood gleamed from his latest wound – to his upper arm. In his hand he held a length of copper piping he must have found in the van. His face was a mess of swollen, bruised flesh. Breath whistled through his broken nose. But he managed a smile. "Come on, Es," he whispered, stooping to pick up Derek's gun.

She helped him back towards the van, conscious of the hostile looks from the faces staring down at them.

To her surprise, Sandor mounted the little traffic island and hauled himself into the driver's seat.

"Sure you can drive?"

He nodded. "Blackshirts will be here in a matter of minutes," he warned. "We'll have to make a quick getaway. I've never seen you drive, Es, but my guess is you'll be way too cautious."

Estelle climbed into the passenger side, stifling the urge to add to his wounds for that remark. With a crashing of gears, Sandor hastily reversed off the island, drove around it and turned right, away from the high street, wincing as he applied his injured leg to the accelerator.

"Wait!" said Estelle, remembering something. "Pull in here!" She indicated a quiet, residential side street one block on from the church.

Sandor skidded to a halt near the corner. "What is it?"

"I made a promise to my shadow that I'd come back for her."

"You're kidding! We don't have time for this."

"I just need to reassure her – tell her that we're going to get help. She needs to know she's not being abandoned."

Estelle was as desperate to escape as Sandor. But when she thought of Shadow-Estelle and her naïve faith in her spirit-mother, she was reminded of herself at fourteen, and the misguided trust she'd placed in her mum – the belief that underneath she really loved her, wanted the best for her. She couldn't leave the girl to rot, as her mother had done to her. Before Sandor could stop her, Estelle jumped out of the van and began racing back towards the church.

Leaping over a low wall, she found a brick path leading to an arched side entrance. She twisted the handle and pushed the oak door. To her relief it squeaked open. Her eyes gradually adjusted to the dim light as she passed between the rows of wooden pews to reach the narrow aisle. The church was plainly decorated with clear windows and a simple, wooden roof. There were no clerics or worshippers in sight. She spotted a small doorway at the base of a set of steps to the left of the altar – the entrance to the crypt.

Unfortunately, the door was locked.

"Can I help you?" came a dulcet voice behind her.

She turned to see a middle-aged man in black wearing a clerical collar. He seemed kind.

"Yes," she said quickly. "I'd like to visit your crypt, please."

He gazed at her quizzically. "Are you alright, my child? I see you've hurt your arm."

She covered the burn mark defensively.

"You weren't involved in that little fracas out there, were you?" he enquired – he spoke as if referring to some minor case of public disorder.

"No, but I believe someone was hurt. You ought to call the police."

The vicar looked displeased. He turned and began to walk away. "We have our own security service in Delhaven," he said. "I'm sure the matter will be dealt with appropriately."

She snorted, astonished at such a display of unconcern, especially in a priest. "Can you at least let me into the crypt?" she called out to him.

"Why?" He sounded much less sympathetic now, almost suspicious.

"I – I'd like to visit the tomb of… Reverend Edmund Craven. He… I think I may be a descendant of his."

The vicar gave a satisfied nod, and his smile reappeared. "I fear your ancestor was a rather troubled soul." He disappeared into a side office and returned with a bunch of keys. "Would you like me to show you where he rests?" he asked, unlocking the door.

"No thank you. I know where… I mean I'm sure I'll find it."

She felt his eyes watching her back as she descended a twisting stone staircase to the crypt. As soon as she was sure the vicar was out of sight, she ran over to the corner where Edmund's coffin lay, squeezed through the gap behind it and knocked on the door. Seconds later, it opened and Shadow-Carl's nervous face appeared.

"You!" he cried, stepping back in surprise.

Estelle quickly slipped past him and into the annex.

Shadow-Estelle put down a book she was reading and ran over to her, eyes twinkling with delight. "Spirit-Mother! You are returned! I knew you will!"

Estelle accepted her embrace, then stepped back so she could look into her eyes. "I have good news and bad news."

"Shadow-Sandor is dead," said the girl, looking down.

"He died bravely," Estelle told her. "He saved my life."

The girl began sobbing into Estelle's shirt.

Estelle turned to Shadow-Carl. "I'm afraid Carl is dead, too."

Shadow-Carl gazed steadily back at her. "I was ready for this," he said. "Carl knew he was going to die the moment he left this chamber… What is your good news?"

"Sandor and I have a van and a gun. We're going to get out of this village. We'll head straight to the police and they'll come back and arrest all the bad people from the Facility. I'll tell them about you two and we'll make special arrangements for you. I want you both to live long, happy lives."

Fear shook Shadow-Estelle. "Spirit-Mother not leave us

again," she pleaded. "Spirit-Mother take us with."

Estelle's shoulders slumped. She prised herself from the girl's embrace. The pain of this was far worse than any bullet burn. "I can't take you," she said gently. "You'll die out there in the sunlight."

"You can take us," said Carl calmly. He walked over to the corner of the room where the bookshelves were, unhooked a lamp-like device from the wall and returned to Estelle. The device had a long box-shaped body with a series of dials at the top and a beam of yellow light projecting out of one end.

"You say you have a van. Well, the zeta-pro radiation from this portable transmitter will be easily enough to sustain us in the back."

Estelle nodded to herself. Yes, this could work. This could work!

"OK," she said. "Let's go then. Take a blanket or something to protect you during the run from the church to the van."

The flexible shadows had no trouble squeezing through the narrow gap between door and tomb, and Estelle was soon running back up the little stairway to the main church with the other two in her wake.

Unfortunately, the vicar was still standing there. "Did you find the tomb?" he asked. Then his face froze as Estelle's identical double came into view, and behind her a man he immediately identified as...

"Carl Henrison!" The vicar grew purple with indignation. "Don't presume that a man of your wickedness can hope for sanctuary within these walls. I – I shall inform the authorities at once."

"I wouldn't do that if I were you, Father," said Shadow-Carl, placing a calming hand on his shoulder. "Or we'll have to tell them about where exactly we've been hiding, and who's been hiding us. And the Facility won't take kindly to that. You'll be stripped of your office, turned into a pariah like me, hounded out of the village. So why don't we keep this as our little secret and say no more about it, eh?"

The vicar was visibly quaking by the close of this speech. "But I didn't hide you," he gasped. "I had no idea…"

"Do you really think they'll believe you?" smiled Shadow-Carl. "That a priest isn't aware of who is living in his own crypt?"

The priest said no more, only stared at them as they made their way out of the church.

Before stepping across the threshold into the open air, the shadows placed the large blanket they'd brought with them carefully over their heads, with the zeta-pro transmitter held by Shadow-Carl beneath it. They followed Estelle down the path and into the street. Once or twice she glanced behind her to check they were following. They certainly made an odd spectacle – a mobile grey tent with a yellowish interior glow, conveyed on two pairs of disembodied running feet.

Reaching the corner of the side road, Estelle was dismayed to find the van was gone. Instead she saw a white car moving slowly along the road towards them. As it came closer, she spotted blackshirts inside it.

"Get back!" she hissed at the shadows, and pushed them against some railings. "Crouch down." They did so, and now resembled nothing more incriminating than a shapeless heap covered by a blanket. Estelle threw herself behind some plastic bin bags. The car paused at the T-junction for a long moment, before turning left towards the high street. When the coast was clear, Estelle returned to the corner of the side street, where she spotted Sandor and the van emerging from a driveway. She beckoned to the shadows and ran to open the rear doors. Once they were safely inside, Estelle slammed the doors shut and climbed into the front passenger seat.

"Drive!" she commanded Sandor as she buckled up.

He glanced through the little viewing window at their cargo, raised his eyebrows in mute surprise, then screeched away.

"They have a portable transmitter to sustain them," Estelle explained, before adding with a note of bitter triumph: "Those two are the living proof of Carl's work. We'll show the world what he's done, and there's nothing the Facility can do to stop us!"

Sandor took his eyes off road-duty for a moment to flash her an ambiguous look – half respect, half surprise. Then his eyes snapped back to the front.

They hit the road heading south out of the village, and already it seemed that Estelle had spoken too soon. About two hundred metres ahead of them, at the point where the last houses petered out and the landscape opened into wide, flat fields, there was a roadblock. Red-and-white-striped barricades barred the road, manned by blackshirts. Three white cars were parked in front of the barrier for good measure – it seemed they were expected.

Sandor skidded to a halt and embarked on a hurried three-point turn. As they reversed, Estelle spotted two white cars racing towards them from the village centre.

"Stop, Sandor!" she cried. "It's no use! They're coming at us from both directions!"

Sandor glanced to his left and right, acknowledging with a grunt that the three cars at the barricade were also now approaching them at full speed. Then, to Estelle's astonishment, he put his foot down and drove the van straight off the road, through a hedge and into a field. The van bounced crazily along the furrows of the freshly ploughed earth.

"Are you crazy?" Estelle cried as she gripped the dashboard to avoid concussing herself on the roof.

"This is why I knew I should drive," Sandor muttered, squinting purposefully ahead through his red, puffed-up eyes.

The window between the front and rear parts of the van was suddenly shoved down and the driver's cabin was flooded with zeta-pro light.

"What the devil is going on?" demanded Shadow-Carl, sounding remarkably like his progenitor. He was clinging to a ceiling strap with one hand while shielding the transmitter from damage with the other.

"We're having to take a slight detour," said Estelle, trying her hardest to be calm.

"We're being chased, aren't we?"

"I'm afraid so," Estelle admitted. All five of their pursuers had now joined them in the field, fanning out to the left and right with the aim of cutting them off in either direction. Their only hope was to continue in a straight line, and that meant...

Estelle's heart sank as she saw the line of dark trees

looming out of the horizon. They were heading for the forest.

"Why they want chase us?" Shadow-Estelle wanted to know.

"They're bad people," Estelle told her, attempting to keep her voice steady. "But we'll get away from them, don't worry." She reached through the little window to squeeze her hand.

Sandor emitted an agonised croak. His face had become constricted with pain.

"Is it the leg?" Estelle asked. "The nose?"

"No, it's my arm," he managed. "Took a bullet back there, and I can feel it with every jolt. See if you can find any painkillers."

She did a quick search in the side and glove compartments, but found no first aid kit or any pills. She did, however, spot a smartphone on a shelf below the dash. Her own phone had gone missing earlier that day or the day before – she couldn't remember. She picked up the phone and pressed the button at the bottom. It lit up, and she expected to see the "no service" signal at the top of the screen. To her surprise, it seemed to work.

"I think we have a working phone," she said.

"Even better," grimaced Sandor. He leaned out of his window. "You'd better call the cops quick. Those scuzzbags are gaining on us. Our only hope is to lose them in the forest."

Cradling the phone as though it were some kind of holy relic, Estelle pressed the relevant icon and a touchpad appeared. For the second time in two days, she keyed in the three-digit number for emergency services.

A male voice answered. "Emergency. Which service?"

Estelle was stunned. Her tongue became stuck. Her brain turned to soup.

The man repeated his question.

"Police," she cried, and then the floodgates opened. "We need the police. We've just witnessed a murder. We're in a van being chased across a field. They're going to kill us. Send helicopters. Send the army. Send –"

"Transferring you," cut in the voice.

Sandor smashed the van through another hedge and then careered to the right onto a narrow, stony track. Unfortunately, this was leading them directly into the path of the three cars now closing in from the south. A left turn into the forest suddenly appeared, and Sandor skidded onto it. They sped through the cool gloom, as strobe-like flashes of sunlight winked across their windscreen. Very soon, the trees thickened around them. The brief snatches of daylight became less frequent and tinged with a deeper gold, while the prevailing light took on an unhealthy glow.

Their pursuers were, as yet, nowhere in sight. It was possible they'd not seen them turn into the forest. Estelle, still on hold, stared anxiously at the phone, but the connection with the outside world had not yet been broken.

A matter-of-fact female voice came on the line. "Hello. Sergeant Reynolds here. How can I help?"

"I want to report a murder," said Estelle, trying to keep a lid on her excitement.

"Can you give me your name and location?"

· "My name is Estelle Grant and I'm here with a friend, Sandor Watts." Estelle briefly considered mentioning their passengers, but quickly dismissed it – too complicated! "We're in Delhaven Forest, near Edgebourne in Wintershire. We're being pursued."

"...Pursued? ... Are you currently in danger, Madam?"

"Yes!"

"Can you give me any more details. Who is pursuing you?"

Estelle glanced at Sandor. "It's a... like a private militia or something. They wear black shirts. They're –"

"Securicus," Sandor told her.

"They're called Securicus, apparently. They provide security for this place called the Facility."

"We've put a trace on your phone, Madam, so don't worry. We'll get someone to you as quickly as possible. You're in a vehicle I take it."

"Yes."

"And the people following you?"

"I counted five white cars."

"Coyote Interceptors," Sandor shouted into the phone.

"You're being chased by five white Coyote Interceptors?" Amazement was steadily creeping into the policewoman's professionally calm tones. "Madam, before I go on, can I say that if you have to break off this call at any time, please do so. You can redial the emergency line and give them the following number and you will be put straight through to me. The incident number is four zero five. Repeat, four zero five. Now can you tell me if members of this Securicus organization carried out the murder?"

"The murderer was a physicist called Derek Atkins. He works for the Facility."

"Thank you. And do you know the name of the victim?"

Estelle grabbed at the dashboard, as Sandor took a bend too fast. "Carl Henrison," she said, once she'd got the phone back in front of her mouth.

"Where and when did this take place?"

"In Delhaven village high street, about half an hour ago."

"How was Mr Henrison killed?"

"Derek Atkins shot him with a... with a Walther P99 handgun."

"Were there any other witnesses apart from yourself?"

"Lots. They were staring out of their windows. It happened right in front of them."

"We haven't had any other reports of this."

"No, well the Facility has a sort of hold over the whole village. They're scared if they speak out, they'll lose their jobs at the plant – or maybe worse."

"OK, well we have response cars and a helicopter currently en route to you. They should be with you in the next twenty minutes. Please do all you can to protect yourselves in the meantime. And if you want to call us for whatever reason, quote the incident number I gave you earlier. Good luck!"

Estelle stared at the phone. Her whole body was shaking with tension and excitement and a desperate kind of hope.

"I think I saw them," said Sandor.

She checked her wing mirror, but could see nothing except trees and twisting, empty road.

"Just before we took the last bend, I thought I caught a flash of headlights, but maybe not." He was sweating and looked feverish. His driving was becoming increasingly erratic.

"The police are sending a helicopter and some fast cars," she told him. "Should be here in twenty minutes."

"That'll mean an hour at least," he said with a bitter chuckle.

"Look, if you want me to take over…"

"No time," he gasped.

The window behind their heads was lowered again. "Everything OK?" enquired Shadow-Carl.

"Just fine," said Estelle. "I've called the police. They're on their way."

"Hooray for that… Listen, I've figured out how this thing works."

She twisted her neck to see what he was referring to. He was holding up Derek's remote control device. She'd forgotten they even had it. "That's great!" she said with fake enthusiasm.

"It's really simple, you see –"

"Would you mind telling us about it later, dear?" she interrupted. "We're rather preoccupied with trying to survive the next twenty minutes, OK?" She pushed up the window before he could say any more.

"There's something up ahead," grunted Sandor.

She peered through the trees and caught a glimpse of sunshine glinting on metal. "What is it?" she asked tremulously. "Cars?"

"Not sure."

Sandor slowed as it came into view: a barrier cut across their path, disappearing into the trees in both directions. Next to the gate that spanned the road was a small concrete structure similar to the one Estelle had encountered outside the Facility. Beyond the barrier lay a large clearing, but no sign of any buildings, just a large rocky outcrop at the base of which was the entrance to a tunnel. The road they were on continued past the barrier and on into the tunnel.

Sandor slowed the van to a halt some fifty metres short of the barrier, where they were still thickly sheltered by trees.

"Perhaps we should turn around," Estelle tentatively suggested. "There may be another road we can –"

He gunned the engine, and the van lurched forwards. Suddenly they were racing at full speed towards the barrier with no chance of stopping in time. Once again, Estelle clung for dear life to the dashboard – once again, she regretted ever letting Sandor near the wheel of this van. She shut her eyes as a strident megaphone voice sounded somewhere above. There was a loud crash and an impact that threw her forwards in her seat. She could hear the agonised screech of metal being dragged along beneath their wheels, more shouting to their rear, then merciful quiet. Reopening her eyes, she found they were cocooned in darkness, with just the thin yellow beams of their headlights lighting the road and the narrow tunnel walls ahead. The road was straight and slightly downhill and they were moving very fast. Behind them, in the distance, were the specks of a pair of pursuing headlights.

The gradient gradually eased and the road grew more level. Shortly afterwards, the tunnel opened out into a vast underground chamber, which Estelle roughly calculated to be the size of a football pitch. Sandor had slowed the van to a crawl – she wanted to scream at him to speed up, but her lips had suddenly gone very dry. Every instinct, every fibre within her, told her they should get out of there, and fast. The road ran through the middle of the chamber and about halfway along its length was a tall mast topped by a globe emitting the now familiar greenish-yellow zeta radiation. In the light of this radiation, they could see, on both sides of the road, row upon row of motionless, black-shirted soul shadows, each one with a red light glowing in their foreheads. Estelle gaped, astonished, at the awesome, chilling sight to either side of her. There were hundreds of them, maybe over a thousand, in perfectly straight lines, their faces impassive, coal-black eyes staring straight ahead.

eight

Sandor drove on to the far end of the chamber. He spotted a narrow turn-off to the left and took it. They followed the curving, unlit track for twenty more metres, taking them out of sight of the main road. Then he stopped and doused the headlights.

"Is this part of the Facility, do you think?" he asked.

Estelle let out a long-held breath. "I guess it must be. But it looks like a – like an army back there!

"I agree."

"Somehow, I don't think this has anything to do with growing spare organs."

Sandor turned in his seat and slid down the little window. "Shadow-Carl? Did you say you'd mastered that remote control?"

"Indeed I have."

"What are you thinking, Sandor?" queried Estelle, not liking the sound of this.

"I'm thinking we could turn that shadow army back there against our pursuers. They'd be powerless to stop us. At least until the police get here."

"The device is not very powerful, I'm afraid," said Shadow-Carl. "We can control a maximum of just four soul shadows with these switches. I'm sure they have much more powerful control systems at their disposal. Any disruption we could cause would be limited, and temporary."

"All the same, it's worth a try, don't you think?" Sandor's eyes looked feverishly bright. Estelle wasn't sure he was thinking rationally.

"I have another idea," offered Shadow-Carl. "It's a little risky, but the rewards could be far greater."

"Go on," said Sandor.

Shadow-Carl cleared his throat. "Before he died, Carl gave me the formula for zeta-pro radiation. I know the exact time interval and diffraction angles of the two radiation beams required to create the interference pattern we need. I could go back to that mast we just saw and adjust the controls on the panel at its base…"

"You'd be affected by the light in the chamber."

"I'm confident I could complete the task before it starts affecting me."

"Then the whole army would become like you," breathed Sandor.

"Precisely. You could give them orders, just like humans, and they'd obey you. You could organise a mutiny."

"No," said Estelle, unnerved by the growing enthusiasm of the men for this crazy scheme – terrified by the thought of going back into that chamber. "There's not time to organise a mutiny. Besides, Shadow-Carl might be killed, or poisoned by that light." She glared at him. "Remember, you're the only one left on Earth who knows Carl's formula for zeta-pro. We can't allow you to take that risk."

Sandor leaned back and sighed. "OK then, Es. Let's hear it. What's your suggestion?"

She ground her teeth, trying to think. Her only desire was to get out of this dark, scary place, back to the surface. "While we've been sitting here, our pursuers have probably continued further up the tunnel. That's where they think we've gone, too. So why don't we double back on ourselves, go back out of the tunnel the way we came, then hide out somewhere in the forest until the police get here?"

Estelle, Sandor and the two shadows took a vote on their options. Shadow-Carl's idea won by three votes to one. Shadow-Estelle apologised to her spirit-mother for voting against her proposal, but said she really did believe Shadow-Carl's was the best idea. Furiously, Estelle slammed shut the van's little communicating window, cutting her and Sandor off from the Shadows.

"Earlier today you didn't believe these people had a right to exist," she bawled at him. "Now you want to give them the vote!"

"Hey, don't you believe they should have a voice in this debate? It's their flesh and blood on the line here as much as ours." Sandor glanced back through the window. "Or their equivalent."

"I'm starting to think that maybe Derek had a point about the Pandora's Box thing," sighed Estelle. "This decision should be up to you and me alone."

Sandor raised his hand placatingly. "I swear, if Shadow-

Carl's idea fails, we'll immediately revert to your plan."

"Oh, I won't mind if it fails. Failure would be fantastic! My fear is that it might succeed! You're talking about waking up an army of soul shadows, Sandor. Do you have any idea of what we might be unleashing, and how we can possibly control it when we do?"

"You're looking at it all wrong, Es. It's an opportunity. We can really turn the tables on the bad guys." His eyes shone with excitement, or it may have been fever. "Can you imagine the faces back at the Facility when they see what we've done?"

Estelle shook her head. "Why is it that time spent with you is like jumping from a series of frying pans into ever hotter fires?"

"Fun though, isn't it?" he smirked. She felt his fingers brush her chin. "You know, you look pretty with your cheeks all flushed. I should get you angry more often."

She flung his hand away. "Don't patronise me," she said, angry and a little confused.

Sandor looked hurt by her reaction, and it surprised her that she had that power over him. Then she wondered if maybe she'd been a little harsh. After all, he'd paid her a compliment – of sorts! But before she could try to make amends, Sandor began climbing out of the van.

She noticed he was moving very stiffly – not only did he still have the limp in his left leg, but his left arm and shoulder had also seized up, giving him a very unbalanced look. She feared for him, and it made what they were about to do seem even more reckless.

Shadow-Estelle was about to follow Shadow-Carl out of the van's rear exit, when Estelle stopped her. "You must stay here. It'll be dangerous."

"No. Shadow-Estelle go with her Spirit-Mother."

Estelle shrugged, and helped her out. She was getting used to being over-ruled.

At the entrance to the chamber, they stopped and peered cautiously into the vast, cavernous space. There was no sign of their pursuers. The same serried ranks of dark-uniformed shadow soldiers stood there in the evil yellow light, motionless, unblinking. Their big black eyes made Estelle think of a colony of predatory insects.

Sandor gave Shadow-Carl an encouraging pat on the back. "This is very brave of you," he said. "I doubt your progenitor would have had such courage."

"My progenitor," replied Shadow-Carl, "was brave in his own way. I am but a reflection of him, after all. The Carl you met had been cowed and beaten into submission by his former friends and colleagues."

"In that case," said Sandor, "by your actions today, you do great honour to his memory… In fact, from now on, if you don't mind, I'm going to call you Carl."

"Thank you," said the shadow, and a rare smile flashed across his face. "That would indeed be an honour." They watched as he embarked swiftly along the road that ran through the centre of the chamber. He had to be quick. The zeta radiation would already be penetrating his skin, subtly affecting him. Estelle peered from their shadowy recess at Carl's diminutive figure hunched over the controls at the base of the mast some 50 metres away, but it was hard to make much out through the foggy light, which rendered everything blurry.

Suddenly, a megaphone crackled from somewhere

high up near the roof of the chamber. Accompanied by a whooping alarm, a grating, metallic voice shrieked: "Alert! Intruder in the Cave! Intruder in the Cave! Intercept and destroy! Intercept and destroy!"

To Estelle's horror, the shadow army began to stir. The lights on their foreheads flashed red, and their mouths opened in a thousand sharp-toothed snarls. Their eyes locked onto Carl and they immediately began converging on him. Those closest quickly surrounded him, while the ones further away wheeled towards the central mast where Carl was crouched, as if planning to use their combined mass to crush him.

With Carl no longer visible beneath the seething mass of bodies, Estelle was about to grab Sandor and urge that they retreat to the van. But Sandor had, by now, limped forwards into the great hall and was pointing his gun straight into the crowd of awakened soul shadows. The shadow army had yet to complete its encirclement, and those immediately surrounding Carl could still be seen through a rapidly narrowing corridor of converging bodies. It was down this corridor that Sandor was aiming.

She wanted to scream at him to stop, but too late: shots were fired, the sound ricocheting off the chamber's rocky walls.

Estelle heard grunts and howls of surprise and pain. A great throng of shadow soldiers nearest them twisted their heads right around on their shoulders so they were now glowering at Sandor, and beyond him at Estelle and her shadow.

"Intruders in the Cave!" screamed the megaphone. "Eliminate! Eradicate!"

A group of shadow soldiers advanced swiftly on Sandor, their eyes now beady with murderous intent.

"No!" wept Shadow-Estelle, grabbing Estelle's hand.

Sandor fired the gun once more, and the closest soldier fell back, but the others simply slid past it. Just as it seemed as though Sandor was about to be engulfed, something changed in the shadow soldiers. They slowed. Their movements became hesitant. The beady look in their eyes was replaced with a flickering uncertainty, and the tight-lipped snarls faded from their faces.

Estelle noticed that the light now emanating from the globe at the top of the mast was different. Still of a yellowish hue, it had lost its sickly pallor and had become warmer in tone, more homely – more like the light in the Sustaining Room.

"Carl has make good light?" asked Shadow-Estelle.

"I think so," whispered Estelle.

Sandor limped stiffly through the sea of bewildered-looking shadow soldiers. They parted passively, allowing him access to the slumped figure of Carl. Estelle saw him squat down next to the fallen shadow, then help him to his feet. The two of them, like a pair of war wounded, supported each other as they made their way back to where Estelle and her shadow were standing. Carl had deep holes in many parts of his body. "This is the stuff I'm made of," he explained when he saw Estelle stare at the grey patches surrounding each hole. "Carl made me strong by building me from this mouldable plastic – not like the wild shadows, which are made of whatever the progenitor happens to be standing next to at the time."

"Are you in pain?" she asked.

"I'm not sure if I understand pain," he said. "What I feel is... diminished. Yes, I think that describes it. But if I can find some suitable material from somewhere, I will repair myself."

"Attack the intruders! Kill the intruders!" blared the megaphone.

The shadow soldiers seemed to rouse themselves from their confused state. They turned in lumbering fashion towards the four figures at the chamber exit. Estelle felt the burn of a thousand stares.

"Attack them! Kill them!"

Once again, Sandor raised his gun, taking aim high into the chamber's dim upper reaches, where the chilling orders were coming from.

He fired.

"Attack them! Ki–"

Silence.

There were grunts of something like surprise. Again, the shadow soldiers wavered and became listless.

Then Sandor spoke.

"Friends!" he shouted, as he looked out across the restless horde. "I am Sandor. I am your friend. I have come to you today with a message. My message is this... You have been created as slaves to do the work of humans." His voice, weakened by tiredness and constricted by pain, was much softer than the megaphone, but it retained enough power to quieten the chamber. "The people who made you are bad. They want you to kill for them. That is the only reason why they have created you. If you listen to me, I will lead you to freedom."

There were grunts and a few whispers in the crowd he

was addressing, but it was impossible to tell if they had understood even a word.

Sandor turned to Carl. "Hey, am I wasting my time here?"

"I'm not sure," answered the shadow.

"Keep going," encouraged Estelle. "At least they've stopped trying to kill us."

Sandor turned back to face the shadow army, who were still murmuring unintelligibly. "The bad people will come and attack us here," Sandor croaked at the top of his voice. "But we must not leave this… Cave. If you leave the Cave, you will be infected by the bad light, and you will become slaves again. We must defend ourselves here against the bad people. Soon, good people will arrive and they will take us all to safety. Do you… understand? Do you follow me?"

There was more low-level muttering. Again, there was no telling what they were saying or thinking.

Sandor turned briefly towards Estelle. He was frowning. Then he staggered slightly, before suddenly keeling over onto his side.

She ran to him. He was shivering, his face coated with sweat. Estelle turned to Carl. "We have to get him out of here," she said urgently. "We can't waste any more time with this. Can you help me get him to the van?"

But Carl's eyes were elsewhere, looking above the heads of the shadow army towards the left-hand side of the chamber. "My lady, I fear we may be too late."

Estelle followed the direction of his gaze and saw a small, glass-fronted room built into the rocky wall of the chamber. Armed blackshirts were pouring out of the room, forcing a path through the ranks of shadow soldiers. Within seconds they had formed a circle around Estelle, Sandor and the two shadows. The dozen or so blackshirts pinned their eyes to the sights of their rifles, the muzzles of which were now pointing at the heads of the four intruders.

One of the blackshirts barked: "You lot! Follow me!" He turned and began marching back towards the glass-fronted room. The other blackshirts closed in menacingly, kicking at Estelle and telling her to get up.

"He can't walk!" Estelle snapped at them. Sandor was muttering to himself feverishly, making no sense.

"Just get going, you!" thundered one of the blackshirts. "You're lucky we don't kill you right now!" He pushed her and she staggered forwards, joining Carl and Shadow-Estelle to form a ragged line heading for the glass-fronted room. Glancing back, Estelle saw two of the blackshirts roughly dragging Sandor along behind them.

The room reminded Estelle of the bland interior of the Facility – all brand-new furniture, fittings and carpet, surrounded on three sides by joyless walls of no describable colour. Seated at one of the desks was a surprising and most unwelcome figure…

Derek Atkins appeared entirely recovered from the bash on the head and was not even wearing a bandage. It didn't take long for Estelle to realise why: located discreetly in his upper forehead was a small diamond-shaped red light. This was not Derek, but his soul shadow.

Once Estelle, her three companions and the twelve guards had entered the room, Shadow-Derek rose to his feet. His eyes scanned each of them. Sandor, dumped unceremoniously on the floor between the boots of two blackshirts, was moaning deliriously. Shadow-Derek nodded to one of the blackshirts, who then kicked Sandor viciously in the ribs, making him groan. He made no further sound after that.

To another blackshirt, Shadow-Derek said: "Go and fix that light out there, will you?" He nodded at the globe at the top of the mast. "I want good old-fashioned zeta rays coming out of there A-S-A-P. Understand?"

"Sir, I –"

"Here," said Derek, handing him a sheet of paper. "Follow the instructions on this. And if you even look at what the current settings are, I'll shoot you. Understand?"

"Yes sir!" The guard saluted and went out.

"Nice to see you again, Estelle," grinned Shadow-Derek. "Forgive me if this time I choose not to meet you in person. I'm channelling my voice through the lips of this soul shadow. The cameras implanted in his eyes are sending real-time images of you straight back to me. You see, I couldn't resist gorging myself on your loveliness one last time, but I'm sure you'll understand that I'd rather keep my distance from that rottweiler of yours." His eyes flicked towards the heap in the corner that was Sandor. "He may be somewhat indisposed at the moment, but animals are at their most dangerous when wounded, as I found out this afternoon to my cost."

"You have to help him," begged Estelle. "He could die."

Shadow-Derek laughed – or at least a gust of Derek-like laughter burst from between his lips. "You amuse me, Estelle, to suggest I should help this man, after what he did to me. Besides, I'm not here to help you people, I'm here to kill you. You should know by now what I'm about.

You should know that I'm nothing if not relentless in the pursuit of the task at hand, and the task remains as it was this morning: to eliminate all evidence of Carl Henrison's unfortunate little secret. And that, I'm afraid, means you, Sandor and your little shadow friends."

Estelle looked desperately at Sandor and then back at Derek. "You haven't always been like this," she pleaded. "Only yesterday, you tried to help me escape."

Again that self-satisfied laugh, and a pitying shake of the head. "I wasn't trying to help you escape, my dear. I was actually bringing you here to the Cave – my main base of operations. I'm afraid you were marked for death the moment you told me you knew about the soul shadows. But I don't mind admitting I was torn – finding you so attractive, as you know. I couldn't bring myself to kill you before… enjoying you, and here we would have had far more privacy than at the main site. Such a shame that wild shadow went and spoiled the party."

"I so wish I'd left you to die in that car," spat Estelle, letting all her hatred for the man burn from her eyes. "Anyway, it's over, Derek," she added. "I called the police from the phone I found in your van. They'll be arriving at the Facility at any moment."

To her surprise and disappointment, this news didn't seem to faze him in the slightest. In fact, he looked delighted.

"Ah yes," he said. "Thanks for reminding me! How careless I was to have left my phone in the van. That could have been quite disastrous for us. Luckily, our professional eavesdroppers informed me of your phone call and we've put a plan in place to deal with it." Shadow-Derek walked over to a TV screen attached to the rear wall and switched it on. The screen showed a monochrome image of two uniformed police officers – one male, one female – waiting in a room that Estelle remembered as the reception area of the Facility. From the camera's angle, which was high up and in one corner, showing almost the entire room, it was clear these images were being streamed from a security camera.

"The police arrived about quarter of an hour ago," said Shadow-Derek. "They asked to speak with you, Estelle. As you can see, they're getting a little impatient now, but they needn't worry. You'll be along very shortly."

As he said these words, there was a movement on the left-hand side of the screen: a door opened and in walked… Estelle couldn't yet see the girl's face, but from the rear view the resemblance to herself was unmistakable. The girl sat down on a chair facing the two police officers, and now her profile became visible, and there was no escaping the reality of who she was and what game the Facility were playing.

"You can't!" cried Estelle. "You can't get away with this!"

"We can, and we will!" laughed Shadow-Derek.

"But where did you get her from? I never generated a –"

And then she remembered: yesterday morning in the woods – it seemed such a long time ago now – that horrid mirror image of herself, which she'd shot and thought she'd killed.

"We found her last night," Shadow-Derek said. "A half-dead wild shadow who'd got snared in one of our traps.

Lucky for us, eh? We patched her up and lobotomised her, so what you're seeing there is little more than a zombie. She can move and walk unaided, but can't speak. She's currently channelling the voice of Barbara Wallace, which is fine, as these people don't know what you sound like. Here, have a listen." He turned the sound up.

The policewoman was speaking in a testy voice: "So you're now saying that you weren't pursued?"

"No I wasn't, and I'm very sorry," replied the girl in the deep, posh-sounding tones of Barbara Wallace. "I have a history of mental illness. You can check with my psychiatrist, Dr Kirby. I may have taken too much medication this morning, and perhaps I was hallucinating."

Estelle listened, horrified by these lies coming out of her own mouth.

"You told us you were being chased by five white cars," said the policeman.

"Did I?" said the girl – Barbara had made her voice sound a little vague and dreamy. "It may have been five white rabbits... You see, I was walking in the forest, and I got lost. The people at the Facility have been very kind. They took me in and gave me tea. I'm sorry if I said anything rude about them."

Estelle found it hard to stop herself screaming. The knowledge that somewhere very close by, the police – the real police – were sitting listening to this rubbish, when just a word or even an appearance from her would change everything, was almost too frustrating to bear.

"And what about this man, Carl Henrison?" the policewoman was asking. "Our colleagues have been asking people in Delhaven and no one claims to have witnessed his or any other murder. Neither are there any signs of violence. Did you hallucinate that, too?"

"Carl Henrison?" Barbara's voice became pensive. "Now I believe I may have seen that name on a wall somewhere hereabouts. Maybe that was where I got it from. Why? Has he been murdered?"

The police officers said nothing to this, but Estelle thought she detected a roll of the eyes from the woman. At this point a man stepped into the camera shot. It was Derek – the real one – sporting a head bandage. He gave a little cough and said with his usual greasy charm: "I can confirm that Professor Carl Henrison used to work here, which is why the young lady might have seen his name about the place."

"Do you know his current whereabouts?" the policeman asked Derek.

"I'm afraid not," he said with a little dip of the head.

The police officers stood up. They looked inclined to leave as soon as possible.

Estelle felt like tearing her hair out. "You stupid fools!" she cried. "Can't you see it's all a sham? Talk to the woman I spoke to on the phone. She'll tell you that puppet sounds nothing like me!"

But the officers were already departing. It was agonising watching them exit through the glass doors into the waning sunlight, and disappear from view. Back in the reception area, the soul shadow of Estelle slumped backwards in her chair like a discarded toy, while Derek, the master manipulator, strode into the centre of the room and gave a little bow to the camera. He grabbed a microphone and said to the people watching the screen: "That went rather well, wouldn't you say?" The words, uncannily, came out of his shadow's lips, who was standing right next to Estelle. "OK, showtime's over, folks!" Derek grinned. "Now it's time for you to die!" His shadow leaned forward, pushed a button, and the screen went black.

Estelle was shoved roughly to the other side of the room, where Shadow-Estelle, Carl and Sandor formed a miserable little group. Once again, rifles were raised to shoulders and trained on the four of them. At the end of each gun, a muzzle's dark circle stared down at them, implacable as a soul shadow's eye.

Avoiding Shadow-Derek's scornful smile, Estelle focused instead on Sandor. She mopped his damp forehead with the hem of her tee shirt. He was still shivering and seemed in a lot of pain. She was thankful that he was not really aware of what was happening, and that his torment would soon be over. Bending forward, she kissed him on the cheek, then wrapped her arm around Shadow-Estelle, who was crying softly into her shoulder.

Estelle closed her eyes – she believed for the last time. As she did so, she heard a sound like an explosion.

The sound was enormous, ear-splitting. She recoiled, then glanced up in time to see a black-shirted guard flying through the air amid a shower of tiny, glittering glass shards. It was an uncanny sight, beautiful almost, and it held her mesmerised for what seemed like minutes. Then the guard landed, and so did the glass, in a painful bombardment, like piercing hail, snagging itself in her hair and clothing and slicing through her skin.

The guard landed face down at the feet of the firing

squad. Estelle, while trying her best to shield herself and Sandor, managed at the same time to glimpse the squad's own desperate efforts to protect their faces from the sparkling storm. The biggest joy, however – and worth every minor skin abrasion – was the face of Shadow-Derek, which displayed the same petrified, rabbit-in-headlights look she'd seen on his progenitor, when she'd charged at him that afternoon.

Behind the black-shirted guard and the shattered glass, there followed a giant soul shadow, who strode into the room like some sort of dark avenging angel – at least to Estelle's fanciful way of thinking. He stood amid the crystal debris, which was piled centimetres deep in places, and coolly surveyed the scene. Virtually the entire glass wall behind him had been destroyed. Beyond the remains of this wall, in tight, military formation, stood the shadow army. The soldiers were bathed in the warm golden light of zeta-pro radiation – the lately airborne guard, now groaning face down on the carpet, had clearly failed in his mission to change the settings on the mast.

"Where is the one who is called Sandor?" boomed the mighty soul shadow.

No one spoke. Estelle shifted surreptitiously to her left to try to shield Sandor from view.

The colossus moved further into the room and picked up one of the blackshirts as though lifting a bag of groceries. "Are you the bad people who are come to attack us?"

The petrified man stammered something incomprehensible.

"Speak! Are you the bad people who Sandor say created us as slaves?"

Again the man could only mumble and drool, and the mammoth soul shadow, tiring of him, hurled him violently to the floor.

At this point, Shadow-Derek seemed to rediscover his voice and his wits. He came forwards, a friendly grin dawning on his face. "It's Jethro, isn't it?" he said amiably. "My, you're a big shadow, aren't you? I remember your progenitor, Corporal Jethro Hadrick. Sadly, he's no longer with us – killed by some wild shadows while out on patrol. It took eight of them to kill him, mind. He was the biggest and strongest man I ever met – and one of the nicest. He'd have liked you, Jethro." The giant shadow stood motionless seeming to listen to every word of this, as Shadow-Derek's expression grew soft and tender. "You see, Jethro, we aren't the bad people. We're your friends. The bad people are over there." He pointed towards Estelle and Sandor. "They're the people you need to kill."

The giant's head swivelled one hundred and eighty degrees. When he saw who Shadow-Derek was pointing to, the red light in his forehead flashed urgently. "That is Sandor!" he roared as he glided in alarmingly close to Sandor's prone figure. Estelle tried to interpose herself between them, but the giant didn't seem to be acting aggressively. In fact, he then rose to his full height and made a deep bow. "Sandor," he boomed solemnly, "is our friend!"

He then turned on Shadow-Derek, whose triumphant smile was now rapidly crumpling. "You lied to me," the giant raged. "You must be bad person." And in one swift movement he picked up Shadow-Derek and ripped him in two. The movement was so sudden and its result so shocking, Estelle couldn't be sure at first that she hadn't imagined it. Yet the evidence was in clear sight: Shadow-Derek's lower half dangled lifelessly from the giant's right hand while his upper half drooped from his left. Estelle watched, stupefied, as the giant flung the two halves against the opposite walls of the room. The waist area of each section – the ripped part – had become cement grey, and the greyness spread swiftly through both dismembered parts. At the same time, they began to lose the form and substance of Derek. His head and face melted into his neck and shoulders, and his legs and feet dissolved into each other, so that in a very short time, Shadow-Derek was no more than two shapeless grey lumps on the floor.

The giant now looked menacingly at the other blackshirts, who immediately dropped their rifles and backed fearfully into the far corner of the room. "I am Jethro," he thundered, "commander of the Shadow Army... Are you bad people?"

"No!" a few of them cried.

"Then why you want hurt my friend Sandor?"

"They not bad people," said Shadow-Estelle. Her nervous voice piping up at that moment took everyone by surprise, especially Estelle.

Jethro rounded on her, suspicion narrowing his eyes. "How you know this?"

"They do what bad man tell them," said Shadow-Estelle, cowering a little beneath his accusing stare. "Bad man make them hurt Sandor. But they not want hurt Sandor."

"She's right," said Estelle, feeling the need to help her out. "Those men are not bad. Please don't kill them."

Jethro seemed to relax. The light on his forehead, which had been glowing bright red, faded to a soft blue. He looked again at Sandor, and his expression became sad. "Sandor not well. Sandor die?"

"We need a doctor," said Estelle, biting her lip.

"I have some surgical skills, inherited from my progenitor," said Carl. "But I will need supplies: tweezers, antiseptic, swabs, bandages, surgical scissors, a suture kit, and some kind of anaesthetic."

The guards, now that their lives were no longer in danger, proved obliging. One of them located a cupboard containing a field surgery kit with most of the equipment Carl was asking for. Two others placed some desks together to form a makeshift operating table upon which Sandor was carefully laid. Carl then set to work, overseen by an anxious Estelle and the watchful gaze of Sandor's latest friend, Jethro the Giant.

As time slipped by, Estelle began to worry about the ominous silence from the original Derek back at the Facility. He had to know by now about their little coup. What could he be planning?

Estelle had, of course, tried to contact the police again, but Derek's smartphone could locate no signal in the Cave. She reasoned that the guards must have a means of communicating with the surface and she asked one of them for his phone. When she tried pressing the "phone" icon on the touch screen, no keypad appeared. Instead there was just a list of names such as Lab 1, Lab 2, Recreation Room, Meeting Room and Professor Atkins' Office. "The phone can only dial pre-programmed numbers," the guard explained. "It connects to different parts of the Facility. None of us are allowed to carry normal phones."

Sighing, Estelle returned to her vigil beside Sandor. There was no anaesthetic to be found in the surgical kit, and Carl was forced to operate without. She held Sandor's hand through the pain. He looked so vulnerable as he lay there mumbling to himself. At one point he cried out for his mum, reminding Estelle that this big, strong man had once been a little boy. Briefly, in those tender, flinching cheeks, in those dark eyes blinking back tears, she caught a glimpse of a much younger Sandor.

He was eleven when they first met. His face was softer and rounder then. He had long, unruly hair, and scabbed knees from forever crashing his bike. She was two years younger, and from the moment he moved in, two doors down from her, she'd always looked up to him. He became her mentor, her protector, the big brother she'd always wanted – he'd filled a void, especially after her dad left.

When Sandor arrived at the cottage two nights ago, she'd stepped right back into her past self, and he'd been only too happy to play along. But things had changed, even if she had trouble seeing it at first. Now she realised that this "victim" act was not her at all. Of course there would be times when she needed his help, but there would also be times when he needed hers. If they ever got out of this thing alive, they would have to find a new way of being with each other. He had to realise that she was older now – and stronger. And he was…

She held his hand tightly as he let out another groan.

… he was more vulnerable than he cared to admit.

Sandor was mumbling something. She put her ear close to his mouth. "Guard... the light," she heard him whisper. Then his eyes closed and his muscles went slack.

"He has lost consciousness," said Carl. "It is a mercy."

Guard the light? Estelle queried to herself. *What does that mean?* Then it suddenly hit her. She passed the message onto Jethro.

Outside, in the main chamber of the Cave, the giant had deployed his troops to guard both entrances. Now, following this advice, he assigned a detachment of them to protect the mast with its golden globe. "Our friend Sandor say we must guard the light," he told them in hushed tones, and, as one, the awestruck soldiers gazed up at it, eyes agleam. The "light", Estelle realised, had become a sacred symbol, to be protected at all costs. Sandor's instincts had been spot on – of course, this would be the first thing the Facility would set out to destroy.

The whole question of "light" and "shadows" had started to puzzle Estelle and she decided to ask Carl about it.

"Carl, you need the zeta-pro radiation to live, am I right?"

The shadow, deeply engaged in his work on Sandor's arm, did not look up. "That's right, Estelle."

"So if the Facility managed to destroy the light in the main chamber, you'd die?"

"Yes."

"How long would it take?" she asked.

"A while. If we resort to eating human flesh, maybe never." He looked up. "Think of us as plants, Estelle. We use the energy from zeta or zeta-pro radiation to convert the chemicals within us into organic compounds, similar to photosynthesis. The radiation nourishes us. But just like plants that must get through the winter with little sunlight, we can survive periods without zeta-pro. And like some carnivorous plants – the venus flytrap for instance – we have found an alternative source of nutrition: in our case, the meat of humans."

He saw her stare. "But my lady, I would never…"

"Let's just hope it doesn't come to that, shall we?" she said.

She looked at Sandor, sleeping peacefully, while Carl carefully wound a bandage around his newly sutured arm. As she watched him, Shadow-Estelle approached and nestled herself at her feet. "Spirit-Mother like Sandor, yes?"

"Yes," nodded Estelle.

"He make your heart go bump-bump-bump."

Estelle grimaced and looked down at her. "It's complicated," she said.

"What means complicated?"

"I don't know how he feels about me."

"Then you must ask him," said the girl, and Estelle was forced to admire the simple wisdom of her words.

"We were best friends when we were younger," she said. "But then everything changed. I went through some very bad times, and so did he. I'm not sure if we'd be so good for each other now."

"You must ask him, Spirit-Mother."

"I just want him to get better. That's my only wish."

"If he get better, will he…" She hesitated.

"Go on," prompted Estelle.

"Will he make another Shadow-Sandor… for Shadow-Estelle?"

Estelle chuckled sadly and stroked the girl's hair.

"Can we be friends, Spirit-Mother?"

"Of course."

"Will you show me your home? Where you live?"

The girl seemed impatient for answers Estelle didn't know how to give. "I would love that… But even if we escape from this place, I don't how you can survive out there in the world."

"Excuse me for intruding on your conversation," said Carl, looking up. "But you might be interested in a line of research Professor Carl was pursuing in the weeks before his death. It was always his dream, you see, for mature soul shadows – I mean the ones who were at least a few months old – to be able to live in normal daylight with the help of some kind of orally administered supplement."

"You mean like a pill?"

"That's right."

Before Estelle could pursue this interesting revelation, they were interrupted by one of the blackshirts, who approached Estelle with his phone. "It's Professor Wallace," he said. "She wants to speak with you."

Barbara Wallace?

A shiver ran through Estelle at the mention of her name. She took the phone from the guard and placed it cautiously to her ear. "Yes?"

"Estelle, my dear!" said the posh, slightly husky voice – the same voice that had flowed through her double's lips just an hour earlier, entirely fooling the police. "You've done very well for yourselves, surviving this far. And how ingenious to convert the lighting in the Cave... Was that your idea?"

Despite the compliment, her voice was harsh and cold, without any hint of Derek-style charm.

"What do you want?" said Estelle through gritted teeth.

"To call a truce, my darling girl. We're in a stalemate, wouldn't you agree? You have our army, but you can't move anywhere with it. Which means that you're stuck and we're stuck. So where does that leave us?"

"Who says we're stuck?" said Estelle, trying to banish the tremor from her voice. "We can leave the Cave any time we want."

"Without the zeta-pro radiation, the Shadow Army will quickly revert to mindless flesh-eaters, like the wild shadows in the forest – you must have realised that."

Estelle hadn't got quite that far with her reasoning – she'd forgotten that the forest was still full of zeta rays – but she wasn't going to admit it. "We can take them as far as the tunnel entrance and fight our way out," she said tentatively. "Then at least we'll be free, even if your army turns wild."

"We've filled both tunnels with zeta radiation," said Barbara. "We've trapped you in the Cave like butterflies in a jar, my dear. However, we do want our army back, and so we're prepared to do a deal."

"What are you proposing?"

"We'll allow you and your friend to leave the Cave, and providing you both agree to submit to a small medical procedure, you will be free to return to your homes."

"What sort of medical procedure?" asked Estelle, eyes widening with alarm.

"A minor operation to remove your memory of the past couple of days. After that, you have my word that you'll be allowed to leave."

"I've learned not to trust anything you people say," Estelle answered stiffly. "You said you were in the spare organs business. Now I see you're building soul shadow armies. Derek promised me we'd be allowed to go free, but then he said we'd never leave this place with our lives."

"Derek has been taken off this assignment," said Barbara. "His methods were altogether too... extreme. Understandably, we have secrets we wish to protect, but he managed to turn a minor threat to our privacy into an unholy mess. I don't mind admitting that this has been a very bad day for us, as I'm sure it's been for you. The last thing we want, my dear, is to make things even worse by having to cover up the deaths of two young people. Our only desire is that you leave this place, and if you are willing to trust me, I can make that happen."

Despite these reassuring words, Estelle remained on her guard. "I've not heard of an operation that can delete the memory of a particular period of time. That sounds like something out of science fiction."

"Had you heard of soul shadows before you came here?" rebutted Barbara. "Science has made advances in many areas, my dear, but not all of it is deemed suitable for public consumption. Trust me, the procedure is quick and perfectly safe. If you do as I say, you and Sandor can be on a train home tomorrow."

"And if we say no?"

"Then I'm afraid you'll just have to rot down there. I'm not sure which will run out first, the food in your little kitchen or the energy feeding that light. I hope for your sakes it will be the former. It would be better to starve to death, I should think, than to be eaten by your army – and when the light goes, they will need to obtain their sustenance from somewhere, and that can only mean your flesh and blood… I look forward to hearing your decision soon, Estelle."

The phone clicked off.

Estelle remained sitting there for a while, thinking over the conversation, when a commotion outside made her look up.

"I'm on your side, for heaven's sake!" cried an indignant male voice. "Now put me down!"

Jethro stepped into the room, his boots crunching on the broken glass. In his huge hand was suspended a long, lanky figure in a white coat.

"My men find this one moving slippery like fox in dark parts of Cave," announced Jethro. "Is this man friend or shall Jethro kill him?"

"Professor Mitchell!" Estelle cried, getting up and moving closer to him. "What are you doing here? I suppose that Wallace woman sent you."

Mitchell looked a pathetic sight dangling from Jethro's fist – a far cry from the proud, aloof character she'd met at the Facility the previous morning. "No!" he bawled. "I swear by the laws of Newton that Barbara Wallace is now my enemy!"

"Have you checked to see if he's armed, Jethro?" Estelle asked.

"He carry no weapon."

"OK, you may put him down."

Jethro opened his hand, and Robert Mitchell fell the ten metres or so to the glass-strewn carpet. He let out a cry of pain, before clambering clumsily to his feet. His chin was bleeding, his coat dirty, his hair was sticking up at odd angles and his once-smooth face looked creased with stress.

"OK, you'd better explain yourself, Professor," said Estelle, "starting with why you were slinking about down here."

Mitchell patted down his hair in a vain attempt to reclaim his dignity. "I have come here," he began, "to inform you of certain things. Things that have recently... that have recently come to my attention." He sighed and allowed himself to collapse into a nearby chair.

If the last few days had taught Estelle anything, it was that no one could be trusted. However, she had to concede that the Professor was doing a passable impression of a thoroughly miserable human being.

"I was wrong," he said bitterly. The fist supporting his cheek clenched as if he wanted to punch himself. "I supported Barbara against Carl. Now I see that Carl was right. He saw the danger signs – I didn't. But all along, I swear, my intentions were honourable. My only ambition was to use the soul shadows to develop a production line of spare organs for transplant. It was good, humanitarian work. I agreed with Barbara that we had to make them stronger if they were to be of any practical use. It never occurred to me that by doing so, we were also making them more dangerous. And by the time I realised that, it was too late." He slammed his fist down on the table in frustration. "But of course the most dangerous monsters were never the soul shadows. They were the humans – Barbara Wallace and Derek Atkins. Between them they created that..."

He stared out of the room's broken glass wall at the expanse of the Cave. "You may find it hard to believe, but until today I had no idea that this 'Shadow Army' even existed. So preoccupied was I in my lab, hard at work on my experiments, that I was completely unaware of this other project. Of course, I should have realised long ago that something was up, what with all those mysterious visits from that madman, Major Harlon Black. He's an ex-soldier turned private military entrepreneur, who no doubt bankrolled this entire operation. Barbara would have told him about the soul shadows, and of course he must have seen their military potential. I'm sure Barbara didn't take much persuading. She's a first-class scientist, that woman, but she has the morals of a jackal."

"So why come here, Professor?" asked Estelle. "Why not get straight onto the police? After all, creating a private army of monsters beneath a forest sounds at least slightly illegal."

"I couldn't do that," said Mitchell, shaking his head tiredly. "Perhaps it's hard for you to understand, Miss Grant, but I've spent the best part of my career on this work. From the start, we committed ourselves to a vow of silence, knowing that to open our doors to public scrutiny could very well invite disaster. If people were to look at us now, they wouldn't see the good things we're achieving, they'd only see... monsters." He fastened her with his pale blue eyes. "I'm so close. With Carl's breakthrough on zeta-pro, I'm sure that within six months we'll be ready to undergo clinical trials. This work could transform the field of organ transplantation. I'm simply not prepared to see the destruction of my entire life's work because my less scrupulous colleagues have messed up."

"So? Why have you come to us?"

He spread his hands in a gesture of openness. "Because, Miss Grant, together, we can defeat them. Yesterday, as I was driving through the forest, I saw a strange-looking tree. I investigated and discovered that it wasn't a tree at all. It was a mast disguised as a tree, and at the top of the mast was a zeta-ray transmitter just like that one." He nodded towards the globe at the top of the mast out in the main chamber. "My suspicions aroused, I hacked into Barbara's computer and found a map detailing the location of about twenty of these masts, dotted all around this part of the forest. I was forced to accept a horrifying truth: the radiation leakage into the forest, which I'd always assumed was an accident, was deliberate! Barbara and Derek must have set up these transmitters in order to create the wild shadows. I don't know why they would do such a thing. Maybe a monster legend was useful to drive away casual snoopers. Maybe they wanted to field-test their shadow army in the woods. Who knows? But the point is, I have the map. I know where the transmitters are. You have Carl's formula for zeta-pro radiation. Between us, we have the tools to defeat Barbara and Derek. We can change the settings on the transmitters in the forest, then lead this army out of the Cave and march on the Facility. We'd be unstoppable. What do you think?"

The man sounded plausible, but then so had Barbara, and Derek, at first. Estelle couldn't forget the way the professor had treated her when she'd arrived at the Facility yesterday. "But you kidnapped me!" she reminded him. "You imprisoned me and then left me at the mercy of that monster Atkins. Why should I trust you? Barbara Wallace has just offered us a way out of here. Why should we believe you any more than her? For all I know this is just a ploy to tempt us to leave the Cave, and you're going to lead us straight into a trap!"

"Miss Grant – Estelle – you have to believe that I'm on your side," said Mitchell earnestly. "I hate these people as much as you do. Our only hope of defeating them is to act together."

She refused to look at him, keeping her eyes fixed on Sandor's sleeping form. Estelle was tired. Her watch read 10.15. She had rather lost track of time, but presumed that had to mean "PM". Their day had begun an eternity ago, before dawn, in Barbara Wallace's cottage, and they had lurched from one crisis to the next ever since. It was hard to think clearly, and it didn't help to have Mitchell yammering on at her.

"Look, here's the map I was telling you about." He flapped a piece of paper in front of her exhausted eyes. "Now, the shaft by which I entered the cave emerges at this place in the forest." He pointed to a spot on the paper. "From here we can easily make it to –"

"I'll decide in the morning," cut in Estelle. "I need to sleep on it."

"But surely it would be better to act now while it's dark?"

"I'll decide in the morning! And stop pestering me!"

She took herself off to another part of the room and turned her back on him.

nine

A short while later, a couple of the guards served up an evening meal of bread, cold beans and sausages. Estelle discovered she was ravenous, and comfortably managed a second helping.

Her shadow stared at her as she ate. "This is what eat humans?" She wrinkled her nose in disgust. "Humans smell good, but what they eat smells bad."

"We smell good?" Estelle was surprised. She hadn't showered in days.

"Yes, good to eat!"

"Oh! You want to eat me then?"

"Oh no, Spirit-Mother." The girl looked horrified. "Shadow-Estelle would never... Carl teaches that this is bad thing to eat humans. We must find other ways to get our energy."

"Quite right!"

She eyed her shadow as the girl curled up next to her and went to sleep. It was strange to think that this sweet, gentle creature had it in her nature to eat her spirit-mother. Estelle hoped she would never have to face that temptation.

Estelle spotted Carl nearby, repairing the holes in his torso inflicted by his earlier encounter with the shadow army. He was using the soft grey residue of Shadow-Derek. He picked up a handful of the stuff and smeared it on a hole in his chest as though spreading plaster on a wall. When he removed his hand, the grey patch gradually changed, over a period of about thirty seconds, to the colour and texture of his yellow shirt.

"That's amazing stuff," Estelle commented.

"This?" replied Carl, grabbing another portion of the material. "This is just mouldable thermoplastic – a useful medium, but not amazing. It is we soul shadows who are amazing. We have the ability to transmute one chemical element into another just by touching it. The process takes about half a minute for a mature shadow like me, but a brand-new one can do it in seconds."

"How come?"

"Looser molecular bonds. It makes them weaker in some ways, but also highly acquisitive in terms of component materials. A forming soul shadow can and will absorb literally anything it comes in contact with – including walls, floors or even people. So remember not to touch one that's forming, Estelle, or you may find yourself becoming part of it."

On that rather disgusting note, Estelle pushed aside the remains of her food, returned to her corner of the main room and tried to settle down to sleep. The carpet was unyielding, and rough against her skin, yet she was so tired she felt herself dropping off within seconds.

She awoke feeling stiff-limbed with a crick in her neck. Blinking in the harsh electric light, she read the time on her watch: 6.25. Next to her watch was the smartphone she'd found in the van. She looked at it and her face dropped. It was smashed! Had she rolled onto it in the night? But she wasn't heavy enough to inflict that sort of damage, even if she had overdone it on the bread and sausages. Massaging her neck, she raised herself to a sitting position. Across the room, seated against the far wall, his head flopped forwards onto his chest, was a sleeping Robert Mitchell. Angrily, she got up and walked over, kicking him hard in the leg and making him wake up with a start.

"How dare you break my phone," she said, holding the shattered device up to his face.

He squinted at the phone and then at her, dazed and shocked. "I – I didn't break your phone."

"You were worried I'd sneak out of here during the night and call the police, weren't you?"

"It never occurred to me. Perhaps someone stepped on it while you were asleep."

She glared at him, jaws clenched, and was suddenly struck by how guileless he looked, with sleep in his eyes and stubble on his cheeks. Maybe he was speaking the truth.

"I've decided to trust you," she said on a whim. "Let's go."

Mitchell shook his head in confusion at this sudden change of attitude. Then an eager smile lit up his face. "Good! Good!" He clambered to his feet with all the grace of an overexcited giraffe.

Before leaving, Estelle took Jethro and Andreas Becker, the leader of the blackshirts, aside. She could tell at once that Jethro remained steadfastly loyal to Sandor, ready to act on any sign or pronouncement from his still-sleeping leader. Nevertheless, Estelle was nervous about leaving Sandor and Shadow-Estelle at the mercy of the blackshirts, whose loyalty was less assured. "Sandor remains your leader," she said to Jethro and Becker. "Any attack on Sandor or Shadow-Estelle is an act of mutiny and punishable by death." She turned to Jethro. "I believe Andreas is good. But if he tells you Sandor is bad, then he is lying and you must kill him."

Jethro nodded. "Sandor is good. He is our friend. He will make us free."

Before setting off, Estelle armed herself with a pistol, procured from one of the blackshirts. She also took one of their intercom phones. The phone could connect her with any of the locations within the Facility complex, including the Cave, so she could call on Sandor or Jethro for help if necessary. Sandor remained asleep for now, but Carl assured her he was comfortable and would probably wake soon. Mitchell said that Carl, with his knowledge of the zeta-pro formula, should come with them, so Carl instructed Shadow-Estelle on how to care for Sandor, including, if necessary, the provision of painkillers. Estelle looked at Sandor one last time. She couldn't resist kissing him on his bruised cheek. Then she hugged Shadow-Estelle and told her not to worry. "This should take no more than three hours," she said – Mitchell's estimate of the time it would take them to convert all the forest transmitters to zeta-pro. "We'll be back in time for lunch."

Mitchell led Estelle and Carl back out into the main chamber of the Cave. Further along on the left-hand side was a dim, barely visible recess in the chamber's rocky wall. Within the recess was a narrow stairwell that spiralled upwards into the gloom above their heads. "I learned about this shaft when I hacked into Barbara's computer," explained Mitchell. "It's about 200 steps, I'm afraid, but it'll take us directly into the forest, quite close to the first transmitter."

"Lead on," said Estelle.

They mounted the stairway, Mitchell in front, followed by Estelle, with Carl bringing up the rear. It was a long climb, and by the time they reached the top, Mitchell and Estelle were exhausted. Carl, by contrast, appeared unaffected. At the top of the stairway lay a small room with concrete walls. The only light came through a thin crack at the edges of a wooden door set into one of the walls. Estelle thought the light looked white rather than yellowy green – perhaps they were in a clearing.

"Out there is the forest," panted Mitchell, pointing at the door. "And it's full of zeta radiation. The first transmitter is about 50 metres from here. Think you can make it, Carl?"

"If I run, maybe."

"OK, open the door and off you go," said Mitchell.

Carl twisted the handle and pulled, then pushed. It wouldn't budge.

"Ah yes," said Mitchell. "Here, let me unlock it for you." He leaned forward and placed a key in the lock beneath the handle.

A key? Where did he get a key from?

The key turned with a click, and this time the door opened. Carl rushed out into white emptiness. Before Estelle could scream at him to stop, she felt Mitchell's hand shoving her after him. She stumbled forwards into a room. Surrounding her and Carl were blackshirts with guns. One of them roughly removed the gun and the phone from her belt. Before her stood the tall, immaculate figure of Barbara Wallace. Her dark eyes sparkled like lasers slicing through metal, and her face gleamed, stone-like, under the harsh glare of striplights. Estelle felt as a fly might, trapped in the web of a black widow.

"Welcome back to the Facility, my dear," said Barbara in her low, smoky voice. Her gaze flicked towards Mitchell. "Thank you, Robert, for delivering me this pretty little package."

"I've done what you asked," said Mitchell. "You have Miss Grant. Now let me have Henrison's shadow."

Estelle cast a brief, hate-filled glance at the treacherous Mitchell. He didn't meet her eyes.

"Half of what I asked," Barbara replied sternly. "Where's the other one – Sandor Watts?"

"He's still recovering from his injuries. He couldn't have climbed these stairs."

Barbara returned her attention to Estelle. A thin, vindictive smile appeared on her lips as she studied her. "We'll see about that," she growled. "Once he hears how much we're hurting his girlfriend, he'll soon find the strength to come and rescue her. Then, of course, we'll be waiting for him."

Estelle watched helplessly as manacles were placed around Carl's wrists and he was led through a doorway by two of the blackshirts. Before following them out of the room, Mitchell hesitated and turned back to Estelle. "I didn't lie about everything, Miss Grant," he said quickly. "I still wish I'd sided with Henrison against these people. I don't care for what they're doing. But the temptation of working with Carl's shadow on zeta-pro was too great... I'm sorry."

"And the forest transmitters?" asked Estelle.

"Shut up!" screamed Barbara, but she wasn't able to stop Mitchell from nodding his head. He left the room, and Barbara turned furiously on Estelle. Then her expression softened. "It doesn't matter that you know about the transmitters. You won't be alive for much longer anyway."

"I thought you were going to remove our memories rather than kill us."

Barbara laughed. "You were right to be sceptical about that one, Estelle. Of course there is no such procedure. We could lobotomise you, I suppose, but that could lead to even more difficult questions than a disappearance or a carefully staged death. Our sole aim is to be allowed to pursue our work in secret. I bear you no personal malice, young lady. It's simply bad luck. You were in the wrong place at the wrong time... But we'll have to keep you alive for just a little longer – long enough, at least, to lure your boyfriend up here."

"You can do what you like to me," said Estelle with more bravado than she felt. "Sandor won't come."

"Don't be so modest, my dear," said Barbara mockingly. "You underestimate your power over that young man.

When he starts to hear your screams on the phone…" She chose not to finish the sentence, but turned to one of the blackshirts – a senior one to judge from the stripes on his sleeve. "Escort Miss Grant to Professor Atkins' laboratory," she instructed him.

Manacles were pressed into the flesh of Estelle's wrists. Her stomach ached with fear at what was to come. She was shoved forwards, her legs almost too weak to support her.

A corridor, more stairs, another corridor, and a familiar metal door painted with yellow and black diagonal stripes. A card was slid through the entry scanner and the door hissed open. Once again, Estelle found herself in Derek's underground lair: the enormous room with the steel-barred, zeta-irradiated cage at its centre. On the cage's straw-matting floor slept the three captured wild shadows that Estelle remembered from her last visit. Their naked bodies were covered with burned, blistered flesh where they'd been exposed to natural light. Derek, who had been standing behind a control panel opposite the cage, turned as she came in and approached her. She couldn't believe she'd once found his smile charming. Seeing it now, creasing up his face, only intensified her nausea.

"Estelle, good to see you! I knew you wouldn't be able to resist me for long!" He eyed her lasciviously, making her squirm inside. All the loathing she felt for him returned, mixed this time with deep unease at his plans for her.

"The tragedy of our relationship," said Derek, looking quite serious for once, "is that you'll never get to know what I'm really like – the man under the white coat, so to speak." He wheeled a large reclining chair – disturbingly like a dentist's chair, Estelle thought – to a position just next to the soul shadow cage. "Away from all this, I'm really quite pleasant. Witty, intelligent – 'GSOH' as they say on dating sites." He pushed down a lever, locking the wheels beneath the chair, then looked at her. "I think you'd have been surprised, Estelle. I'm knowledgeable about all sorts of things, I mean apart from radiation. I'd be much better company than that grunt downstairs who you've formed such an inexplicable attachment to."

He signalled to one of the blackshirts, who escorted her to the chair and forced her to lie down on it, her feet protruding from the end. "I know about wine and jazz, to name but two of my interests," Derek continued. "It makes me sad to think that I'll never get to share these things with you." Her hands were already manacled in front of her, and now straps were placed across her chest and legs, restricting her movement still further. "You're the sort of woman my mother, God rest her soul, would have liked for me." With great gentleness, he began removing her shoes and socks. He stared at her naked feet, and swallowed. "If only we could have met under different circumstances." He moved behind her, stroking her hair as he went. She heard the brake lever being pulled and felt the chair inching forwards, so that her feet were now positioned between two of the vertical steel bars of the cage. The brake was reapplied, then Derek's footsteps retreated across the shiny, echoey floor. Twisting her head, she saw him at the desk manipulating controls. A narrow beam of light shone down from the ceiling, slicing through the yellow mist of zeta radiation inside the cage. It lit up the flank of one of the sleeping soul shadows. The creature started and let forth a howl of pain. The beam of light disappeared. The awoken shadow glanced fearfully aloft, cowering at the prospect of another searing flash. When none came, it raised itself cautiously to a standing position. It didn't take it long to notice Estelle's feet, inserted enticingly through the bars of the cage. It cocked its head warily, perhaps suspecting a trap. Then it licked its lips and Estelle caught a glimpse of razor-edged teeth.

She tried desperately to bend her legs and draw her feet in, but the strap across her knees was too tight.

"Very soon you're going to wish Sandor hadn't stopped me killing you yesterday, Estelle," said Derek. "A bullet in the head would have been quick. I'm afraid this won't be. I don't know how long it'll take, to be honest. But I hope for your sake that Sandor is able to climb those steps fast, despite his injury. Because until he gets here, my orders are to keep going. They'll eat your tiny toes first, and then we'll see how things progress from there, shall we?"

The creature was slowly approaching her, its yellow eyes never leaving the two juicy prospects poking into its cage. Estelle struggled against the tight constraints. She wriggled her feet like crazy, but could do nothing to pull them out of range. She felt the onset of madness, as her mind became consumed with the coming pain and mutilation – her soft, vulnerable flesh hanging out there like meat in a butcher's shop, and those fangs, shiny with saliva, aching to rip into them.

The thing was on its knees before her, its long black tongue snaking outwards. She felt its clingy wetness on her heel.

"No!" she sobbed. "Please –"

The soul shadow opened its jaws, revealing in full its evil dentistry.

Behind her, like a buzzing insect, she was vaguely aware of Derek's voice. "Hello? Who's that? Captain Becker? Professor Atkins here. I wish to speak with Sandor Watts. … Asleep? . Well, wake him up! There isn't much time."

Then, for some reason, the shadow froze, as in the moment of a camera flash when everything goes white and still. Indeed, the entire cage seemed suddenly to pop in a blinding flare of light. The soul shadow probably didn't even feel his own extinction. It just became rigid in that position, forever anticipating its first bite. Very soon it started to crumble, like a sculpture in sand gone dry and brittle in the sun. Its lower jaw fell off, then its ears, followed by its nose and arms, until it became a featureless form that slowly collapsed in on itself.

She blinked and tried to make sense of what had happened. It seemed that the tower of yellow zeta radiation that had been pouring into the cage had, for some reason, slid off to the right, to be replaced by the brilliant light that was now bathing her feet and had brought instant death to the three shadows. The light didn't fade as flashes do, but remained steady, only losing its intensity as her eyes became accustomed to it. She twisted herself as far as possible to her right to see where the shaft of zeta radiation had gone, and discovered that it was now enclosing Derek. He was standing there, in the misty yellow glow, frowning at the ceiling as if wondering who was playing around with his lighting system. The yellow beam hit Derek at an angle of about 60 degrees, so that his body cast a shadow, and that shadow, Estelle could see, was beginning to stir.

The shiny, dark grey floor behind him was softening and undulating, rising up and forming itself into a vaguely human shape. When Derek finally looked down and saw what was developing at his feet, he emitted a small squawk of surprise. Trying to retreat backwards, he stumbled on the base of the control panel and instead stepped on the forming mass on the floor. His foot and ankle disappeared into the shiny grey goo and when he raised his leg again, the stuff came up too, like slimy, sucky mud, adhering to his shoe. He tugged at it to free himself, but couldn't. Instead, his foot seemed to get dragged back into the figure. "Damn!" muttered Derek, as he put ever more frantic efforts into separating himself from the squishy shape, and Estelle was reminded of Carl's words that morning:

A forming soul shadow can and will absorb literally anything it comes in contact with – including walls, floors or even people.

She shuddered as she watched Derek's increasingly desperate battle to remain distinct from his sticky shadow. He was now up to his left knee in the thing, and, foolishly, he tried to lever himself out with his hand, which then also became stuck. Derek yelled at a blackshirt to help him. Keeping well clear of the shadow, the guard ran over and grasped Derek's free hand. He pulled with all his strength, clutching at the control panel for balance, but the shadow's attractive power was astonishing, and the guard's shoes kept slipping. It seemed that nothing could prevent Derek's leg and arm from disappearing further and further into the billowing grey mass. The other three guards joined the effort to free Derek, all pulling urgently at his remaining two limbs, but Estelle could tell from their despairing faces that they were losing the battle. Soon, all but the very tops of his right arm and leg had fused with the shadow and Derek was looking utterly terrified. He screamed at the guards to destroy the thing. One of them fired his gun at the shadow's head, but when he did so, Derek cried out in agony, as if his own nervous system had become entwined with his shadow's. The hole in the thing's head swiftly disappeared – in fact, the monster seemed to swell and grow ever stronger as it absorbed Derek inch by inch. It wasn't long before Derek's trunk started to merge into the grey mass. Derek blubbed like a baby, but refused to passively accept his fate. He thrashed around and strained his neck forwards to keep his head clear of the shadow for as long as possible.

Estelle felt sickened by the spectacle, yet a darker part of her – a part she would almost prefer not to acknowledge – felt a gruesome satisfaction that some sort of natural justice was playing itself out.

The shadow, which was now bigger than any Estelle had hitherto encountered – including Jethro – was beginning to detach itself from the ground, though its surface remained shiny grey, like a living piece of floor. Its arm rose up and the guards backed away, scared that they too might be dragged into it. The shadow grabbed Derek's flapping left arm and folded it into its torso. It did the same with Derek's leg and the remainder of his torso, so that all that remained of the physicist was his head, protruding from the monster's chest. Derek looked insane, eyes wild, mouth – better known for its grin – now open in a scream, but without the physical equipment to generate sound or breath. He seemed to be looking directly at Estelle, though she doubted by this time that his brain could even process the information its eyes were feeding it. That was her last view of Derek Atkins – scientist, wine lover, jazz enthusiast and murderer – before the shadow's hands closed over his face and buried the remainder of him in its colossal chest.

With their boss now gone, the blackshirts stood around looking directionless and scared. They gaped at the towering shadow as it gradually took on the colours and textures of its progenitor. With the white coat, the chubby face with the receding hairline, it was as if Derek was reappearing before them at double his original size.

At that moment, there came a loud metallic crash to Estelle's rear. She couldn't see what had happened, but all four guards now turned towards the far end of the room as a booming voice echoed through the hall.

"I am Jethro, commander of the Shadow Army!"

Hearing this, Estelle almost laughed with exhilaration and relief.

"I am here on orders of our friend Sandor. You bad men. Must die."

She saw him then, as he swooped like a giant raptor on the blackshirts, who scattered, taking shelter behind cabinets or desks and drawing their weapons. One wasn't fast enough and was grabbed from behind. He was raised from the floor by Jethro's fist and then flung against a wall six metres away before falling unconscious to the floor. Gunfire crackled and pinged around the room. Jethro's body shook as bullets thumped into him. Estelle saw holes appear in his chest and arms and grey patches spreading outwards from them. He may not have been as fast or powerful without the nourishing light of the Cave, but he didn't cease in his advance. Descending on the guards one by one like a vengeful force of nature, he hauled them from their hiding places, twirled them around his head and flung them to various corners of the room. They lay where they fell, too scared, dazed or wounded to move.

All the while, Estelle was conscious of the giant Shadow-Derek acquiring ever finer detail in its appearance, as well as strength and suppleness in its limbs.

Jethro, having despatched the last of the guards, approached her. "You friend of Sandor. I help you be free.... Arrrggghhh!" He stepped back with an angry roar as some of the brilliant light from the cage interior fell on his forearm.

After pulling the chair she lay on clear of the light, he ripped the straps from her chest and legs. With one flex of his muscles, he broke open the manacles binding her wrists. "Thank you," said Estelle sitting up and rubbing her legs where the straps had bitten. "But do be careful, Jethro!" Behind him, the Shadow-Derek was looking menacingly in his direction, bearing a mouthful of nasty-looking spiked teeth. It was almost twice as tall as Jethro, and thicker through the chest and shoulders. Jethro turned his head around in that disconcertingly flexible way of soul shadows and whipped out an extra long arm, burying his fingers in the monster's throat. With a roar, the Shadow-Derek seized his arm and tore it clean off. It then dragged Jethro by his stump into its circular beam of zeta radiation. Jethro clawed at the thing's shoulder with his other hand, while it pushed Jethro's head right back against his spine at an angle that would have snapped a human neck. They seemed locked in a fight to the death, and at any moment Jethro, now exposed to the evil rays, might turn bad. Estelle didn't intend to hang around to find out. She leapt off the chair and ran for the exit door, which had earlier been ripped from its hinges by Jethro, then scooted into the corridor. She almost collided with Carl, who was running in the opposite direction.

"My lady, come quickly!" he exclaimed. "We are escaping!" He grabbed her hand and whisked her back towards the stairs that led to the Facility's main site. It was like being borne along by the wind – she barely felt her feet touching the ground as she flew along at shadow-speed.

"Who's we?" she gasped as they went. "And how come Jethro's here?"

"No time to explain now," he replied. "We must move fast before we are discovered."

At the top of the stairs they turned left, then sped down another corridor, taking them to a location directly above the chamber Estelle had just left. Carl pulled her into a room. To her delighted surprise, Sandor was there with a big grin on his face. He looked fresh and full of vitality, notwithstanding the bandaged arm and leg. Shadow-Estelle was also there, and she immediately rushed to Estelle, embracing her like a long-lost sister. "Spirit-Mother, I so happy you alive!"

Not so welcome was the sight of Robert Mitchell, seated in a swivel chair before a control panel not dissimilar to the one Derek had been piloting on the floor below.

"What's that man doing here?" blurted Estelle, breaking away from her shadow.

Mitchell didn't look up from the controls. "What's going on downstairs, Miss Grant?" he asked.

"Is Atkins dead?"

"Yes... I mean, sort of." She was struggling to express herself, fazed as she was by the sight of Mitchell suddenly acting like one of the good guys. "He was kind of... I mean, he generated this shadow, and –"

"A shadow!" interjected Mitchell. "Then we'd better turn off the zeta ray beam." He flipped a switch. "There, that should weaken it. Where's Jethro?"

"Fighting the shadow."

"How's my big friend doing?" asked Sandor.

"Well, he didn't look like he was winning... Listen, can someone explain to me what –?"

"No time for explanations," said Sandor, starting towards the door. "We have to get out of here fast."

As they left the room, an alarm began to sound and a red light pulsed. A calm, female, computerised voice announced: "Intruders at large in the Facility. Lockdown. Intruders at large in the Facility. Lockdown."

Carl accelerated towards the reception area and pushed at the main entrance door. It failed to open. The alarm and the looped voice continued, as they tried the window. That too was locked.

"My office. Quick!" called Mitchell, and they followed him down a different corridor. But his window was also locked. A rapid check in the canteen and the recreation room told the same story: a centralised command must have secured every outer door and window in the building, leaving them trapped.

Booted footsteps approached from a nearby stairwell.

"Blackshirts!" said Estelle.

Mitchell beckoned them to follow him back into

the rec room.

"It has to be Barbara," frowned Mitchell once they were all safely inside. "She's the only one with the access codes to carry out a lockdown."

"Where is she?" asked Sandor.

"She could be anywhere. All she needs is a computer and there are dozens of them in this building." He slammed his fist against the wall. "She's trapped us, and I know she'll do whatever it takes to prevent us escaping."

Estelle peered into the corridor through the door's little viewing window, while keeping herself hidden. She couldn't see anyone about.

"We have guns," said Sandor. "We could shoot our way out of here."

Mitchell shook his head. "The windows are bullet-proof. And even if we get out, there's the electrified fence to deal with. Our only hope is to find Barbara, before her blackshirts or that shadow downstairs find us."

"The shadow should not be a threat, now that you've switched off the zeta radiation," pointed out Carl.

As he said this, Estelle, who was still looking into the corridor, noticed an odd change in the lighting: the strip lights in the ceiling went out and, simultaneously, the corridor became filled with a distinctly yellow-hued light, from no discernible source: the sallow, insipid glow of zeta radiation.

"I don't think we can say that now, Carl," she said, and pointed.

Mitchell had already seen fingers of yellow light shooting through the gap at the bottom of the door and pouring through the little window in the door, casting a patch on the carpet. He took his white coat off and threw it at the base of the door before any of the rays could touch Carl or Shadow-Estelle. Some pages ripped from a magazine, were sufficient to block out the little window.

"What the devil is the woman playing at?" hissed Mitchell. "Any blackshirt wandering around out there is going to generate more shadows. Not to mention Derek's shadow downstairs. She'll wind up killing us all – herself included!"

"Um, about that shadow downstairs," said Estelle. "There's something I perhaps ought to tell you. It's not ordinary. I mean, it absorbed Derek."

On hearing this, Mitchell groaned and sank into a nearby armchair. Carl wore an expression that reminded her of his progenitor after a visit from the blackshirts.

"What exactly are you saying, Es?" asked Sandor.

"What she's saying is that the shadow downstairs is a Super Shadow," said Carl.

"And now it can travel anywhere in the building," murmured Mitchell. "Barbara probably doesn't have a clue what she's unleashed."

"What the devil is a Super Shadow?" asked Sandor.

"Derek stepped on the shadow while it was forming..." Estelle told him.

"The idiot should have known better," muttered Mitchell.

"...And sort of got stuck in it," she continued. "Three men couldn't drag him free. It was pretty gross watching him get sucked in bit by bit."

"Super Shadows are about twice as big and strong as ordinary shadows," said Carl.

"Which means twice as deadly," added Mitchell.

"They also acquire some additional intelligence and personality from their human component," continued Carl.

"And with Derek's personality, that's going to make for one mean brute," Mitchell finished.

"So long as the creature doesn't try flirting with me while it's killing me, I don't care," grimaced Estelle.

Sandor looked at her, bemused.

"Derek was coming onto me even while he was strapping me into his torture chair," she explained. "Telling me he liked jazz and wishing he could have introduced me to his mother. It was so weird and sick..." She looked up. Shadow-Estelle and Carl looked blank and uncomprehending. Mitchell had his head in his hands, not even listening. Sandor was looking a little shocked, but not half as angry or jealous as she'd hoped. "But enough about me," she said quickly, and with a touch of irritation. "How about explaining how you, Jethro and my shadow ended up here if you were still asleep in the Cave when Derek called you just now?"

"Because I wasn't asleep in the Cave," answered Sandor with a wry smile. "I was upstairs in that control room, along with everyone else here, trying to figure out a way of rescuing you. It was Mitchell's idea to manipulate Derek's lighting system. Had to fry those poor wretches in the cage, unfortunately, but it was the only way to stop you being eaten alive. Then we sent in Jethro to get you out of there."

"But that blackshirt captain that Derek spoke to, Andreas Becker. He said –"

"He said what he had to to stay alive. One of Jethro's henchmen was standing very close by when he took that call."

"But why did you even come here, Sandor? How did you know it was a trap?"

"It's amazing what you can learn while pretending to be unconscious. I was lying there on that table soon after you left, listening to two blackshirts whispering."

"Clever you! What were they saying?"

"About how you'd been duped by Mitchell."

"You can say that again," Estelle frowned. "Speaking of which, why are we even still talking to that treacherous scumbag?"

Mitchell raised his head from his hands and pointed to Carl. "You can thank Henrison's shadow for that," he told her. "He's a very persuasive fellow. Said if I ever wanted to learn anything from him, I'd first have to help you lot. That's the only reason why I'm here with you now."

"Oh, so it wasn't out of common human decency then?" said Estelle sarcastically.

"As I told you before, Miss Grant," sighed Mitchell. "I'm a humanitarian, but my mind operates on larger scales than individual lives. If I can only bring my life's work to fruition, I'll be able to count the lives I've saved in the millions, most of them as yet unborn. It happened that, on this occasion, it was in my interests to intervene on your behalf, but it was a purely rational act, I assure you. Of course, as a fellow human being, I wish you a long and healthy life, but in the greater scheme of things, in a choice between your continued existence and the success of my project, I would not hesitate to let you die."

Charming! But honest, at least.

"So it was you who smashed my phone?"

"Guilty as charged," he confessed.

A distant howl echoed from somewhere in the Facility.

"The Super Shadow's on the move," said Mitchell.

"You don't think Jethro might have killed it?" suggested Sandor.

Mitchell shook his head. "Not a chance. Our only hope is that it finds Barbara before it finds us."

Suddenly a phone rang inside the room. They all stared at the red office-style phone, previously disregarded, sitting on a table.

"That'll be Barbara," predicted Mitchell. "No doubt offering her demands."

Estelle, who was closest, went and picked it up. "Hello?"

An avuncular Scottish voice replied: "Estelle? Is that you, lassie?"

"Doctor Kirby!" She was so surprised she nearly dropped the receiver.

"Estelle! I'm so glad to have found ye. Your aunt and I have been worried. We couldn't get hold of you on your mobile. Then we went to the cottage and could'na find you there." The line was crackling, his voice growing indistinct. He kept fading in and out. "The police told us... called the Facility... top-secret government place... weren't even allowed to tell us where... could'na find it on any maps... found this number on the internet... tried it on the off-chance... so relieved that I've found ye! Are you OK, my dear?"

Estelle drank in these words, faint and broken up as they were, like a sweet, reviving beverage. It was so wonderful to hear that deep, rich brogue, so familiar from their many sessions together – she could almost smell the pipe smoke – and to know that the nightmare must now, surely, be nearly over. She was so overcome, she started to cry.

"Doctor... Doctor Kirby," she sobbed. "I'm not... I'm really not OK. This place is evil. The police were fooled... We're trapped here... There's this crazy woman, Barbara Wallace... And this Super Shadow... And..."

A commotion broke out behind Estelle as she said this. She turned in time to see Mitchell trying to reach for the receiver, but being restrained from doing so by Sandor.

At the other end of the line, Dr Kirby was sounding confused. "What? Estelle, I can't make out what you're saying. Are you in trouble?"

"Call the police!" she cried, forcing herself to be clearer. "Tell them they were tricked. That wasn't me they spoke to. We're trapped here, Doctor Kirby. They have to come back here and get us out. There isn't much time!"

"I'm sorry, lassie... hear you properly. I'll call the police... get the address... come and get you." There was a click, followed by the dialling tone.

Mitchell was now back in his armchair, shaking his head, a resigned expression on his face. "Congratulations," he said to Estelle, giving her a mock round of applause. "You've just single-handedly destroyed my career."

"Screw your career!" shouted Estelle. "This is about survival."

"We could have got out of here by ourselves," he said. "There was no need to call on the police. There's five of us against one woman. We can take her."

"You've forgotten about the blackshirts," said Sandor.

"And the Super Shadow," added Carl.

"The guards won't stick around while there's a Super Shadow on the loose," said Mitchell. "By now, I'm sure they're either dead or cowering in the basement somewhere… The Super Shadow, admittedly, is a danger. But it's a danger to us if we stay here as well. The key is to find Barbara. Once we've located her and forced her to end this lockdown, we can get out of here… And I have a pretty good idea of where she might be."

"Oh? And where's that?" asked Estelle sceptically.

"There's a fortified safe room behind her office. She had it built in case of a soul shadow attack on the Facility. It's totally secure and contains food and water for thirty days. I'm certain that's where she is."

"Can you get in there?" asked Sandor.

"No, I don't have the password. But we have some explosives in the armoury. If she doesn't open the door, we could threaten to blast our way in."

They heard a scream – it sounded human, and not far away.

"The Super Shadow's found itself a snack," commented Sandor.

"We should get a move on," said Mitchell. "Before it's too late."

"I'm staying right here until Doctor Kirby or the police arrive," insisted Estelle.

"What do you think, Carl?" asked Sandor. "Carl!" He ran to the shadow, who's head had slumped forwards onto his chest.

Carl roused himself. "I'm sorry," he said tiredly. "I'm

feeling a little weak in this light."

Estelle noticed that her shadow was also looking decidedly worn out. "Are you OK?" she asked her.

"Yes, Spirit-Mother," she assured her croakily. "Please don't worry about me."

"I'm not sure we have the luxury of waiting for the cavalry this time, Es," said Sandor. "Not if we want to keep the shadows alive."

Estelle was tempted to suggest feeding Mitchell to them, but held her tongue. Instead, another idea came to her. "Where's the building's electrical room located?" she asked.

"In the basement," said Mitchell. "We could turn the power off from there, I suppose, and that would weaken the Super Shadow eventually. But it wouldn't solve our problem: we'll still be stuck in here, while Barbara, with her separate generator, will remain as secure and untouchable as ever."

"What about that lighting control room we were just in?" suggested Sandor. "We managed to manipulate the basement lights from there. Couldn't we do the same to the lights up here? With Carl's help we could convert it all to zeta-pro."

Mitchell shook his head. "No chance. The lockdown mechanism not only secures every door and window in the place, it also disables all internal and external computer and telecommunications systems – unless, that is, you have the access codes. People, like your Doctor Kirby, can still call us, but we can't make any calls, and we can no longer mess around with the lights. Needless to say, the person in charge of setting up the security system for this building was Barbara Wallace." He shook his head, almost admiringly. "Funny, I've worked with that woman for twenty years, and I don't think I ever understood her fully until today."

They heard a low growl from further down the corridor.

Estelle felt a liquid fear in her insides. Mitchell paled, muttering incoherently, his fists clenching and unclenching. "I-I don't think we'll be able to go anywhere now. It's too late! We should t-try to block the door."

They looked around for furniture to use as a barricade – there wasn't much: a sofa, a few chairs, a table. Sandor began one-handedly dragging the table over to the door. Estelle jumped up to lend a hand, and Mitchell pushed a chair over. Soon every item of furniture had been arranged in a haphazard pile in front of the door.

Sandor's eye was caught by something above Estelle's head. She turned to see what he was staring at and noticed a large mesh grill high up on the wall, just below the ceiling. To judge by the size of the grill, the shaft behind it had to be wide – wide enough for a person.

"What are you thinking?" she asked him.

"Your idea," he said to her, "about switching off the building's power." He turned to Mitchell. "That would also kill the power to the external electrified fence, wouldn't it?"

Mitchell nodded warily.

"If we could sneak through that ventilation duct, it might take us into the basement. Then we could switch the power off and go back up the shaft to the roof. From there we could escape, right?"

"What about the shadows?" asked Estelle.

"Don't worry about me, Spirit-Mother," said Shadow-Estelle weakly. "You must save yourself."

"I could get the van from the Cave," said Sandor. "It's still got zeta-pro lighting inside it. I'll bring it to the entrance of the Facility while you lot make your way out through the ventilation duct."

"N-no," stammered Mitchell. "We should use the duct to get to the armoury, and then to Barbara's safe room." He banged his chair arm in a state of high excitement. "Th-the priority has to be the safe room. That's where she's controlling the lighting, the doors, the computers – everything. Both the armoury and the safe room are on this floor and shouldn't be hard to find. I wouldn't know how to navigate the duct to find the electrical room."

From outside, they heard another menacing growl. It seemed like no more than a few metres from the door. Sandor and Estelle exchanged glances. Mitchell's hands began to shake.

Ten

As they stood there, trying to decide what their next move should be, the light in the room faded and then changed to yellow. Estelle immediately bundled her shadow under a nearby table, which had been pushed up against the door, and joined her there. Meanwhile, Mitchell crammed his long, lanky body into the shade provided by an overturned sofa. Sandor began pushing Carl towards the same piece of shelter, but by the time Carl reached it, he had already received several seconds of exposure. Sandor squeezed in next to him.

Estelle peered through the thicket of chair and table legs. Carl had his head down on his knees, showing only the dome of his bald cranium, with its tufts of gingery hair. His narrow shoulders were shaking.

"Is he OK?"

Carl said something muffled.

"What is it, Carl?" asked Sandor.

"Kill me," whispered Carl. There was a harsh, grating quality to his voice.

"We're not going to do that," said Sandor. "We're going

to get you back to the Cave so you can bathe in some good-quality light."

Estelle noticed that Sandor's hand had moved to the gun in his underarm holster.

Carl's breathing sounded strange.

Mitchell placed a hand on Carl's arm. "You didn't catch more than a few millirems, my friend. Not enough to affect you."

Carl's head rose. His tear-filled eyes were totally black. "Kill me!" he pleaded. As he spoke, Estelle noticed that his mouth bristled with sharp teeth.

A gunshot exploded in the confined space, and Carl's head, now misshapen and mostly grey, slumped forwards.

"No!" cried Mitchell.

Sandor replaced his pistol.

Shadow-Estelle began to cry. She clutched at Estelle, who stroked her hair absently. Carl was gone – in the space of a heartbeat, his quiet, dignified presence was no more.

"Carl's formula died with that shadow," lamented Mitchell. "Now we'll never know how to manufacture zeta-pro."

"The formula was lost the moment he got exposed to those rays," said Sandor.

There came a great howl from the corridor outside. A massive bang on the door rocked their furniture fortifications.

"We have to get out of here," said Estelle.

Sandor slid himself out from under the sofa. Once back on his feet, he aimed his gun at the vent cover on the wall and fired. After three shots, and a shower of plaster dust, the cover dangled loose. Sandor limped back to the pile of furniture and extracted a chair, which he dragged to a position below the vent opening. Climbing onto the chair, he reached up and ripped away the damaged cover.

"Mitchell, pick up your coat and give it to Shadow-Estelle," Sandor ordered. "She'll need it to make the dash across the room."

The morose professor plucked up his discarded white coat and passed it through the furniture legs to Estelle, who draped it over her shadow.

"Off you go, my dear," she whispered to her.

The shrouded figure of Shadow-Estelle flitted like a ghost across the floor and then up and through the dark hole in the wall. Sandor barely had to help her on her way.

"You alright?" he asked after her.

"Yes, thank you," her quiet voice echoed back.

"You next, Professor," said Sandor.

"Shouldn't I go?" queried Estelle, thinking that her shadow might want her close.

"We need the Prof near the front to show us the way," said Sandor.

Outside the door, the Super Shadow howled, and the furniture pile wobbled under the impact of another crash. Spurred on by terror, Mitchell clambered out of his hiding place, leapt onto the chair and then scrambled head-first into the duct entrance. With his good hand, Sandor helped him slide in.

"You'll have to help me up there, Es," said Sandor.

She crawled out from under the table and stepped up onto the chair. Between her and Mitchell, they managed to lift Sandor through the gap.

Another explosive pummelling behind her made her

turn in fright. She watched in horror as the left-hand door of the rec room rose clear off its hinges and then crashed down onto the furniture barricade.

The sight behind the door was hellish. Atkins' Super Shadow seemed to fill the corridor – so big it had to crouch, with its head thrust forwards through the doorway, beneath its massive shoulders. The head was a horror: she recognised vestiges of Derek – the round face and receding hairline – but the grin, which had repulsed her even on its original owner, now split the face from ear to ear like a Halloween pumpkin head, displaying a thick forest of jagged, blood-smeared teeth. Its eyes stared at her like gleaming, jet-black stones.

The strength drained from her limbs, and she felt herself collapsing. Luckily, Sandor's sinewy right arm caught her and hauled her up into the duct.

The space inside the square-sectioned duct was cramped – just a little wider than her shoulders. She used her hands and feet to slither along the smooth, frictionless metal interior, trying to keep up with Sandor's retreating form. Behind her, the vent opening they had just come through darkened.

The thing was close! If it managed to get into the vent, it would all be over very quickly.

"Hurry, Sandor!" she called, as she pushed herself ever more urgently along.

Then something fluttered against her ankle. She felt a tug, and a sharp pain like knife points digging into her skin. Trying not to panic, she pushed her hands flat against the metal walls, levering herself forwards with all her might. But the force pulling her back was unrelenting.

Her ankle was being squeezed as much as pulled, until it felt like it might break.

"Sandor!" she screamed.

He looked back. "Let go of the sides," he shouted. "Let it take you!"

She stared at him, not wanting to believe what she was hearing. Her arm muscles cried out – she was using every ounce of her strength to resist. But her hands began squeaking against the duct walls as the Super Shadow slowly dragged her backwards. Behind her she saw the giant grinning jack-o-lantern head, which had somehow squeezed itself into the duct, mouth opening wider than seemed possible.

"Let go!" Sandor's voice echoed, further away now.

She could no longer fight it. One of her hands momentarily slipped, and she felt herself being sucked backwards at terrifying speed. Then came the loudest noise she'd ever heard. It was like a thunderclap inside her head, and it made her ears scream. The searing pain in her ankle faded as, behind her, the Super Shadow's head fell out of the pipe and the arm slid away after it.

Sandor reholstered his gun. He was speaking to her, but she couldn't hear a thing.

"What?" she tried saying.

Eventually, she heard his voice, very faintly: "I'm sorry. With your hand in the way, I couldn't get a clear shot... Now come on, before it recovers."

They continued forwards, slithering along like a procession of caterpillars through the narrow duct. Estelle's ankle felt sore, the bullet graze on her arm burned and her ears were ringing from the gunshot – but she was alive!

A dozen metres further on, they passed a second vent cover. Through its latticework, Estelle saw another room – a meeting room, to judge from the large table, chairs, notepads and presentation screen against one wall. The lighting in the room was normal. It was also normal in the next room they came to, which Estelle figured out before she got there, from the white light streaming through the holes in the mesh grille.

How did Barbara Wallace know to change the rec room lighting to zeta radiation, while leaving the others normal? Was she able to track their movements?

Mitchell stopped crawling when he came to this room. He stared into it, then exchanged some words with Sandor, which Estelle couldn't hear because of the jangling in her head.

Eventually, Sandor turned and said to her: "Andreas Becker's in there, with a couple of other blackshirts I recognise from the Cave. They look pretty scared. I don't think they'll harm us. We might be able to use their help. Do you think we should make ourselves known to them?"

Estelle was surprised and gratified to be asked her opinion for once. Sandor usually just did the first and most dangerous thing that came into his head.

"Yes," she said after a moment's reflection. "But be careful. We haven't got Jethro to protect us any more."

Sandor passed this advice onto Mitchell, who tapped on the grille and announced himself to the people in the room. Again, Estelle couldn't hear what he said.

A few moments later, they were being helped down, one at a time, into the canteen.

Andreas and the other two blackshirts had bolted the canteen's swing doors, and then strengthened their defences with an impressive barricade of upturned tables and benches.

The three men were dishevelled. They looked jumpy, and their eyes frequently darted towards the doors, as if expecting the monster to barge its way in at any moment.

"Captain…" began Mitchell.

But Andreas put up his hand. "Call me Becker. After everything that's happened today, we're dispensing with formalities." With a glance at Mitchell, he added: "And we're not taking orders from anyone either. It's every man for himself." He nodded towards the short, stockily built man to his left. "This is Corporal James Kaplan, better known as Kappo."

"And I'm Private Edward Paskey – but everyone calls me Paz," said the other man, who was tall and sandy haired with a freckled face.

"OK, how come you lot are here?" asked Mitchell.

"Things got pretty chaotic down in the Cave after you all left," Becker said hollowly. "With Sandor and Jethro gone, the Shadow Army was effectively leaderless. I tried to keep order, but a couple of my men must have been in secret communication with Professor Wallace. Acting on her orders, they fostered dissent in the ranks. Pretty soon, the shadow soldiers had formed into rival factions. One of the factions took against the zeta-pro light. There was an almighty set-to, during which the light and our office got destroyed. I don't think that was Wallace's plan. I suppose she wanted the men to restore the zeta radiation, but it didn't work out that way, and she may have lost as much as half her army as a result. Me, Kappo and Paz managed to escape the wreckage, but I reckon the rest of my unit copped it."

"I'm sorry," said Sandor quietly.

So even the lab-grown shadow soldiers were becoming uncontrollable, let alone the wild ones. Estelle was reminded of the story of Pandora's Box, and, not for the first time, she wondered at the vanity and stupidity of humans, to believe they could bring such creatures into the world and then control them. She thought once more of the silent, deserted forest: the animals had known instinctively that something malevolent was about. And now that thing in its most horrifying manifestation – the Super Shadow – was here, inside the Facility, hunting them down.

"Who else is in the building besides us?" asked Sandor.

"We've seen lots of bodies," said Paz. "You're the only other living people we've seen – on this floor at least."

"And there's Barbara, of course," said Mitchell.

"If you ask me, that Wallace woman has gone mad," said Kappo.

Mitchell nodded solemnly. "She's actually been crazy for the past five years, though I've tried to pretend to myself otherwise. She's been mad ever since her husband and both her children died in a car crash." His eyes clouded and his head shook at the memory. "Such a senseless waste of life! And while most people would grieve, she refused to. She just closed right up inside and carried on with her work. She never talks about it – almost acts as if it didn't happen. She's preserved her cottage absolutely as it was on the day of the accident. It's as if her personal life has been frozen in space and time, and she exists now only as a scientist. It's insane, because she's denied a whole part of herself, and of course that sort of thing has consequences. There's this unexpressed rage inside her. She hates the world, although you'll never see her get angry. Instead, she makes deals with megalomaniac ex-soldiers to build shadow armies. And she kills anyone who opposes her." He looked at each of the others in turn. "That's what we're dealing with: hatred, driven by cold, ruthless logic."

"A sad story, and it explains a lot," said Sandor. "But it doesn't help us much in our immediate predicament. We need a plan to get ourselves out of here. I suggest that one of you fit lads get back into that ventilation system and head for the electrical room – knock out the power to the electrified fence. Then we all head for the roof and escape that way. Agreed?"

No one spoke.

"Volunteers, please form an orderly queue," Sandor said disappointedly.

"What's the matter?" he coaxed. "I'd do it myself if I had four functioning limbs."

"The thing is," said Becker slowly, "the electrical room is in the basement, which is now zeta irradiated and crawling with hungry shadow soldiers. Going down there would be a suicide mission."

Sandor nodded to himself and flexed his jaw muscles. He looked reconciled to the defeat of his plan.

"Which brings us back to Barbara," said Mitchell, with a pointed glance at Sandor. "As I've said all along, she's the key to all this, not the shadows, not even the Super Shadow. If we can only defeat her, all our problems will be solved." He explained to Becker, Paz and Kappo about the safe room behind Barbara's office where he was sure she was currently hiding.

Paz, who in a former incarnation had been employed on the construction of the Facility, drew a sketch of the ground floor layout on a paper napkin. He traced a line with his finger to show the route of the ventilation ducts. "The pipe continues from here into the kitchen, then across the corridor and behind various storerooms and offices, before it turns a corner here, and we get to the armoury –"

Mitchell interrupted him. "We should stop there and pick up some explosives. Hopefully we'll only need to threaten their use to encourage Barbara to open the door."

"Nice idea, Professor," said Paz, energised by the plan. "From there," he continued, "we'll need to climb a shaft to the rooftop AHU – that's the air handling unit. We'll have to smash our way through the filter, the heating coil and the fan. After that, it's just a short distance to Professor Wallace's office."

Plan agreed, they climbed, one by one, back into the dark, claustrophobic vent. Paz went first, followed by Becker, Mitchell, Sandor, Kappo, Estelle and Shadow-Estelle.

"Spirit-Mother," called Shadow-Estelle softly, once they were crawling.

"What is it?"

"You must save yourself. Not worry for me."

"We're all going to get through this, my dear. Including you."

"I hope so," murmured the girl. "Carl give me hope

when he speak about pill I can take to keep me alive in daylight."

"We'll find a way," Estelle assured her.

"But if we don't," persisted the shadow, "you not worry for me. I so happy just to know you and Carl and Sandor. I don't mind for dying now."

The duct widened after they turned a corner, and they could now crawl on their hands and knees. Through a vent cover in the floor of the duct, they saw they were passing above the kitchen. Kappo suddenly stopped, forcing Estelle and her shadow to do likewise.

"What is it?" she asked him, unable to see much past his bulk.

"Not sure," he said. "Why have we stopped?" he asked Sandor.

The answer came back that Paz thought he'd heard a tapping sound up ahead. They remained where they were for a moment, all of them listening intently. Then the procession began to move once more.

They hadn't crawled more than a few metres when they heard a low rumble. It might have been the metal joints of the ventilation duct groaning under their combined weight, except that it didn't sound like that. It sounded like a deep, rumbling sigh.

Again, everyone stopped.

"I think it m-may be beneath us," said Mitchell, his voice tight.

"In the kitchen?" whispered Becker. "How could it get in there? We barricaded the canteen."

"Through the washroom next door," said Paz.

"Quick!" hissed Mitchell. "Let's get out of here."

Estelle couldn't see a thing in the gloom, but she imagined Mitchell pushing at Becker's rear.

"No," came Sandor's voice. "If we move, it'll hear us. We have to stay absolutely still… Es, is there any way your shadow can crawl very quietly back to that vent cover we just passed, and check if she can see anything?"

Estelle relayed the message, and her shadow slid silently on her tummy back to the grille, and peered through.

She shook her head. "I see no one."

When this message had been passed on, the line began to move slowly forwards again.

A growl stopped them in their tracks. It was low and sustained, like the warning snarl of a giant guard dog.

"It's in front of us," howled Mitchell. "Ohhhh!! It's in the pipe." His panic echoed through the confined space. Kappo skidded backwards into Estelle, presumably pushed into reverse by the now hysterical Mitchell. "Let me out!" cried the Professor. "Get out of my way, you stupid people. It's coming for us!" She caught a flash of the whites of Mitchell's eyes. He looked mad with fear.

"Calm down, Professor!" shouted Sandor. "It's not in the pipe. It's below us."

"It's not below us. I've seen it!!! It's in the pipe I tell you."

"What can you see, Paz?" asked Becker.

"I'm not sure," came the hesitant reply. "It may have been nothing."

"Let me out of here! I can't breathe!" sobbed Mitchell. But his cries were drowned out by a sudden immense hammering that shook the pipe. The hammering was accompanied by a tremendous, screaming howl.

"Get moving, Paz!" cried Sandor. "It knows we're here!"

"No!" shrieked Mitchell. "We're heading straight for it."

The hammering and howling continued. There was no way of knowing which direction it was coming from.

"I think it behind us," snivelled Shadow-Estelle. "I think it get me first!"

"It's not behind us," snapped Estelle, her own growing panic making her tetchy. "We just have to keep moving."

But they weren't moving.

Mitchell was refusing to budge, despite being pulled by Becker and pushed by Sandor.

They were going to die in a pipe because of one crazy man.

"I'm not going there, you idiots!" Mitchell cried.

Then Kappo said: "Shhhh!"

Everyone went quiet.

The hammering had stopped.

"Professor," whispered Kappo calmly. "There's nothing up ahead, I promise. A thing that size could not have got into this pipe. You just have to start crawling, one hand and one knee at a time. I promise you, nothing will happen."

Estelle waited for Mitchell's response, hoping Kappo's calm voice had had the desired effect.

"That's it, Professor. One hand… and one knee…"

A bulge arose in the metal floor beneath Kappo. He didn't see it. Estelle tried to warn him, but before she could, the bulge became a hole, and zeta light pierced the darkness. The metal tore and a hand burst through. It plunged deep into Kappo's muscular torso and grabbed at something inside him. It yanked downwards, and he flopped with a bang to the floor, sinking into the metal, warping it. Then his body was gone, and zeta yellow poured through a much bigger hole.

Estelle screamed and pulled at her hair. Sandor was shouting at her, but all she could see was the beast below them gorging itself on Kappo.

Sandor reached out across the gap, telling her to take his hand. She leaned forwards, tremblingly, feeling that at any moment she would crumble like a shadow in sunlight. Worse, she might fall into those blood-soaked jaws. Her mind had turned to jelly, but by forcing her eyes from the horror below, she eventually found the will to obey him. Taking his hand, she let him support her across the hole made by Kappo's body. Shadow-Estelle, once more shrouded for protection in Mitchell's voluminous white coat, swiftly followed her.

The next few minutes passed in a zombie-like blur. Estelle was vaguely aware of them moving steadily forwards through the ventilation duct. Mitchell must have become quieter – at least she didn't hear any more from him.

Eventually they stopped again and a message came back from Paz that they had reached the armoury.

They waited in the cramped darkness for a few more minutes while Paz checked that the coast was clear. They emerged from the pipe one by one into a small room lined with racks and shelves of weapons and ammunition.

There was an atmosphere of clench-jawed determination. No one spoke much, being too affected by what had just happened. Estelle gradually emerged from her benumbed state. "Just continue with the plan," she told herself. "Focus on the next step, and soon we'll be out of here." She looked disdainfully at Mitchell, seated on a chair, fist supporting his cheek, looking down, not meeting anyone's eyes. Estelle wondered whether in the ocean of self-pity he was currently wallowing in, he might spare a thought for Kappo, and the part he'd played in the man's death.

On the bottom shelf, Becker found a box filled with brown sticks of gelignite. He loaded half a dozen of them into a rucksack, along with an electric detonator – a small metal cylinder attached to a length of wire. Then his eye was drawn to the racks of high-powered rifles and shotguns. "While we're here lads…" he murmured.

Becker, Sandor and Paz began considering what weaponry they might usefully purloin. Meanwhile, Estelle's attention was attracted to the room's door, which was ajar, offering a view into a short corridor. Off the corridor was another room – perhaps an office. Offices contained phones.

"Wait here," she whispered to her shadow. "I won't be long."

She moved stealthily into the corridor and peered into the other room. It was, indeed, an office. There were two pictures on display: a framed photo on the desk showing a severe, plump-cheeked woman, and a large poster-sized monochrome image on the wall of a famous jazz saxophonist. From these clues, Estelle concluded that this must have been Derek's office. She fervently hoped his Super Shadow didn't possess a homing instinct. Near the photo on the desk lay a mobile phone. After listening for a moment and assuring herself that all was quiet, she stole into the office and picked up the phone. To her relief, it was working. The first number she tried was Aunt Lucy's. She let it ring ten times before giving up. She toyed with the idea of calling the police, but decided that might just take too long, and she wasn't certain she'd even be believed this time. So she called Dr Kirby, whose number she had luckily memorised.

"Helloo?" came his chirpy voice.

"Doctor Kirby, it's Estelle."

"Ah, helloo lassie. Ah'm on my way to ye now. Can ye tell me where ye are from Delhaven?"

Estelle recalled their madcap chase across the fields. There'd been a bit of south, but it had mainly been east.

"East," she told him. "Head east into the forest and you should find it – it's an ultra-modern building with white walls and tiny dark windows, surrounded by electrified fencing and a guardpost by the gate."

"Where are ye right now? Are ye in the white building?"

"Yes, we're under attack from this... Well, I can't say it or you'll think I'm madder than ever. But our plan is to move through the building's ventilator ducts. We're going to crawl through the air-conditioning unit on the roof to reach a safe room where the bad woman, Barbara, is hiding. We're going to force her to end the lockdown so we can get out of here."

"Goodness me, that all sounds mighty dangerous. Are ye sure –?"

"Call the police, Doctor. Tell them to send a helicopter to pick us up from the roof of the Facility. There'll be six of us... I think that'll be our only way out of here if we can't switch off the fence. We'll still try to reverse the lockdown in case the police refuse to help, but please do your best."

"A helicopter! Ah, well, I'll see what I can do, Estelle."

She noticed Sandor looking at her from the doorway.

"I have to go now, Doctor. But please... call the police."

"I will, don't worry. And I'll be seein' ye very soon."

She switched off the phone and looked up at Sandor.

"Well done you for finding a phone," he said.

"I feel like going up to the roof right now and waiting for the helicopter," she sighed. "Do we really have to confront that awful woman?"

"I think we do," he said. "It's not that I don't trust your doctor, but I wonder if the police are going to think he's been hoodwinked by a delusional patient... after what happened yesterday."

She moved towards the door, planning to follow him back to the armoury, but Sandor remained where he was, looking intently at her.

"You OK Es?"

"No," she said. His staring was making her feel vulnerable, like he wanted her to face up to stuff she really wasn't capable of dealing with right now. Her shoulders slumped as she leaned against the door frame.

"That was horrible – back there," he said.

"I know... I'm trying to blank it from my mind. Just move on, you know? Do the next thing on the list!" She hadn't meant to sound angry. "I'm sorry," she added with a half smile.

His own answering grin was made crooked by his swollen cheek and the bruise by the side of his mouth. Despite this, and the blackened eye, he looked weirdly handsome.

"Your face is quite a work of art, you know," she told him.

"What? You mean like a Picasso?"

She giggled. "Yes, I'd say it would fetch about ten million at auction."

"I'd say yours would fetch twenty," Sandor said.

"I didn't get beaten up to achieve this effect," she joked. "I was born with it." This banter was already making her feel a bit better, but Sandor didn't look inclined to continue with it. He was still staring at her, but now he was looking serious, as if he was building up to saying something important. They were standing very close together in the doorway. She could smell his leather-and-gun-oil scent. "You know, Es. If we ever get out of here…"

"Yes?" Her heart slowed, and then began to beat again, loudly in her ears.

"I'd like it if we could spend a bit more… time together. You know, like we did in the old days."

"I'd like that, too," she heard herself say.

"Of course it wouldn't be exactly the same."

"Of course not."

"I mean, we're older, wiser."

"Surely not wiser," she grinned, aware that she was blushing like a beacon.

"Perhaps you could come down and see us in Edgebourne."

"Sure!" And then she stopped. "Us?"

"Yeah. Me and Marie. Did I not mention her?"

"Marie?"

"My girlfriend."

Everything stopped then. The flow of her blood was interrupted, like the scrape of a needle breaking into the music on an old-fashioned record player. That word girlfriend casually dropping from his lips – it made everything suddenly wilt inside her. He continued to talk – about "me and Marie", how they met during military training and discovered a shared interest in "guns and stuff" and la-di-da-di-da – but she hardly heard him. How could she have been so stupid? A gorgeous guy – a soldier. What did she expect? That she could call him up after four years and he'd just fall into her arms? Of course that wasn't why she'd called him, but so much had happened since then. There was this – she didn't know what to call it – this beautiful tension between them. She could feel it. Couldn't he?

"You OK, Es?"

She squeezed out a smile. "Yeah!"

"You're cool about this?"

"Why shouldn't I be?" Then the smile cracked. "Why the hell shouldn't I be?"

"Hey, you guys!" It was Paz, leaning out of the door to the Armoury. "They're all back in the vent. We're only waiting for you."

BANG!

The door to Derek's office caved in as his Super Shadow burst into the room. Sandor pushed Estelle behind him and raised his shotgun. He blasted a hole in the creature's neck, causing it to stagger backwards into some filing cabinets.

They rushed back into the armoury and hastily climbed through the hole and back into the duct. Estelle went first, then helped Sandor up. Paz was following them in when they heard another crash in the corridor just outside. The creature lurched in, its head sitting lopsidedly on its half-obliterated neck. Paz shot at it, but managed only to graze its shoulder.

The creature lashed out and grabbed his thigh.

Sandor tried to pull him up, but was no match for the monster's strength.

"Come on!" he cried through gritted teeth, as his hold on Paz began to slip. If Sandor had had his other arm available, he could have attempted to fire at the creature. Estelle could only watch helplessly, being too far from the vent cover to offer any help. She saw the veins popping in Sandor's temple, the desperate grimace, as Paz slowly slid from his grasp.

Mitchell's panicky tones broke in from further up the pipe. "Let's go!" he screeched. "He's dead, isn't he? If you stay there, you'll be next!"

Paz fell, and, with a fading gasp, was gone.

Despairingly, Sandor reached for his gun, aimed and fired three times. From his look, Estelle knew he'd saved the last shot for Paz.

She tugged at him. "Come on," she urged.

They began to move on through the duct, and Estelle tried, once more, to do the blanking out thing – just continue with the plan, she told herself. But it was getting harder. She'd seen Paz's face as he was caught in the tug of war between Sandor and the monster. She'd seen the dread in his eyes, mingled with this little spark of hope, as he'd gazed up at Sandor. And she'd witnessed the gradual extinguishing of that spark as their limbs had slowly untwined.

A short distance on, the duct twisted sharply upwards. Becker called back: "This must be the shaft leading to the AHU."

Small handholds in the shaft wall enabled them to ascend it. Lines of afternoon sunshine glimmered down from above. Estelle could smell the forest air. They were close to the roof. Shadow-Estelle, immediately above her, didn't need warning of the dangers and quickly covered her head and body in the white coat.

Beyond Shadow-Estelle and Mitchell, Estelle could see Becker climbing into a cramped cube-shaped compartment.

"There's an obstacle in front of me," he called down. "It's got horizontal lines. Looks like the back of a fridge."

"That's the heating coil," said Mitchell. "We'll just have to blast our way through it. And the cooling coil behind it."

"OK, block your ears everyone."

Becker donned some ear mufflers grabbed from his rucksack, then took aim with his shotgun and fired.

Estelle was ready for the noise this time, but it still felt like a firecracker going off next to her ear.

Becker tried to push back the singed edges of the hole he'd created, before swiftly withdrawing his scorched hand. Using his jacket sleeves, he made the hole wide enough to climb through. His blast had knocked through both air coils, allowing them access into a second compartment. Another blast from the shotgun dealt with the air filter, which left only the blower, which was seated in a drum inside a large slatted cage through which the rooftop and sky could be glimpsed.

"Fan's not working," Becker reported.

"Maybe Barbara switched it off," speculated Mitchell. "Even so, we'll still have to find some way past it."

Becker cautiously placed a hand on one of the motionless blades. The blower suddenly erupted into noisy life. Estelle was spattered with blood. She heard Becker scream and clutch his hand. He cursed violently and protractedly, his eyes squeezed tight. Finally, pulling his injured hand out from under his arm, Estelle saw that about half of two of his fingers were missing, ground to mincemeat by the fan.

"How in the blue blazes did that happen?" Becker wanted to know. "Does that bitch know we're up here or what?" He let forth a howl of pain and rage. With his good hand, he ripped off part of his shirt sleeve and wound it tightly around the blood-soaked stumps of his fingers.

"Everyone move to one side," said Sandor, popping his head through the hole Becker had blasted earlier. Estelle pressed herself against one wall of the AHU and made sure her shadow did likewise. Sandor aimed his gun at the centre of the whirling blades. Another ear-splitting discharge, a smell of cordite and smoke, and the blades were stilled.

Becker kicked at the thing angrily. He kicked again and again, until the blower's drum began to poke through the slatted wall on the far side of the cage. Soon it had been shoved far enough out to allow the party to move past it and into the shaft that lay directly below.

After a descent of five or six metres, the ductwork made another right-angled turn to the horizontal.

"This should lead us straight to Barbara's office!" said Mitchell, excitement returning to his voice.

One by one, they got back onto their hands and knees and moved into the horizontal pipe. Just ten metres further on, they reached a dead end.

"We're inside the wall of her office," said Mitchell quietly, peering through the grille next to him. "Of course, the safe room isn't on the main ventilation circuit – that would make it too accessible – so this is where our journey inside the building's ventilation system ends."

Estelle noticed a dark hole about eight inches wide to her left. "Where does this lead?" she asked.

"Oh, that connects the main circuit to a smaller one that runs through the central part of the building, ventilating the labs," said Mitchell. "I'm sure it also connects to the safe room, but it's of no use to us. Look how narrow it is… Right, who wants to be first out of here?" He began pushing at the ventilator cover.

"I can get through it," said Shadow-Estelle timidly. She was pointing at the narrow duct. "If I make self very thin, can get through small long hole and go to bad lady's room."

Mitchell brightened at this suggestion. "Why, that's true. I hadn't thought of that."

Estelle eyed the small aperture of the pipe with alarm. "It'll be so tight and dark in there. What if you get stuck? And even if you make it, you're no match for that woman."

"She'll have the advantage of surprise," said Sandor. "And she'll have a gun."

"I don't like it," said Estelle, anxiously noting her shadow's excited look. Leaning closer to Sandor, she whispered: "She told me earlier she didn't mind dying. I'm worried about what might be motivating this."

Sandor shook his head. "It sounds to me like a better plan than trying to smoke Barbara out with the threat of gelignite." He turned to Shadow-Estelle. "You really think you can get through that hole?"

The girl nodded enthusiastically.

"You're very brave."

"I do it for you and Spirit-Mother."

"You're not to die for us, understand?" Sandor said sternly. "We want to see you again."

"I want see you, too."

Sandor turned to Estelle, and she nodded.

"This pipe will end in a T-junction," Mitchell explained to Shadow-Estelle. He placed his hands in the shape of a T to show her what he meant. "When you get to the junction, you must turn right. Right! Understand?" Again, elaborate hand movements seemed to help, and she nodded her understanding. "Continue through the pipe for a bit longer, then turn right again at the next junction. OK?" He drew three sides of a square in the air to show her the basic route he wanted her to follow. "That will take you to above the safe room over there." He pointed at the metal wall marking the duct's dead end.

Sandor handed her a pistol and demonstrated the safety catch and trigger. "When you open the vent cover, point the gun at her and tell her to open the safe room door," he told her. "Don't listen to anything she says. She'll try and persuade you to put the gun down. Don't listen. Just keep the gun pointing at her until she opens the door."

"And if she not open door?" Shadow-Estelle asked.

Sandor stared at her. "Then you'll have to shoot her."

Shadow-Estelle didn't blink. "I hate to do that... But I do it if I must to."

Estelle embraced her. "Take care, my dear. If you get lost or scared, don't worry. Just come straight back. If you get stuck, call to us. We'll hear you."

Shadow-Estelle kissed her on the cheek, then slid herself into the tiny black hole. Her body seemed to flow into the pipe in a manner that was unlike anything solid or even liquid. It was more like vapour, except that she remained entirely opaque and separate from the surrounding air. In truth, she looked like nothing other than what she was: a three-dimensional shadow.

After Shadow-Estelle had departed, they waited a few more minutes in the pipe, ensuring that all was quiet outside, before descending. One by one, they climbed down onto a desk and then the floor of Barbara's office. The four of them slid some heavy filing cabinets in front of the door, in case the Super Shadow decided to pay a visit during their wait for Barbara and Shadow-Estelle.

"The door to the safe room is behind there," said Mitchell, pointing to a wall of shelves containing books, journals and box files. He crouched down and slid his hand beneath the bottom shelf. There was a small click, then he got back to his feet and pulled a handle on the right-hand side of the bookshelf unit. The hinged unit opened smoothly outwards to reveal a shiny metal door behind. It reminded Estelle of a bank vault entrance, complete with spoked wheel and combination lock in its centre.

The four of them stared at the door. "For all we know Barbara isn't even in there," said Estelle quietly.

"She's in there," said Mitchell confidently. "There's no way she could have instituted the lockdown, changed the lighting and switched on that fan on the roof without being inside the Facility – and this is the only secure place in the building."

"Is Shadow-Estelle there yet, do you reckon?" asked Becker.

"I would assume so," answered Mitchell.

Estelle glanced at the ceiling, wondering where exactly her shadow was, and anxious for her safety. She was brave, but so very innocent. Did she really have a chance against that ruthless arch-manipulator Barbara Wallace?

They waited in silence, watching the door. Estelle had deliberately placed herself a good distance from Sandor, with the other two men between them. She did this because she was now feeling angry with him. She had no justification for this, besides a vague feeling that he might have led her on a little (he probably hadn't), and that he could have shown a little more sensitivity in introducing the "me and Marie" thing.

After all they had been through, her jealousy seemed an extremely trivial concern, and she wondered why she couldn't rise above it when faced with the life-or-death enormity of their current plight. She thought it might be a symptom of her damaged personality – the fact that she found rejection harder to accept than the likelihood of imminent death. How was it that she could deal with the existence of a Super Shadow – but not with a girl called Marie? She was sure Dr Kirby would have something to say about that. Dr Kirby! Would she ever even see him again? What she'd give right now for the sound of spinning chopper blades on the roof.

"This is taking too long," said Sandor.

"I don't like it," Becker murmured.

"Let's give it a little longer," said Mitchell. "They're probably talking."

"They shouldn't be talking," said Sandor anxiously. "I told her, if Barbara doesn't open that door, she should kill her."

Another minute went by.

Mitchell strode up and knocked sharply on the metal door. "Barbara?" he said loudly. "Can you hear me?"

No response.

And then the wheel on the door began to turn. With a small hiss, the door opened. Inside the room was Shadow-Estelle.

She was alone.

"Where is she?" cried Mitchell, dashing in. The room contained a desk with a computer, a bed and a kitchenette, with a door to a tiny bathroom. Mitchell checked the bathroom before stamping his foot in frustration. "Where the devil is that woman?"

"The computer's on," said Sandor. "She probably only just left." He turned to Shadow-Estelle. "Did you see anything?"

She shook her head. "It just like this when I come. I sorry for delay. I find it hard open door."

"She must have known we were coming and got out while we were still up in the vent," said Becker. "Just like she knew when we were in the AHU unit." He glanced ruefully at his hand.

"And she knew we were in the rec room, too," said Estelle. "That's why she switched it to zeta light."

"Are there motion sensors in the building?" asked Sandor.

Mitchell shook his head. "I drew the line at that," he said. "Too intrusive."

"Security cameras?"

"Only outside and in reception."

"Somehow she knew where we were," said Becker. He looked at the screen, as if expecting to see security camera images of other rooms in the building. The screen was blank except for six small boxes with a flashing cursor in the first one, and some green numbers in the top corner.

"Without Barbara, we can't end the lockdown," said Mitchell. "It's still in force, so she must be somewhere in the building. We should split up and look for her."

"That could be very dangerous with a Super Shadow on the loose."

"I find this on desk," said Shadow-Estelle, showing them an envelope. "It is for you, Spirit-Mother." She handed it to Estelle, who saw it had her name handwritten on it. She ripped it open and extracted a single sheet of folded cream-coloured paper. The letter was written in a flowing, girlish script. She read it out to the others:

Hello Estelle,

Congratulations on getting this far, my dear. Despite all my efforts to kill you, you remain stubbornly alive. You are a survivor and no question. It's simply too bad, despite your great talent for eluding death, that this is where you finally run out of road.

Let me take you back to the beginning – I'll be brief, for as you'll soon learn, there isn't a lot of time. You were always a marked woman, Estelle. From the day you moved into that cottage next to the meadow, you were in our sights. We had been looking for a way of testing our shadow soldiers on a live target, to see how they fared in the field. And there you were, living alone in that isolated place – the perfect bait for our zeta-fortified warriors.

It was fortunate for us that your friend Sandor arrived just as things were getting interesting. Now we had two live targets for the price of one. It was a little problematic that he'd brought a car, but Derek Atkins dealt with that by stealing the battery.

What we hadn't bargained for was your luck and ingenuity. Finding Carl Henrison was unfortunate. Happening on the Cave was even worse. And turning poor old Derek into a Super Shadow was just plain tiresome. Nevertheless, here you finally are, together with that coward and traitor, Robert Mitchell, just where I want you. And now there can be no escape.

You see, I've activated a time bomb. It's a very big bomb, and should destroy the entire building. To deactivate it, you will need a six-letter code. I'll be sporting and give you a clue. It's the name of someone I lost. Mitchell might know who I'm referring to. But he had better be very sure of himself, because you only get one chance to enter the correct code. If you get it wrong – kaboom! By the way, the clock in the top right of the computer screen tells you how much time you have before it detonates.

Bon voyage, my little survivor. Let's see if you can get out of this one.

Barbara Wallace

xxx

They all crowded round the computer screen. The numbers in the top corner were clicking steadily downwards:

02.56… 02.55… 02.54… 02.53

Estelle felt herself shaking. The letter fell from her hand. She wanted to run, but her feet were stuck like glue. Biting her lip, she looked at Sandor, desperate to hear that he had some clever scheme to get them out of this.

But Sandor, cursing under his breath, could offer no crumb of solace. He turned to Mitchell. "You said she lost a husband and a couple of kids. What were their names?"

Mitchell's mouth was flapping open and shut like a fish as his eyes stared wildly at the flashing, ever decreasing, numbers in the corner of the screen. Sandor slapped the professor's cheek, making him blink. But his eyes never left the numbers.

"Barry Wallace was her husband," he croaked.

"Barry – that's only five letters. What about the kids?"

"Th-the girl was… now let me see. Amber. No. Ambrosia. No no no. Am-Amelia. That was it."

"OK. And the other one?"

"The boy also had a name starting with A. Now what was it? Um… Adrian. Yes, I'm pretty sure it was Adrian."

Sandor sighed. "Two six-letter names. It's a coin toss."

"Look at this." Becker was on his knees under the desk, tracing the route of a wire from the back of the computer.

The wire disappeared through a hole in one corner of a removable floor tile.

"Be careful," warned Sandor. "It may be booby-trapped."

Becker inserted one of his undamaged fingers into the hole and raised the tile to reveal a metal floor about a metre below where they knelt. Within the metal floor was a hatch with bolts on it, currently standing open. Beneath the hatch was a long ladder, plunging some 20 metres to the floor of Derek's basement chamber.

"So that's how she made her escape," gasped Sandor.

The wire plugged into the back of the computer trailed endlessly down the ladder.

"The bomb must be somewhere down there," said Becker. "I know a little bit about bomb disposal, I might be able to defuse it."

"There are shadow soldiers roaming around, and time is running out!" Sandor reminded him.

"I know," breathed Becker, wiping a bead of sweat from his brow. "And there's always the chance I'll cut the wrong wire. But the odds are still better than trying one of those codes – if you ask me!"

Estelle was still mesmerised by the screen.

02.04... 02.03... 02.02

"W-we've still got time to get to the roof," she stammered, finding her voice at last. "The police will be here soon, with a helicopter. It's our best chance!" She grabbed Sandor's shoulder to make him look at her. "Please!" she cried.

"Adrian," murmured Mitchell through dry lips. "I'm sure she would have chosen Adrian... Although

on the other hand…"
  01.56… 01.55… 01.54…

eleven

01.53… 01.52… 01.51…

Estelle stood with her shadow at the door of the safe room. She was urging Sandor and the others to follow them to the roof. Mitchell was at the computer, fingers poised to type "amelia" or "adrian" into the keyboard. Becker was on his knees under the desk, about to crawl through the hatch beneath the floor to try and find and defuse the bomb. Sandor stood in the midst of them, and all their eyes were on him. Somehow the final decision had become his to take. Estelle observed the conflicting currents in his normally decisive face, and for a brief, objective second, she felt sympathy for him. But this was soon submerged beneath an ever more suffocating panic as the merciless numbers on the screen continued to tick downwards.

"Becker," said Sandor through parched lips. "It has to be down to you, my friend. Get down there and defuse that bomb!"

Becker nodded. He wriggled through the hole beneath the desk to land on the steel floor beneath.

"Got a phone?" Sandor asked him.

"Only this," answered Becker, indicating the intercom phone nestling in his belt.

"Can you call Barbara's office on that?"

"Yes."

"Call us when you find the bomb."

Becker nodded, then placed a foot on the top rung of the ladder below the hatchway. They watched him descend as rapidly as his injured hand would allow.

Estelle and Mitchell began to speak at the same time, both objecting.

"Shut up, both of you!" said Sandor viciously.

Estelle flinched as if she'd been slapped.

"The decision's been taken. Now all we can do is wait. And pray!"

01.32... 01.31... 01.30

In Barbara's office, Sandor found a cordless phone on the desk. He grabbed the handset and returned to the safe room. He slid his legs through the hole and got painfully into a kneeling position on the steel floor so he could peer through the hatch.

Into the empty silence, Mitchell whined: "So the boy's done Bomb Disposal 101, and suddenly he's the master of our fate. Well isn't that just wonderful?!"

Sandor turned his cold eyes on him. "If you want to make yourself useful, Professor, I noticed another computer in Barbara's office. Why don't you try hacking into it, like you did before, and see if you can deactivate the lockdown."

"In 75 seconds?" moaned Mitchell, as he shuffled off to the outer office.

Estelle barely noticed him go. She felt frozen inside. Shadow-Estelle's arm was linked in hers. The girl's body was close, touching her, and shadows were normally warm – but she couldn't feel any warmth now. Since Sandor had told her to shut up, a doorway of hope had closed in Estelle's head. The panic had subsided and she'd fallen into a stasis of thought, feeling and action. She felt numb, emotionally as well as physically.

01.05... 01.04... 01.03

Perhaps this was a natural response – the thing that follows fight-or-flight – when you become resigned to your own extinction. The numbers on the screen no longer held power over her. They simply marked the countdown of her life, like leaves falling from a branch, like years spinning by.

00.54... 00.53... 00.52

Barbara's phone began to ring. Sandor switched the handset to speaker. Becker's breathless yet triumphant voice blared: "Good news! I've located the bomb and opened the fusebox cover. It's a standard detonation device. I should be able to stop it, no problem. I just need to cut the wire."

Estelle's heart began beating again. Life surged back into her limbs, and heat returned to her face. She clutched her shadow's hand.

"Fantastic," said Sandor. "Go ahead and cut it."

"There's only one problem," replied Becker sheepishly.

"What's that?"

"I've got nothing to cut it with."

00.32… 00.31… 00.30

"You're kidding me!"

"Is there something you can chuck down: scissors or even a letter opener?"

Sandor looked up towards Estelle, who was already scouring the desk and opening drawers. Pens, paper clips, notepads abounded, but there was no sign of anything with a sharp edge.

"Check in Barbara's office," shouted Sandor.

Estelle dashed into the office. As she did so, the door and the filing-cabinet barricade, together with several square metres of surrounding wall, crashed inwards in a thick cloud of rubble and plaster dust. Mitchell, seated at the desk in the middle of the room, was caught in the forehead by a flying piece of rubble and immediately slumped to the floor unconscious.

The dust cleared once more to reveal the terrifying form of Derek's Super Shadow. Its bull-like head, no longer supportable by the remnants of its blasted neck, now flopped uselessly against its chest, so that it couldn't see anything but the floor immediately in front of it.

The Super Shadow emitted a strange, strangled grunt as it staggered further into the room and towered above the desk. On the desk surface, which was now coated with a thick blanket of dust, was a jar containing some biros, marker pens… and a large pair of scissors. Retrieving the scissors would bring Estelle into the monster's sightline.

"Hurry, Es!" came Sandor's voice. "We've got about fifteen seconds."

Screaming with fear and adrenaline, Estelle charged towards the desk. The monster's excited, gurgling growl shook the air as she reached for the scissors. Feeling a rib-cracking force against her sides and back, she was jerked upwards into the air to find herself directly beneath the overhang of the creature's head, her cheek just centimetres from its dripping smile. With her lungs collapsing in the iron squeeze of its hands, she used the last of her strength to plunge the scissors into the Super Shadow's face. The blade encountered a soft pulpiness and her ears were assaulted by a screech like an express train braking in a tunnel. The excruciating pressure on her ribcage lessened a degree to allow another breath. She withdrew the scissors and then used them to slice manically through the thick strand of rubbery tissue connecting the Super Shadow's body to its head.

The giant body, along with Estelle, crashed to the floor, and its head bounced and rolled to the far wall. Extracting herself from the dead creature's flaccid arms, Estelle raced back to the safe room. Sandor was looking grey as he watched the final numbers ticking downwards.

00.09… 00.08… 00.07

"Not enough time," he said quietly, as Estelle flung the scissors through the hatch and watched them fall to the distant floor.

They saw the tiny figure of Becker gather them up and sprint off to his right.

00.04… 00.03… 00.02

Too late.

Estelle closed her eyes and waited….

No sound came. No explosion. She was still alive. Still breathing the dust-clogged air.

She risked opening her eyes a fraction. The countdown

clock on the screen had stopped at 00.01.

Below them, a weary Becker came back into view and raised his thumb in triumph.

Estelle felt Sandor's kiss on her cheek, and she wondered if she was dreaming.

"That was awesome, what you did just now," he whispered.

She smiled and gave him a hug. Then she noticed Shadow-Estelle standing there, still shaking with emotion, and she embraced her as well.

They gathered at the hatch as Becker began the long ascent to the safe room, preparing to welcome the returning hero. He was smiling up at them as he climbed the ladder, and so was the last to see the creature rising up behind him like dark smoke.

They could only watch in horror as the soul shadow enveloped him and dragged him downwards. Others were there, too – former shadow soldiers, turned feral – and they began fighting like a pack of hyenas over Becker's remains, until shots from Sandor's gun dispersed them.

"Oh no! Not Becker," wailed Estelle.

Sandor started down the ladder.

"Where are you going?" she gasped.

"To fetch his body."

"But we have to get out of here, Sandor. It's still dangerous."

"I'm not leaving him here to be picked apart by shadows. Not after what he just did for us."

Sandor was moving fast, despite his injuries. "Check if Mitchell's OK," he called. "I'll be back in a jiff."

"Be careful," sighed Estelle. As she watched him

descend, she was reminded of that moment the previous afternoon when he'd thrown himself backwards out of an upper-storey window onto a van roof to stop Derek getting away. His insane courage both awed and wearied her, and she wished she could rid herself of these pointless and inappropriate protective instincts. Let Marie do the worrying, she told herself. If he really wanted to kill himself, it was an issue for them, not her. Trying to ignore a horrid vision of Sandor surrounded by feral shadows and running out of bullets, she returned to Barbara's office.

Her shadow was already there, helping Mitchell to his feet.

"I'm fine," Mitchell snapped at the girl, shrugging her away. Then he noticed the Super Shadow's headless corpse and gave a yelp. "What on earth...?" Estelle watched as memory and anxiety returned to his face. "What happened with the bomb, Miss Grant?" he asked.

"Becker defused it," she told him. "I'm afraid he was killed."

Mitchell didn't react to this, but simply turned back to the computer. He wiped the screen free of dust, and began typing on the keyboard.

"You know I worked out that six-letter code," he said as he typed. "It wasn't Amelia or Adrian, but Barbie. That was her husband's name for her, and it became our name for her, too. But she dropped it after the tragedy. It suddenly occurred to me that 'Barbie' was the 'someone' she was referring to her in her letter – she lost that happy, loving woman she used to be."

"How do you know?"

"Because I've just hacked into her computer using that

277

name as a password, and I'm sure she would have used the same name for the bomb deactivation code." He turned to Estelle, then his eyes dropped to the floor. "I'm very glad Mr Watts didn't let me type in 'Adrian' or 'Amelia'... And I'm grateful to Becker." He faced her. "I know you despise me, Miss Grant. I've been a fool and a coward, as well as an egomaniac – so obsessed with my place in history, I forgot about the needs of the people around me. I don't deserve to live when better men like Becker have died... But at least let me try to make amends while I'm here. Let me try to unlock the exits."

Estelle could think of nothing to say to this, so she returned to the safe room to wait for Sandor's return.

After ten anxiety-filled minutes watching him climb the ladder with Becker balanced precariously across his shoulders, Estelle helped Sandor up the last few rungs into the safe room. His face, shiny with sweat, lined with pain and exhaustion, and grim with sorrow, nevertheless carried a look of honour satisfied.

"He should be safe up here until the police arrive," he said, closing and bolting the hatch cover. Becker's body had been badly savaged, and Sandor's shirt was covered in his blood. They laid him down on the floor of the safe room, and Sandor closed the man's eyes.

From next door came a shout of excitement from Mitchell.

"What is it?" cried Estelle, rushing into the office. "Have you managed to open the doors?"

Mitchell looked up. "What? Oh that. Yes. Yes. I've opened the doors. But look! This is far more exciting. I've found the formula for zeta-pro on Barbara's computer. The devious woman must have found out about it somehow and kept it quiet."

"She got it from Carl Henrison," Estelle told him. "He gave her the formula, together with living proof that it worked, in the form of her own shadow. She then kidnapped the Shadow-Barbara. We found it living in her garden shed."

Mitchell looked stunned at this revelation.

The printer next to the computer came to life.

"What are you doing?" Estelle asked him.

"Printing out the formula of course."

"No!" said Estelle. She moved towards the printer, determined to rip up the piece of paper as it emerged, but was stayed by a hand on her arm.

"Spirit-Mother wants utop make more good shadows. Why?"

Estelle turned to her shadow. "Because..." But everything she was about to say – that this whole technology was evil and wrong and should never have been developed in the first place – would have been devastating for her shadow to hear. "Because... I'm sorry, but I don't think there should be any more like you."

"Why, Spirit-Mother?"

"Yes, exactly," said Mitchell. "Why are you so against this?"

Estelle kept her eyes on her shadow while pointing her finger at Mitchell. "Because that man wants to breed soul shadows to provide spare parts for humans," she told her. "He has no interest in you as intelligent beings... And because the same technology that created you, my dear, sweet girl, also created that." She moved her pointing finger towards the dead Super Shadow on the floor. "We can't risk that happening."

She grabbed the paper in the printer tray and ripped it up. Mitchell merely chuckled. He waggled his pocket-sized PDA. "I've also uploaded it onto here," he told her, "and emailed it to my PC at home. The technology's out there, Miss Grant, and there's nothing you can do to stop it."

Estelle fumed – and also shuddered.

"Leave it, Es," said Sandor, entering the room. "Let's just concentrate on getting out of here… You've deactivated the lockdown, Professor. But what about the fence?"

Again, Mitchell was distracted by what he was finding on Barbara's computer.

"Unbelievable!" he gasped. "I had no idea the woman was so advanced in her research!"

"What about the fence, Professor?" Sandor repeated.

"She's even got a formula for an orally administered zeta drug here. That would mean soul shadows existing without the need for radiation. This is the holy grail. Incredible!"

Estelle remembered Shadow-Carl mentioning this to her.

Shadow-Estelle remembered, too. "Spirit-Mother, does he mean pill for allow me to live in normal world… with you?"

Estelle turned to her, unsure what to say. She was saved from a response by a noise in the corridor outside.

"Quick!" hissed Sandor. "In here." They all bolted into the safe room.

Sandor pushed the door until it was almost shut,

leaving a sufficient gap for him to peer through into the office.

"Helloo?" came a friendly Scottish lilt. "Is there anyone here?"

"Doctor Kirby!" cried Estelle, pushing past Sandor and opening the door wide.

The psychiatrist stood there in the shattered entrance to the office, blinking through the dust. His craggy face broke into a big beaming grin when he saw her. "There ye are, m'dear! Ah'm so pleased to have found ye."

"Oh, Doctor!" sobbed Estelle, rushing over and throwing her arms around his thin, bony shoulders. "You made it! How did you get in?"

"Ah just walked in, lassie. The gates were open. Seems the whole place is deserted but for you and your friends." He gaped at the damage to the wall surrounding what used to be the doorway. "But what's been goin' on here? There's been some violence and no mistake!" Then he caught sight of Shadow-Estelle and gasped. "You never told me ye had a twin sister, Estelle."

Estelle found that a coherent reply to Dr Kirby's questions was currently beyond her. His sudden appearance here was so overwhelming, her only response was tears and a prolonged hug for the poor man.

Perhaps it was fortunate for the doctor that the Super Shadow's corpse was obscured from his sightline by the desk, the rubble and the dust – there was already rather too much for one man to comfortably take in.

"We can explain everything later, Doctor," said Sandor. "For now, our only desire is to leave this place and return to our homes. Have you called the police?"

"Aye, I called them after I spoke to Estelle the second time. But they said they'd been here yesterday and it had all been a misunderstanding. They told me that you, Estelle, were a delusional young lady, and I as your psychiatrist should have known better than to be deceived by you. Clearly a deception has been accomplished here," he said, looking about him once again, "but not by you, dear lass. I'll call the police again shortly, but first let me get the four of ye out of here. And you, sir," he added, noticing Sandor's arm and leg, "look like ye have need of a hospital as your first port of call."

They followed Dr Kirby out of Barbara's office and into the corridor. The place was deserted, silent – any remaining shadow soldiers were probably in the basement. Lying on the floor by the side of a smashed coffee machine, evidently missed by the short-sighted doctor on his way in, was the badly mauled corpse of a blackshirt. After a short hike, they arrived at the building's wider, main corridor. Sandor moved into the lead and checked both ways before giving the others the all-clear. To their left was the canteen. To their right lay the glass-walled reception – and freedom. Late afternoon light streamed in from the entrance, making the air sparkle as the golden beams caught the drifting constellations of dust. Estelle was too exhausted, too saddened by all that had happened, to smile, but inside she felt an unfamiliar calm settle over her, an unknotting of tensed muscles and an easier rhythm to her heart. They may have been end-of-the-day rays illuminating the corridor, but symbolically they belonged to the dawn, as she sensed a long and terrifying nightmare drawing to a close.

In the reception area was a coat stand on which they found a lady's dark blue cloak with a hood. Perhaps it belonged to Barbara – who cared? – it was ideal for Shadow-Estelle. When she tried it on, it covered her head and body even better than Mitchell's white coat had, and provided an effective shield against the zeta-irradiated forest outside.

"Is your sister OK?" enquired Dr Kirby.

"Suffers from allergies," explained Estelle vaguely.

"Ah, well. If she's ready now, let's be off."

The glass doors slid aside with a satisfying swish, and they stepped out into the silent golden afternoon.

As Dr Kirby had said, the perimeter gate was standing open and the guardhouse was abandoned. Soon their feet were no longer treading concrete or tarmac but the soft grass of the clearing. Before them stood the thick trunks and dark green canopy of the forest. Zeta light, a pallid, ugly cousin of the flaxen-coloured sunshine bathing the clearing, seeped out from the trees.

"Is that your car, Doctor?" asked Sandor doubtfully, spotting a pale blue, ramshackle vehicle of uncertain make and vintage.

"Indeed it is," said Dr Kirby, but he made no decisive move towards it. In fact, he had drawn more or less to a halt.

"What's wrong, Doctor?" asked Estelle.

"Nothing, m'dear," said Dr Kirby in an abstracted tone. "Nothing at all."

As he said this, Estelle caught a glimpse of movement in the nearby trees. She gave a start of alarm, and the exhilaration that had been building within her, hastily drained away. Yes, it had all been too easy. She should have known by now that getting out of the Facility would not be the end of it – not with acres of shadow-infested woodland still to be traversed. She expected to see wild shadows emerging. But the figures that appeared from behind the trees were not the asthmatic, misshapen creatures formed accidentally from bark, leaves and mud that she had encountered on her first venture into the forest. These were big, clean-lined, dark-uniformed shadow soldiers, with a smooth, almost plastic texture to their skin, and small red lights set into their foreheads. Their teeth, however, were just as sharp, just as fierce as those of their feral cousins, and they bared these now, as they advanced – some thirty of them – as a single body into the clearing.

Behind them came the tall, imposing shape of Barbara Wallace. She was holding a remote control device similar to the one Derek had used at Carl Henrison's house.

Sandor grabbed the gun from his under-arm holster and opened fire on the nearest shadow soldier, causing it to collapse. Three other shadows immediately responded by whipping out their long arms. One of the extended arms dashed the gun from Sandor's hand while the other two grabbed him at the elbows. He cried out as one of them squeezed down on his wound.

While this was happening, Estelle became aware of Mitchell making a helter-skelter dash for the forest. He slipped through a gap in the closing cordon of shadow soldiers and, surprisingly, made it past them and disappeared into the trees. Furiously, Barbara pressed some buttons on her remote control, and three of the shadow soldiers darted after him.

At the same time, more shadow arms flickered outwards across the clearing, and Estelle felt herself once again tightly ensnared in their grip. Shadow-Estelle, to her right, was similarly trapped. Strangely, Dr Kirby had been left at liberty. Even more surprising was the expression on his face – or rather the absence of expression: he didn't look shocked or scared, appalled or outraged. Instead he looked entirely accepting of these events – almost as if... he had expected them.

"Thank you, Doctor Kirby," Barbara said to him in her posh, gravelly voice. "A sterling effort on your part."

"Och it was nothing, Barbara," said Dr Kirby.

"And now we have the renegades where we want them," she purred. "Rest assured, the last of them, Professor Mitchell, will be rounded up soon enough."

"Doctor?" murmured Estelle, wondering if the Wallace witch had hypnotised him.

At last Dr Kirby turned to her, and she saw he wasn't in a trance; he was perfectly himself – even smiling. "Estelle, ye might as well know now, I was never the man you thought I was. You should'na placed your trust in me."

"The cottage," she spluttered. "You – you knew about this."

"It's not mine," said Dr Kirby with a mock-penitent shrug. "It belongs to the Facility."

"John Kirby and I go back a long way," Barbara smirked. "I approached him because I needed someone suitable to use as live bait for my shadow soldiers – someone mentally unstable, whose death could be explained away as suicide; someone who, if they did escape, would not necessarily be believed. John was the first person I thought of. I paid him well."

"Extremely well," chortled Dr Kirby. "Ye've made a rich man o' me, Barbara Wallace."

"Well, you provided us with the perfect target," said Barbara, eyeing Estelle as if she were a prize racehorse.

Estelle felt queasy. As she listened to Dr Kirby's breezy laugh, she was reminded of their many sessions together in his consulting rooms high up above the city street. He'd laughed like that sometimes at her little jokes. Had he really been laughing at the prospect of how much money she would earn him?

I was never the man you thought I was. You should'na placed your trust in me.

Her legs wobbled and her vision began to blur. If she hadn't been held fast by a shadow soldier, she'd certainly have collapsed. Dr Kirby's betrayal was so much worse than anything else that had happened to her these past few days. Until this moment, she could blame it all on a particular place – Delhaven village, the forest, the Facility – and her own bad luck in having stumbled on it. But now, like a rapacious weed, the nightmare was extending itself backwards and outwards into her life. Maybe there was no end to it. Maybe everyone, from her mother onwards, had been part of this all-consuming consipiracy against her! Her shadow, with all her simpering talk of "spirit-mother", had only ever seen Estelle as a passport to the outside world and a provider of a shadow boyfriend. And as for Sandor, how did she ever think she could trust him? His reckless decisions had led them ever deeper into this mess, and always against her better advice. And his casual revelation earlier that he had a girlfriend was the final proof that he cared nothing for her. His friendship, like everything else, was an elaborate deceit. She was, she realised, on her own – always had been. She'd never escaped from that attic four years ago. She was still there, living in the dust and the shadows, and all that had followed since then was fantasy. The thought of this was so horrible she felt she had to scream. It began in her head – an almost audible torrent of despair crashing through her brain – and then it became real: an unstoppable energy wave that poured out of her lungs, her throat, her mouth. It was an animal sound – a wordless, senseless cry of anguish that sounded, even to her ears, frighteningly out of control. The scream echoed through the clearing, and if there'd been animals or birds around to hear it, she was sure it would have frightened them all away. She felt her shadow's scared eyes on her, and glimpsed Sandor's look of desperate concern. But she didn't care – didn't care what either of them thought any more. It was Barbara's impatience that finally ended it. She flicked a switch on the remote, and Estelle felt a stinging blow to her face and the taste of blood in her mouth.

The sound of her scream persisted though – it seemed to hang in the forest air long after she'd been hit. Beneath its dying ring she heard her own damp, ragged breath, as she dangled in the grip of her captor. She was exhausted, spent, and heard nothing of the talk continuing around her.

A commotion nearby caused her to lift her eyes. She saw an angry, scared Robert Mitchell being hauled back into the clearing by a shadow soldier.

"Let go of me, you brute!" he cried, struggling to break free. "I'm on your side. Get this creature off me, Barbara, for heaven's sake."

"To be honest, Robert," said Barbara coolly, "you've swapped sides so many times over the past forty-eight hours, I can't keep up."

"Does twenty years as your loyal colleague count for nothing?" he pleaded, as he was forced to join the other three prisoners in a line. Then he caught sight of Dr Kirby, who was now standing alongside Barbara. He peered at him through the twilight gloom. "You! I thought I'd seen you somewhere before. You've been here, to the Facility, haven't you?"

"Aye, on a number of occasions," smiled the doctor. "In fact, I've been here throughout today. It was me in the safe room, not Barbara. She was out here, mustering the remnants of the Shadow Army."

Understanding dawned in Mitchell's eyes. "And from Miss Grant's phone conversations with you, you were able to track our movements around the building. That was how you knew to switch on the zeta light in the rec room, and turn on that fan that nearly took Becker's hand off."

"Robert's a canny old so-and-so, Barbara," said the doctor admiringly.

"And also slippery as a snake," she said. "But now we've caught him by the tail, so let's finish the job. We need to kill these renegades, John. But first…" Estelle heard approaching footsteps. Wearily, she raised her head. Barbara had stopped near Shadow-Estelle and was peering inside the hood of her dark blue cloak. "A zeta-pro Shadow," she chuckled. "The last of Carl Henrison's unholy progeny. Well, well. I think it's high time we turned you wild, my dear. Before we kill you, that is. Unveil yourself."

As she witnessed her shadow shaking with fear, guilt struck Estelle like a cold slap in the face. How could she have doubted her? Even in the dark and cynical depths to which her mind had now plummeted, she had to recognise her shadow as that rare thing – a flower in the desert. And now the poor girl was being forced to expose herself to the bad radiation. Estelle would have to watch her sweet, innocent nature dissolve before her eyes, to be replaced by something brutish, ugly and violent.

"Remove that cloak," ordered Barbara, "or I'll order one of the shadows to do it!"

Tremblingly, Shadow-Estelle pulled back the hood from her head, opened the cloak and let it fall to the ground. She turned to Estelle with tears in her eyes. "Spirit-Mother," she croaked, but had no time to say any more as the shadow soldier holding her shoved her closer to the forest, exposing her to the full dosage of zeta radiation.

From where she stood, Estelle was unable to see her shadow's eyes and teeth change, only the cold smile playing on Barbara's lips.

Farewell, my little shadow. Farewell to your dreams of a life with me in the city.

In a strange way, Estelle felt like she was saying goodbye to herself – her youth, her innocence, her idealism. And what would be left? A cynical, world-weary shell. She needed that girl far more than she realised, especially after Dr Kirby's betrayal. She'd protected her, loved her, but her shadow had given her something precious, too: a sense of hope. And now it was gone…

Barbara's smile faded, to be replaced by a mild frown. She manipulated a control on the remote, and Shadow-Estelle was shoved deeper into the forest so that she literally glowed with zeta light.

Barbara watched the girl's face intently, but her frown didn't ease. Was it Estelle's imagination, or did the zeta light look different? Not sickly pale, but warmer, more golden, like the light from Carl Henrison's Sustaining Room. Barbara's puzzlement gradually shaded into suspicion. She turned on Mitchell. "What did you do?" she demanded. "Just now, in the forest. What did you do?"

Mitchell, though almost bent double in the stranglehold of his captor, managed a weak laugh. "I changed the settings on the nearest transmitter," he wheezed.

"Where did you get the zeta-pro formula?"

"From your computer, Barbie."

Her face went dark – Estelle couldn't be sure if it was because of Mitchell's revelation, or the name he'd called her.

"I'll kill you!" she roared, and she thrust her finger down on another button.

Mitchell emitted a feeble, strangled cry. Then came a horrid cracking as the bones of his neck were broken. His body fell lifelessly to the ground.

Oh, Mitchell, you did a brave thing in the end.

Dr Kirby turned to Barbara. "So ye kept the zeta-pro formula on your computer? I thought the decision was to destroy it."

"That was what Derek wanted," said Barbara. "But I was never so sure. Just imagine how useful it could be. We could use the soul shadows to infiltrate society. They would look just like ordinary humans, but we could deploy them as spies, assassins, moles, saboteurs. The possibilities are endless. And before he died, Carl Henrison developed a formula for a zeta-pro drug, so we'll be able to send our shadow agents out into the world without any need for zeta radiation. This is the most exciting development of all, John." Barbara's eyes briefly shone with fervour at the vision she had conjured, before turning cold and practical again. "But for now we must find and destroy that transmitter."

She pointed her remote at the nearest shadow and pressed a button, but the shadow failed to respond. "Move, you fool!" she shouted at it.

"Move. Where I move?" replied the shadow uncertainly.

"And now they're talking back to me," Barbara sighed as she hurled her remote control to the ground. "Go... and... destroy... the... transmitter!" she ordered the shadow.

"Where transmitter?"

"In the forest. Over there!" She pointed into the trees.

The shadow shambled away.

"You!" Barbara said to the one holding Sandor. "Kill... him!"

"Kill him," grunted the shadow, and its hands began to squeeze Sandor's neck.

Sandor tried to prise the hands from his throat, but he was no match for the shadow, and he began to choke and splutter.

"STOP!"

The voice boomed around the clearing with such

authority that everyone immediately turned to see who had spoken, including the shadow currently engaged in strangling Sandor. Even the shadow soldier that Barbara had just dispatched into the forest to destroy the transmitter, now re-emerged from the trees.

"I am Jethro, commander of the Shadow Army!" rumbled the voice.

It was a phrase Estelle had never expected to hear again. Yet there he stood by the gate to the Facility. Holes were visible in his chest, his left hand was missing, and his body looked as battered and misshapen as one might expect after losing a fight with a Super Shadow. But Jethro was alive, and his spirit seemed as strong as ever.

He strode forwards, slowing as he approached Sandor.

"My friend!" he said, his voice thick with emotion. Then he turned on the shadow holding him. "Why you hurt my friend Sandor?" he thundered. "Release him!"

The shadow immediately did so.

"Kill him!" shouted Barbara. She took a small pistol from her belt and fired it at Jethro. He jerked in surprise, as yet another hole appeared in his torso. Then his head rotated on his shoulders, and he flicked out his right arm at Barbara. His hand smashed her gun away, then grasped her around the neck. He raised her several metres from the ground. Barbara turned an even deeper shade of fury as she wrestled to free herself from his grasp and her legs kicked uselessly at the air.

"I am your commander," she squawked at the bemused shadows. "You must obey MEEE!!"

"No!" roared Jethro. "You created us as slaves to do the work of humans. You are bad people. You created us so that we kill for you. That is the only reason you created us. Thus spoke Sandor. Sandor is our friend. He will lead us to freedom."

"Sandor is our friend!" chorused the other shadow soldiers. "He will lead us to freedom."

As they spoke, Estelle and her shadow were freed from their shadow guards' tight grasp. Shadow-Estelle rushed into her spirit-mother's arms, crying with joy and relief.

Seeing that their position was now hopeless, Dr Kirby made a sudden break for freedom, bolting into the forest as fast as his short legs could carry him. He was hauled back seconds later by a pursuing shadow soldier.

Barbara and Dr Kirby were then dragged to Sandor and made to kneel before him. The two prisoners were pinned by their necks to the ground, with their noses in the dust.

"They bad people," said Jethro. "We kill them, yes?"

Sandor shook his head tiredly. "They're bad, Jethro. But we have laws for them. They will go to jail."

"What is jail?"

"A place for bad people. They'll lose their freedom."

Jethro nodded. "This is good. I take them to jail. Where is jail?"

"No no. First we must call the police, and then –"

"What is police?"

"Ah, well, you see…"

Estelle smiled to herself as she listened to Sandor trying to explain the complexities of the criminal justice system to his friend. She felt the warmth of her shadow's body snuggled up against hers, and she savoured the beauty of the ruddy sky to the west, above the tree tops. Hope, that inextinguishable flame, was flickering once more like the light in those branches. The madness that had overtaken her just now, when she was still reeling from Dr Kirby's betrayal, was subsiding. Of course there was no worldwide conspiracy against her – just one slimy, two-faced toad of a psychiatrist!

She contemplated Sandor, as he stood there explaining things to Jethro. His bruised, handsome face gleamed in the dying light of the day, and he looked as he always had – a hero, and her truest friend. He would never be more than that, she realised. But that was fine. That was OK. She'd been without him these past four years, and she'd not done too badly. She'd survive as she always did, one day at a time.

The two prisoners were tied up with strong cord retrieved from the Facility, and placed inside Dr Kirby's car. Sandor used the doctor's phone to call the police. When he was assured they were on their way, he beckoned to Shadow-Estelle. She detached herself from her spirit-mother and went to him.

"You are now free to live as you choose," Sandor told her and Jethro. "But I warn you: the world of humans is not for you. You and your kind will not be accepted there. They will want to cage you, experiment on you. You should make your home here, in the forest. I'll talk to the police. It's possible some arrangement can be made so you can live here in peace, undisturbed by the outside world. I'll do my best to convince them of that." He crouched down by Mitchell's body and extracted the PDA from his pocket. When he touched the screen, the zeta-pro formula lit up. He showed this to Jethro and Shadow-Estelle. "Here are instructions for converting the other transmitters to the good light. Estelle and I can go into the forest now and change the light for you on the other transmitters. Then you'll be able to move around this part of the forest in safety."

Jethro looked at Sandor for a moment, before turning to Shadow-Estelle. "We think on what you say," said the giant. "I talk with Shadow-Estelle and my shadow soldiers, and then we tell you what we decide."

"Fine," nodded Sandor.

As the two shadows walked away to another part of the clearing, Estelle went to join Sandor. He gazed at her tenderly. "You know, Es, I think this is nearly over."

Estelle hugged him fiercely, placing her head against his chest. "This is just a friendship hug," she assured him. "Marie doesn't have to be worried."

"Marie? Oh, yes..." He sighed uneasily. She closed her eyes tightly as his arms enveloped her. With gentle pressure he pulled her closer to him. That felt nice – almost like floating. And with her eyes closed, it was so much easier to talk to him. They could be anywhere right now. At last it felt OK to say stuff – stuff she'd been bottling up for days.

"Sandor," she said, "the police will be here soon, and there are going to be endless interviews and... and then I'm sure you'll want to get back home. So..."

"So what?"

"So I don't think I'm going to have another chance to say this."

"Say what, Es?"

"To tell you about the way I feel..." – she bit her lip hard – "...about you."

Did she imagine it, or did his heart just skip a beat?

"I love you," she whispered.

Silence.

From somewhere, she found the courage to open her eyes and look at him. He was staring at her, but not in surprise. He looked intense, serious – almost angry. He was breathing hard, concentrating.

The tension of waiting for his response was unbearable. She'd have to break it with more words – any words. "I'm sorry," she blurted. "I shouldn't have said that. It was totally unfair. You've got your life with Marie. I felt I needed to tell you. But really, it's OK. Forget I ever spoke. We don't have to see each other again after this, Sandor. If it's awkward, that's fine. I'll probably... I'll probably leave the country or something... You won't ever have to see me again."

He had muttered something while she'd been saying all this, but she hadn't heard it, being so determined to ease the horrid awkwardness between them.

"What?" she now said.

"I said I love you, too, Es."

Her body shook. "But... what about Marie?"

"It's virtually over between us. A typical Forces romance. It was kind of fun while it lasted, but it never meant too much. Anyway, I don't think me and Marie ever really stood a chance. See, I lost my heart to a girl four years ago. A crazy little child in an attic... when I found you there that night all alone on that grubby little bed, my heart actually broke, and it's never really mended. You needed help, help for your mind, and it hurt me so much that I wasn't the person who could give you that help. That's partly why I joined the army. I needed to get away. But I never stopped thinking about you. I thought I could put you out of my mind and start a new life with Marie. But these… these past few days… They've made me realise that you and me were always meant for each other. I know you've changed, Es. I can see you've grown up and that you're strong – stronger than me, maybe. I'm going to try and change, too, and I think that, maybe, you and me, we could be good together. I love you, Es. I don't ever want to be parted from you again."

The tears had started flowing from Estelle's eyes long before the end of this speech. And by the time he finished, she found she couldn't stop crying. Sobs wracked her body, and her tears mingled with the sweat on his shirt. She felt his kisses on her forehead, and she raised her head so she could enjoy the warmth of those lips on hers. They kissed for ages, and despite the chill evening air gusting through the clearing, Estelle felt full of warm sunshine.

"Spirit-Mother."

Estelle turned to see her shadow standing there, with Jethro a few paces behind. Shadow-Estelle's eyes were darting between Estelle and Sandor, and she was grinning. "You love each other. I very happy!"

Sandor and Estelle exchanged amused, happy smiles.

"Have you decided what you're going to do?" Estelle asked her.

Jethro stepped forwards. "We will destroy the lights," he said.

"You mean you'll change them to the good light?"

"No, Spirit-Mother," said her shadow. "We will destroy the lights. Bad and good. Me and Jethro talk about this with the shadow soldiers and we all decide we not belong here in this human world. We are born of bad experiments. Bad people made us. We should not have been born. It is better to destroy the lights."

"But if you make the lights good –" began Sandor.

"If we make the lights good," said Jethro, "maybe some bad person will come and turn the lights bad again. It is better we destroy the lights."

"But what about the pills," said Estelle. "I'm sure we can find a way…"

Her shadow smiled sadly and shook her head. "It was nice dream for me. That I could live in city with you. But no. My place is here with Jethro. I stay with Jethro to the end."

Estelle noticed her shadow's hand nestling in Jethro's.

"You won't live long without the zeta light."

"We are ready for this," said Shadow-Estelle, gazing up at Jethro. Then she turned back to Estelle. "I love you, Spirit-Mother. I come say good-bye."

Estelle embraced her. "Good-bye… my child." Then she watched as Jethro and Shadow-Estelle led the remnants of the Shadow Army into the forest.

Ten minutes later, distant sirens could be heard coming through the trees, and before long the clearing was bathed in the blue flashing lights of police vehicles and ambulances. Sandor and Estelle watched as the police tape went up around the Facility and a team of white-suited crime scene investigators entered the building. By the time the first of a succession of stretchers emerged bearing the savaged corpses of blackshirts, night had fallen and the scene was lit with the glare of arc lights. As the covered bodies were loaded into the waiting ambulances, Estelle wondered which of them belonged to Kappo, Paz and Becker.

Beyond the range of the arc lights, the forest was pitch black, and she knew with a sinking heart that the transmitters had been destroyed. The soul shadows had this final night together, at least. They would be killed when the first rays of dawn penetrated the forest canopy.

The chief inspector was full of questions, which Estelle and Sandor answered truthfully, however outlandish their answers might have sounded. In any case, the inspector had no excuse for scepticism: he'd seen the corpse of the Super Shadow. Estelle also tipped him off about Major Harlon Black, the "private military entrepreneur" who had apparently funded the Shadow Army. The inspector assured her he would look into it.

As for the two prisoners tied up in the car, Barbara Wallace tried her best to concoct a story that cast herself as the innocent scientist dedicated to solving the world shortage in transplant organs. Robert Mitchell, she declared, was the evil one who had created an illegal Shadow Army without her knowledge. Her story began to crumble, however, when Dr Kirby failed to corroborate it, and it fell apart completely when the letter she'd written to Estelle was found in the safe room.

Some three hours later, as a light rain began to fall in the clearing, Estelle and Sandor were told they were free to leave. More questions would doubtless follow in the days and weeks to come, but for now they were advised to get some much-needed rest, and Sandor to get his injuries checked out in a hospital. The detective inspector offered them a lift in his car, which they readily accepted.

As Estelle was climbing in, she was distracted by the sight of a short, plump, middle-aged woman bursting out from the trees into the clearing. Estelle shielded her eyes from the arc lights to see who it might be and was amazed and delighted to discover it was her Aunt Lucy.

"Auntie!" she cried, rushing over to her.

"Dearie me! Is that you, Estelle?" gasped her aunt.

Estelle embraced her. "Oh, Auntie! What are you doing here?"

"That is such a long story, my girl, I don't know where to begin. I was trying to get hold of you by phone, and when I couldn't, I went to the cottage just to be sure you were OK. When I didn't find you there, I panicked. I called Doctor Kirby and he said I should wait for him at the cottage and we'd look for you together. I waited and waited but the doctor didn't come, so I began searching for you by myself. I've been wandering these woods for days. Well, hours at least. I was quite lost, I don't mind admitting. And then I saw these bright lights through the trees. But what's going on, Estelle? Why are there all these police cars here? Has there been some sort of trouble?"

"Don't worry, Auntie," laughed Estelle. "I'll tell you all about it on the way home. I'm just so glad you arrived when you did. The inspector was about to give us a lift. Why don't you come along with us? You remember Sandor Watts, don't you? He was my best friend from years ago…"

One evening, a few weeks later, Estelle was in her bedroom at her aunt's house. She'd just got off the phone from Sandor. He'd invited her to his flat in Edgebourne that weekend and her head was now full of dreamy anticipation at the prospect. She lay back on her bed and let a feeling of intense joy wash over her. It was so wonderful being back at home with her delightful, eccentric Aunt Lucy. And being in love as well, life could not be better. She was happily contemplating what outfits to pack, when it occurred to her that she didn't even own a suitcase anymore. She'd left her only one at that awful cottage, and of course she'd never gone back to retrieve it.

"Estelle!" cried her aunt from downstairs. "Your soup is ready."

"Coming, Auntie!" she called back. But instead of heading directly downstairs, she slipped into Aunt Lucy's bedroom to see if she could nab herself one of her aunt's smaller suitcases.

She knelt down and looked under the bed. Her eyes immediately lit on one: a small, dark overnight case with wheels and a little pull-up handle. Perfect.

She reached for it and dragged it out. As she was getting back to her feet, she spotted a small bottle of pills on her aunt's bedside table. This was surprising as her aunt was in robust health and she'd rarely known her to suffer ailments. Furthermore, Aunt Lucy never liked to take supplements of any kind, believing that all her nutritional needs could be catered for by a healthy, balanced, vegetarian diet. Estelle examined the bottle of ordinary-looking round white pills, but there was no label to tell her what they were.

Shrugging, she put them down again, carried the case to her bedroom, then went downstairs to join her aunt in the dining room.

"I spotted some pills in your room, Auntie," she said as she sat down opposite her and tucked into the soup. "I didn't know you were feeling poorly."

"Oh, not now, Estelle," her aunt smiled. "Not since I've been taking them."

"What was wrong with you?"

"I wasn't feeling myself, if you must know."

"Who prescribed them?"

Aunt Lucy put down her spoon and looked at her curiously. "No one. I was given them as a matter of fact. You remember that day when I was wandering around the forest looking for you. I never told you this, but during my wanderings, I met this lady. A very kind lady. I told her I wasn't feeling myself, and she gave me those pills. They've really put me right." She frowned. "Funny, she said she'd come and see me in a few days to see how I was getting on, but I never heard from her again."

Aunt Lucy picked up her spoon again and started once more on her soup. Estelle stared at her hand lifting the soup spoon to her mouth. It was her left hand. Surely Aunt Lucy was right-handed... wasn't she?

about the author

Alex Woolf has been "writing" stories since before he could write, crafting narratives while playing with toy soldiers in the attic of his childhood home. He's always been fascinated by the supernatural, and he longs to see a ghost, though he's sure he'd turn to jelly if he ever did. He is, quite literally, scared of his own shadow, and he wrote this book in the hope of curing himself. It didn't work! Alex's debut novel was a science-fiction tale called *Chronosphere: Time Out of Time*, published by Scribo in 2011. Two more Chronosphere novels followed. In February 2013, his fourth novel, *Aldo Moon and the Ghost of Gravewood Hall*, was published. It's about a Victorian teenage ghost-hunter – exactly the kind of person Alex would have liked to be if he'd been a bit braver!

For more exciting books from
brilliant authors, follow the fox!
www.curious-fox.com